INTENTIONALLY

D.W. Hogan

Intentionally

Punctuation & Grammar Note: this publisher deliberately chooses a punctuation light style.

For Book Clubs and other special orders contact:
director@vanvelzerpress.com

A Van Velzer Press Fiction in collaboration with Phoenix Farm

Paperback ISBN: 978-0-9898486-5-7
Hardback ISBN: 978-1-954253-72-8
eBook ISBN: 978-0-9898486-6-4

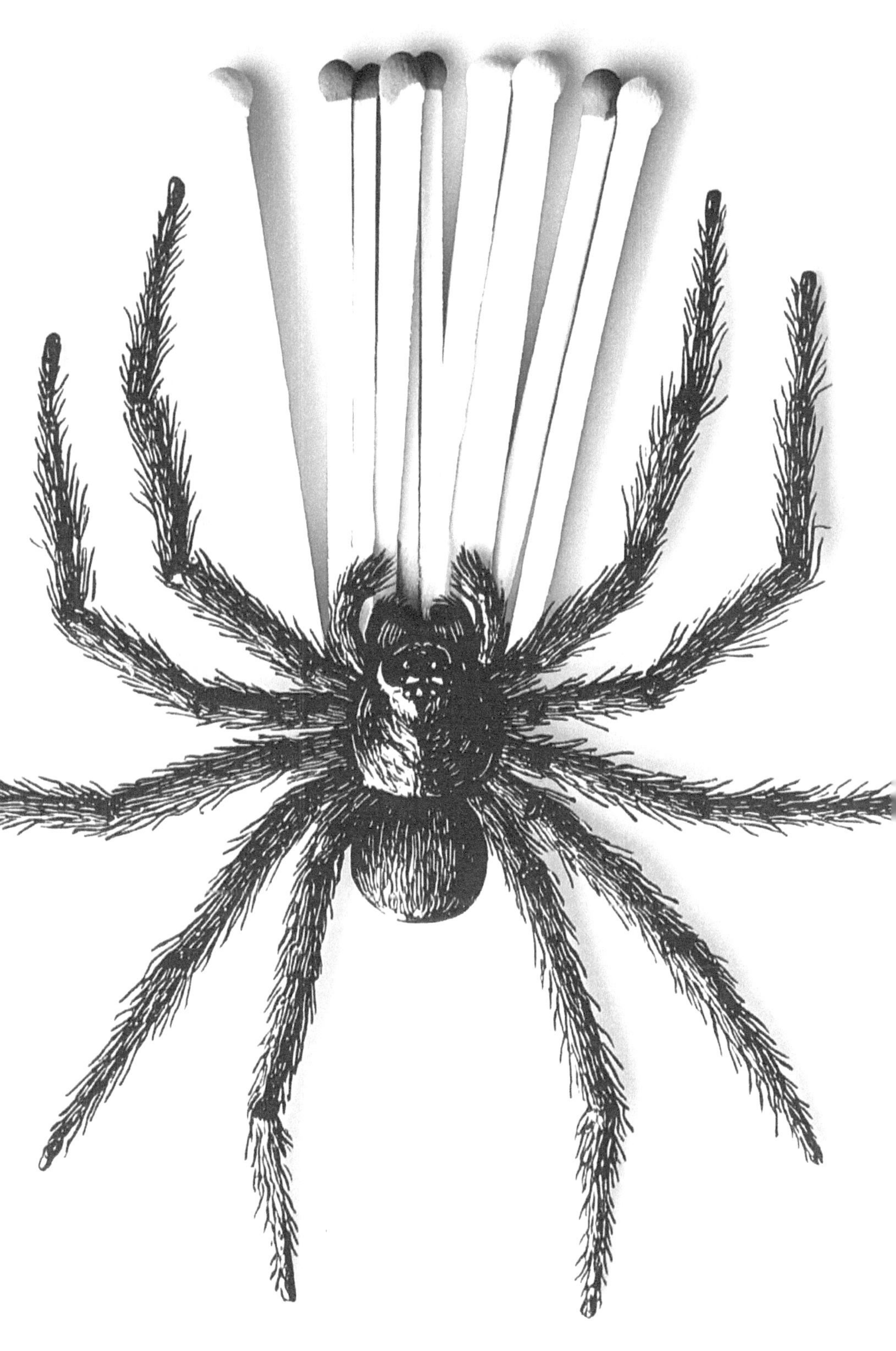

Dedication

This book is dedicated to all the veracious crime readers who can't get enough of twisted serial killer stories –

You're my kind of people.

1

Boston

Agents O'Sullivan and Grant sat in leather armchairs taking in the crowded home office of David Hobart PhD. Packed bookcases lined the walls. File boxes were stacked in various places. On the desk, piles of semi-organized folders in haphazard queues took up all the space leaving a small area clear enough to write or lean elbows on.

The professor joined them, coming through the French doors with two mugs of coffee. As he handed each agent their poison, he said, "I assume you want to talk to me about the serial killer again. Between the interview I gave to the Boston police department and your FBI probe, I gave a detailed report." He side-stepped some boxes on the way to his high-backed chair, rolling it to face the men.

"We have those reports. We just want to go over the events one more time. Given it's been a couple of months, you might remember something new. We're trying to wrap up this investigation," said the younger, clean cut, agent.

David's mind flooded with visions of the night of the fire, Regina's screams, his Abby, covered in soot. The sound of the gunshots still woke him from a dead sleep. No wonder he suffered from insomnia. Now they were asking him to relive it all again?

"So," the older, more distinguished O'Sullivan, grey at the temples, leaned forward taking over. "You're a professor at Boston University in the Psychology Department?"

From experience David comprehended the agents didn't ask rhetorical questions so he elaborated. "Yes, for fifteen years. I started my career as an associate professor and now I both teach and conduct research." He pinched the bridge of his nose with his thumb and index finger. An all too familiar migraine threatened. He'd been to the doctors and undergone the tests. They advised him to reduce stress. He scoffed at that absurdity. His head was going to be throbbing, and soon. The definite symptoms of classic PTSD.

David dreaded what he knew was coming, questions about his marriage. Would he have to tell them again they got married because she got pregnant? That theirs was a loveless marriage?

"Regina Hobart—your wife—and Abigail—daughter, fourteen years old?" O'Sullivan asked, confirming the file notes.

David looked down at his hands, at the scars healing over his burns, and nodded. "Ex-wife, Regina and I, we'd recently divorced." What he didn't say was, *Yes, she found out about my multiple affairs and tried to ruin my career. Then she tried to turn my daughter against me. We shamefully dragged Abby through a custody battle that left her feeling like a rope in a vicious game of tug of war. Am I ashamed? Absolutely! Along with a myriad of other things.*

"We're truly sorry about what happened."

David nodded, not looking up from his palms. His hand unconsciously went to the still tender, mending gash at his temple. It took fifteen stitches to close; the ER doctor warned it would leave a scar.

"I read your book that came out five years ago on the interpretation of body language," Agent Grant put in. "I've found it very helpful during interviews."

Like this one, David thought. Through the sizeable picture window, the bright January light reflecting off newly fallen snow was deceiving. A cold draft seeping through the old windows of the brownstone made David shiver.

"You have two books now I see." O'Sullivan was scrolling on his phone. "Best sellers. Congratulations."

"Thanks, yes, they've done well." *I made a shit load of money and yet, it was never enough for Regina. She had to have the best of everything, including prestigious private schools for our daughter.*

"You and Regina owned the house on Manchester Avenue?"

"Yes. It was quite the fixer upper when we bought it. Regina took on the renovation. To her credit, she turned it into a show place." *We couldn't afford one that was livable in the upscale neighborhood she chose, so she badgered me until I agreed to buy the one that was practically falling down. What a money suck. We fought constantly over money. Turns out, with all that century old wood, it was also a firetrap.*

"Who filed for the divorce, and on what grounds?"

"She did, adultery." *Yes, I cheated on my wife, who seven years ago, banished me from the master bedroom, sighting my rudeness for waking her up when I came in after midnight. I worked my ass off teaching and conducting research. All to be successful enough to afford the push-me/pull-me life we were building.*

"Claire Wiseman was your last research assistant before Darcy Jenson?" O'Sullivan looked up from his phone.

"Yes. We began the study of Intentional Human Behavior. We were interviewing highly successful people to find out what behaviors they all have in common. The head of the Psychology Department, Dr. William Collingsworth, planned to submit it for the National Research Service Award. But..."

"But your relationship with Claire ended your marriage and derailed your project?" Agent Grant asked.

"Yes. Claire left the state humiliated. The research we'd been working on got shelved." *And World War III began with Regina. She set the rumor mill at the university buzzing with gory details of our divorce.*

David sighed long and deep. "Look, in all honesty, Regina and I married and stayed married as long as we did because we thought it best for Abby." David swallowed trying to get the lump of emotion in his throat to go down. His voice caught when he said, "Abby, that girl changed my life. We were so close when she was little. I take full responsibility for my failures. I lost sight of the importance of our relationship. I know now, she should have been my main focus. Regina and I fought a lot. By the end of the marriage, we hated each other. Blamed each other. We were both responsible for the destruction of our family, in different ways." *Hubris. That's what it was. I'd let all the attention get to me. I sure wasn't getting attention from my wife. The requests for interviews: podcasts, internet influencers, Psychology journals, national talk shows. That was heady stuff. The problems started with traveling engagements where women slipped me key cards for their hotel rooms. All that attention blew my mind.*

"Tell us about the domestic violence charge," Grant prompted.

David crossed his arms over his chest. *This wasn't all my fault. Regina was full of ego too. What about her ambitions to be the wife of the Dean of Psychology? Her pushing, her nagging. It was too much. How many times did I give in just to shut her up? She manipulated me. She'd studied psychology too. She'd been betting I'd give her a reason to divorce me and take me for as much as she could get.*

"We had a difficult divorce. Regina changed the locks and kicked me out of our house, putting all my belongings outside, during a thunderstorm. Papers and clothes scattered all over the place in the pouring rain. Then, when I asked for some trash bags to gather my stuff, she motioned me to the library window where she threatened to burn boxes of my research in the fireplace. She had a fire going and files in her hand, she planned to do it. I forced my way into the house. Not my finest moment. I didn't lay a hand on her, I never have. My only concern centered on saving my work. Those charges were dropped."

O'Sullivan cleared his throat. "This was the research Darcy Jenson worked on?"

"No, this work came before I hired Darcy. My research was in a drawer for about a year when Dr. William Collingsworth insisted I resume the work on intentional human behavior." David patted two manuscript boxes on the corner of his desk. "I decided to widen the scope of the data to include negative intentional behaviors. That's when I brought on an assistant. It was Darcy who suggested patients in mental health facilities should be included. I hired her because she was smart. I ignored all the red flags," he said mournfully, shaking his head.

Agent O'Sullivan raised his eyebrows.

"The university was breathing down my neck, wanting results. With my wounds from the divorce still festering, my sharp thinking was off. I was in a hurry, not paying full attention. To be honest, if I knew then what I know now, I doubt I would have hired Darcy Jensen," David said wearily.

"I have to believe she didn't intentionally bring a serial killer into our lives."

Part 1

Life with Purpose

2

Foundations

Darcy Jensen began her life as Victoria Lawrence, the only child of James and Lillian Lawrence, an affluent couple from Evanston, Illinois. For all the thirteen years of her charmed existence, she lived in the same house in a neighborhood with manicured yards with ancient shade trees surrounding enormous executive homes.

The only secret in this family was kept by the mother. Lillian had a premonition on the night she gave birth that Victoria would be shadowed by evil, that her childhood was in danger, that Victoria would not exist as an adult. She couldn't share this; her sanity would be questioned or it would be called post-partum depression. So Lillian kept her secret, yet knew it was real. She began to lay the groundwork to protect her daughter, and one means to keep Victoria from the bad things in the world was to homeschool her child.

Victoria's only friend was her cousin Paige. They had sleep overs often, Paige brought her the world: rebelliousness, energy, hope and makeup.

Realizing Victoria needed more socializing than she was getting, yet fearing traditional schools wouldn't bring out her best (or keep her safe), her parents found a home school group when she turned thirteen that met on Mondays, Wednesdays and Fridays at the Baptist church around the corner. All of the students were gifted like Victoria. Miss Rogers was a brilliant teacher.

The first day of school brought with it excitement and anxiety for Victoria. This was her favorite time of year and she was eager to begin. Yet apprehension about her ability to fit in caused her to change her outfit three times before she settled on brown Capri pants and a cream and brown short-sleeved silk top.

Nervous, Victoria brushed her hair into a ponytail. This feeling of angst intensified when Lillian insisted on walking her to the classroom.

"Mom, I'm a big girl. I'm sure I can find my way to the basement," she said. Sitting in her mother's Lexis, Victoria found it ridiculous they'd driven barely around the block to the church.

"I know you can. I just want to see what it looks like. I promise, after today, I'll drop you off at the door." Lillian turned off the car and put her keys in her purse. She'd arranged her blondish, highlighted hair in a French twist and wore navy blue dress pants and a pale blue silk blouse. Anxiety radiated off her mother as she fiddled with her wedding ring.

"Or I could walk over here by myself," Victoria said, presenting an alternative.

"Food for thought," Lillian said, her usual non-committal response. Victoria followed her mother into the modern-looking brick church and down the stairs to the basement. Lillian's heals clicked with each step. They entered the first door on the right where long folding tables were set up, facing a whiteboard. The florescent overhead lights cast a greenish tint on the white concrete block walls. Several students, already seated at the tables, eyed Victoria curiously.

The scent of fresh paint hung in the air. This room clearly doubled as a Sunday school class because one wall had a mural with cartoon children from around the world with the declaration: We Are All God's Children.

Lillian greeted the teacher. "Miss Rogers, nice to see you again. This is my daughter, Victoria."

"Welcome, Victoria! I'm so pleased you've joined our class."

"I'm happy to be here, Ma'am."

"You can take a seat anywhere you like." Miss Rogers smiled as she whispered, "Don't be nervous, we have several new students this year, so you won't be the only one."

Victoria picked a spot at the second-row unoccupied table, while Lillian and the teacher shared a brief conversation. She was relieved when her mother gave a slight wave and didn't make a big production out of saying good-bye.

She opened her notebook and took out a pen.

The class was a mishmash of personalities and social skills. A consummate people watcher and astute observer, the different nuances in these new people fascinated Victoria. Each night she'd journal about the day. It helped give order to her overactive mind. She sorted out the peculiarities and commonalities between herself and her classmates.

Some students, like Natalie Perry and Bobby Neil, always put their hands up first to answer Miss Rogers' questions. Natalie was fourteen, a thin red head with a peppering of freckles across her nose. A chubby twelve-year-old with a Napoleon complex, Bobby came off as a know-it-all. Across the room, Sarah Birks habitually twirled long blonde hair around her index finger while Malory Phelps never made eye-contact with anyone and scribbled down the lectures in her spiral notebook.

Then came Sean Weeden. He was tall and lanky with shaggy

strawberry blonde hair and the same age as Victoria. He couldn't sit still and chewed his fingernails. His father was a police officer. It occurred to her he might suffer from anxiety due to the danger his father faced daily. Sean chose a seat next to Victoria on the first day of school and continued to sit by her every day.

Larry and Barry Devlin were hard to tell apart. They intrigued her the most. Identical twins, tall for their age, at 5'9" they dwarfed Miss Rogers when they stood next to her. Blonde-haired and blue-eyed, they were handsome. They never dressed identically, although polo shirts and jeans were their main choices.

They paid attention during class, except a few times when Victoria saw one of them pull some dental floss and wooden matchsticks from his pocket and, under the table, construct a sculpture resembling a grasshopper. She suspected Barry as the artist and the other one, who kept stealing glances at her, must be Larry.

Victoria considered herself just another odd shaped, puzzle piece in this group. Each one of the unique students fit better in this assemblage than they would among other cliques of their peers. Victoria realized she wasn't "normal" either. Limited interaction and experience with the outside world didn't quell curiosity. It's impossible to shelter someone who doesn't miss much. Living in the greater metropolitan area of Chicago she knew about drive by shootings and the violence outside her safe environment. She kept up on world news and skimmed the trends in pop culture.

Miss Rogers announced the group would be participating in an area-wide Science Fair after Victoria had been in the group for a few months. First through third place winners would be sent to the state competition. All overachievers, the students leaned in for the details and who Miss Rogers would partner them with.

Miss Rogers produced a plastic bowl containing folded slips of yellow paper. Swirling them around she explained, "I'm going to randomly pair you up by pulling your names. You'll have six weeks to complete your projects. I'm going to dedicate half our class time to this. You're allowed to work on it from home as long as you work together. The more effort you put into the project, the better your chance of moving on to the state finals. For some of you, I know you'll consider this a matter of life or death to win. All I'm asking is for you to submit your very best work. I wish you good luck."

The students laughed at her insight into their competitive natures. Miss Rogers began to pull names and instructed them to stand together at the back of the room. As the pool grew smaller, Victoria worried. She didn't want it to be Bobby; he'd tear apart all her ideas.

"Bobby Neil and Sara Berks," Miss Rogers announced. Victoria breathed a sigh of relief. "Larry Devlin and Victoria Lawrence; Sean

Weeden and Barry Devlin." With the draw completed, the students stood in pairs waiting for further instructions.

The groups claimed their spaces to begin. Victoria and Larry settled in the corner and sat on the hard vinyl floor with their backs to the room. His face flushed pink when he looked her in the eyes. *Is he blushing? No, surely not.*

"How do I know you're Larry and not Barry? I can't tell you apart," Victoria asked.

"That's a blessing and a curse," the boy answered, smiling confidently, making light of the situation.

Victoria smiled back. "You didn't answer my question."

"I'm Larry. If you knew us better, you'd be able to see the differences. I'm smarter and stronger than he is."

"Okay." Victoria responded, as if he'd clarified the issue. But she wondered what he meant. The faint murmuring of the other classmates reminded her of the task at hand, so she set aside her curiosity for the moment and powered up the computer.

"Okay, what do you think we should do?" she asked.

"Beats me."

Victoria sighed; this wasn't going to be easy. "Let's brainstorm categories, then try to agree on one that interests both of us."

She was right, this wasn't going to be easy. Once they settled on a tutorial for younger students about the solar system, it came out that Larry couldn't get on the internet at home, nor was he allowed to call her. His mother was beyond strict. He did find ways to sneak on the classroom laptop which he took home, logging on at odd times to Facetime with Victoria about their project. Then he would rush off at a moment's notice.

Victoria walked into class the next week and found Larry sitting in her usual seat. She hung up her coat and pulled the chair Sean occupied most days closer to her partner.

"I went through our outline one more time and polished the spelling and punctuation," she whispered. Larry opened their project laptop and inserted the USB memory stick she handed him. He scooted his chair closer and with their heads almost touching they both silently read over the finished outline.

Larry smelled like a warm blanket fresh out of the dryer. Disconcerted, she slid her chair slowly away and asked, "What do you think? Any changes you want to make?" The artificial light from overhead made his eyes look glacier blue.

"No," he said, with a white toothy smile. "I think we're perfect."

They waited patiently as the room filled, knowing they were prepared. Everyone showed up except for Sean Weeden. Miss Rogers broke them into their groups and told Barry, "Don't worry about it; Sean's probably running late. He's never absent."

She consulted with several other teams, checking their work, before she got to Victoria and Larry.

"Very good, I like it. You've got the right idea—" her cell phone rang. She put up her index finger, signaling she'd complete her thought in a minute, excusing herself to take the call.

She stood close enough for Victoria and Larry to hear the caller. "Miss Rogers, this is Officer Weeden."

"Is something wrong with Sean?" Their teacher's voice was tense and higher than usual.

"Yes and no. We've kind of had a situation here this morning..."

"I hope it's nothing major," Miss Rogers whispered concerned.

"Sean's pretty shook up. Someone killed our dog and he found him on the back porch," Sean's dad said.

Miss Rogers gasped; her face went from concerned to horrified. "That's terrible."

"You have no idea. Whoever did this is one sick individual. They butchered our family pet and intentionally left him for us to find," Officer Weeden said.

"I'm so sorry, is there anything I can do?"

"Not that I can think of. We're going to keep Sean at home. He's not up to being around anyone today."

"That's understandable. Tell him I'm so sorry to hear about this and he's in my prayers," Miss Rogers said.

"I will, thanks," Sean's father said, ending the call.

Victoria shot a look of disbelief at Larry. His eyes were huge and round, staring at their teacher. He turned and took a long drink from his water bottle.

"Sorry for the interruption," Miss Rogers began, clueless she had been overheard. She went on to finish reviewing their outline and gave them her seal of approval to continue.

"Wow, you heard what he said, right?" Victoria asked when she moved on.

He nodded. "I guess Officer Weeden must have given the wrong guy a speeding ticket."

Miss Rogers went to Barry to see where he and Sean stood on their collaboration.

"We're going to do something on the circulatory system," Barry said, trying to be quiet, but Victoria overheard this conversation too.

"You two aren't as far as you need to be on this," Miss Rogers said, with a frown. "Where's your outline?"

"We don't have one. Sean's not easy to work with. He shoots down all my ideas. Thinks he knows everything," Barry complained almost in a whine.

"You're going to have to work it out, Barry. If he's inflexible then you need to be the one who compromises. Maybe then he'll be more willing to consider some of your concepts. That's all I can tell you," the teacher advised, placing her hand on his shoulder.

"That's not very fair," he grumbled. Recoiling from her touch he scooted away.

"There are a lot of things that aren't very fair in this world. If you can learn to adjust your actions in those situations, you'll stand a better chance of attaining the outcome you're looking for."

Barry didn't say anything else but the glower on his face spoke volumes. The rest of the morning the students worked quietly on their projects, except for Barry who couldn't move forward without his partner.

When Sean Weeden returned to class, his father came into the room with him. A mountain of a man dressed in blackish cargo pants: standard issue for the Evanston police. His open puffy jacket with the police patch and sergeant stripes revealed the well-equipped gear vest with a body camera in the middle. A radio microphone was clipped at the shoulder. His hair was buzzcut and he had the neck of a bodybuilder.

From where she sat, Victoria saw the gun strapped at his hip. Sean stood next to him while they talked with Miss Rogers. The boy's sullen demeanor bore witness to his recent trauma. He looked as if he might break down in tears at any moment. He had dark circles under his eyes.

"We're going to do everything we can to catch the creep who is doing this. We've added extra patrols and after the story in the paper, I'm sure we'll get some leads," Richard Weeden predicted.

"I hope so," Miss Rogers said.

Sean settled in his chair at the table next to Victoria. He looked so sad she felt sorry for him. She ripped a piece of paper from her notebook and wrote down her cell number, then handed it to him. "In case you want someone to talk to," she whispered.

"I don't want to talk about it, but thanks," he said, sliding her number into his pocket.

Barry and Sean finally settled on a circulatory system display for their project.

Victoria noticed Larry's attention wandering after a few minutes. "We talked about the moons on Saturday, about how many we should mention, remember?"

"Yeah, of course. Sorry. I'm dog-tired," he muttered, glancing in his brother's direction. He seemed more interested in the goings on between

Barry and Sean.

Sean had his arms crossed defiantly while Barry drew on a piece of paper. Miss Rogers spent most of her time with them that morning trying to get Sean to participate and speed along the process to get them caught up.

3
Twin Secrets

Except for a mishap involving a utility knife and plastic tubing which required stitches to Barry's palm, the work over the next few weeks went smoothly. Sean and Barry used triangle pieces of foam board to create supports so their display stood life-size.

"I have to admit, their project looks better than I expected it would," Victoria quietly confided to Larry.

"I guess, but it's still not good enough to win," Larry said watching as Barry attempted to pour goopy red liquid into the back of their foam-core, illustrated man.

"What did they use for that blood?" Victoria asked.

"Corn syrup, water and red paint. Apparently plain water ended up too thin," Larry answered with a sarcastic smile on his face.

"Here goes nothen," Barry said, flipping the switch to activate the pump.

Ever so slowly the simulated blood trickled into the tubing. Barry's face dropped in disappointment and annoyance. "I think we need to turn up the pressure on the pump."

"No. Just give it a minute to force the liquid into the tubes," Sean shot back angry as always.

"It's taking too long. I'm telling you we have to adjust the pump," Barry said.

"If you push it too hard, the tubing might not be able to handle it," Sean said, huffing.

Barry crossed his arms over his chest and gave Sean a look that screamed *my partner is an idiot.* After thirty seconds Barry mumbled under his breath, "This is bullshit." Then he stomped around to the back of the display and tinkered with the pump.

"Don't do it," Sean warned.

Coming back to the front, Barry smiled as the crimson fluid coursed through the plastic arteries. The rubber heart pulsed and made the rhythmic sound of a fast heartbeat. "There, what did I tell you?" he gloated, quite satisfied with himself.

Sean didn't respond. In disbelief he stared at the exhibit with his mouth pinched in a trembling straight line. All of the others students gave them a round of applause.

Without warning one end of the plastic pipeline ruptured from the board and began dancing around like a lose fire hose, spurting realistic looking blood everywhere. By the time Sean finally deactivated the hemorrhaging figure, he and Barry were splattered from face to foot with sticky red ooze.

Sean shouted furiously, "You wouldn't listen to me, would you? You're crazy, you know that? A stark-raving lunatic!"

"Oh no," Larry breathed, rushing toward his twin. A wild uncontrolled expression came over Barry's face. Larry placed his hand on his brother's chest, speaking softly, attempting to calm him.

Miss Rogers supplied a bucket of hot soapy water, a mop and sponges and aided in the cleanup effort. Larry went into the adjacent church kitchen to wash his brother's science disaster off his hands. Victoria slipped in behind him.

"That was kind of scary. Barry looked like he wanted to murder Sean," she said.

Larry scrubbed his flesh but the gore stain lingered. "Sometimes, if he's pushed too far, he loses it."

"When he gets that disturbing look on his face?" Victoria asked.

"Yeah. I can always tell when he's about to go off."

"I hope you don't ever lose it like Barry just did," she said.

"No, I told you we might be identical twins judging by our looks but our personalities and temperaments are very different," Larry assured her.

"Good, because I like you and—"

Before her next words left her mouth Larry spontaneously planted a quick warm kiss on her never been kissed before lips.

Taking a step back, her surprise and embarrassment multiplied when she noticed Barry in the doorway. Barry said, "Miss Rogers called Mom to pick us up early so I don't have to sit in this mess for the rest of the day."

"I'll be right there," Larry said impatiently.

As soon as Barry left the room, Victoria faced Larry. "Why did you do that?" Her stiff body language and angry tone made it clear he'd committed a major breach of etiquette.

"Because you're pretty and I like you too. I thought—"

"Look, Larry, our friendship is important to me. But getting romantically involved could only ruin everything."

"I did it on impulse. I won't do it again. I promise."

Victoria breathed a heavy sigh, stared into his lucid crystal blue eyes and saw pain and fear. Remorse hit her like a brick to the heart. "I'm sorry, I'm overreacting."

Larry frowned but didn't say anything.

Victoria considered telling her mother about Larry's overture but decided against it. She didn't want to give Lillian a reason to be concerned.

March arrived as a late season blizzard immobilized the Chicago-land area. With snow falling an inch and hour for three days, even the city, efficient in snow removal, struggled to clear the main roads.

Plowing side streets wasn't on the Public Works priority list. The wind off Lake Michigan whipped wildly, creating massive snow drifts which blocked roads and buried cars. Classes were cancelled for the whole week.

Most teenagers would have been ecstatic about a snow day, Victoria was bummed out. She and Larry were accomplishing the list of time sensitive goals they set for themselves and she worried this setback might cause them to fall behind. The only bright spot in the bizarre weather was that Paige, after a huge argument with Aunt Lisa, spent the night. Now, like everyone else in the vicinity of Lake Michigan, she wouldn't be going anywhere. The snow kept falling.

Paige paced the floor of Victoria's bedroom trying to think of something to relieve her boredom. Victoria stationed herself in front of her computer attempting to contact Larry. Paige's cell chimed alerting her to an undoubtedly urgent text from one of her emotionally crippled friends.

Victoria shook her head as she watched her cousin's fingers fly across the screen as if her response was critical to rescuing the entire world from certain obliteration. How was it the girl texted with the skill of a person who wrote the texting dictionary, but couldn't navigate her way out of a paper bag when it came to English class?

Paige slipped her phone into the back pocket of her jeans and updated Victoria on the latest gossip. "Katie's Busted! I told her to put on her big girl panties and deal with it."

"What did she do?" Victoria asked.

"Her mom found her stash of weed and she's threatened to take her phone away."

"You're not smoking that stuff, are you? You know it's a gateway drug, right?" Victoria's voice went up an octave higher.

"I've tried it, from my mom's stash. I don't see what the big deal is. It made me want to eat junk food and watch Sponge Bob." Paige shrugged.

"Aunt Lisa's smoking pot, now?" Victoria asked, aghast.

"She thinks I don't know about it. She's picked up a lot of bad habits since Dad divorced her and she started hanging out in the bars. Whatever. I'm not going to gateway into crack or anything," Paige said.

"You'd better not," Victoria warned. She knew her mother was concerned about Lisa's recent behavior. It didn't help that Paige's father remarried a much younger woman and they'd just had a baby together. It was as if Lisa was trying to recapture her youth. The negative result was that she was acting more like a teenager than Paige was.

"I know! Let's paint our toenails," Paige suggested, changing the subject.

Ordinarily, Victoria considered that a monumental waste of time. However, since occupying Paige took as much work as trying to entertain a sugared-up four-year-old, she agreed if Paige did the painting. Whenever Paige had talked her into this in the past, Victoria's talent resulted in a polish job which included the knuckles of her toes.

Happy, Paige grabbed her cosmetic bag and took a spot on the bed. Victoria swung her computer chair around and took off her slippers and warm fuzzy socks, placing her feet in her cousin's lap.

"Seriously, Vicky, have you ever heard the term cuticle care?" Paige asked.

While her cousin worked her magic on Victoria's neglected toenails, she rambled on about the words of her favorite song and how they accurately described what she felt about her parents' divorce and her identity as a misunderstood teenager.

As Paige opened the cap of a florescent pink polish, Larry popped up on Victoria's computer. "Hey, I didn't want you to think I'm avoiding you, but I can't get on right now. I have to shovel snow, imagine that."

"You and the rest of the Midwest. Do you think you can get on later?"

Paige stepped up behind her; the web cam now included her image in the transmission. "Hi, I'm Paige, Vicky's cousin," she said.

"Hi, Paige," Larry greeted. "What are you doing?"

"We're painting our toenails," Paige said.

"Really? I would not have guessed that type of bedazzling from you, Vicky." He said her nickname sarcastically, minus any humor. "I've got to go but I'll try to get on later. You enjoy your pedicure." Larry's expression looked condescending.

"That's not my name," she said gently to not make whatever was bothering him worse. "Only my cousin calls me that, and I get her back for it. Listen, I'll be here, it's not like I'm going anywhere," Victoria said, rolling her eyes as he tapped the disconnect, cutting her off. That struck her as odd.

"He's cute. I'd totally be hitting on him if I were you," Paige advised.

"He kissed me last week," Victoria confided. Still bothered by his shortness.

"What? No! For real?" Paige asked. Her mouth dropped open.

"Yep, right out of the blue," Victoria confirmed. She swung toward the bed and rested her feet back in her cousin's lap.

"You liked it, didn't you?"

Victoria shrugged and tilted her head in confirmation.

"Oh, thank God, there's hope for you after all," her cousin applauded. "Tell me all about him!"

"Nothing to tell. We're working on a science project together."

"So, does this mean he's your boyfriend?" Paige asked sing-songy.

"No. I don't want to talk about it. Don't make me regret telling you," Victoria cautioned ending the teasing.

Paige was soaking in a bubble bath when Larry came back online after dinner. His first words were, "You're not still mad at me about that stupid kiss, are you?"

"Absolutely not," Victoria reassured him. "It's forgotten."

"Good. Like you said, you overreacted." He knit his eyebrows making him look angry.

Never experiencing antagonism on Larry's part, this flustered her. *Does he have a temper too, like Barry?* "Let's use our time wisely and not rehash things we don't need to."

"Fine," he said sharply, not looking into the camera. Moving on, they discussed polishing the graphics for the video.

"Okay, so this is what I've been working on," Larry said. He brought up a 3-D cartoon narrator. Using his mouse, Larry navigated the Star-Wars-like drone, sending it flying through the solar system as a self-contained spaceship. "Let me introduce you to Copernicus."

"He's so cute! And kid friendly," Victoria praise, applauding.

"Watch this." Larry tapped a few more keys, giving a voice to his cosmos buddy, he said, "Welcome to your fun filled tour of our solar system!" A red light lit up where the mouth would be in time with his words.

The wrap-up was to make, then to test, the voice/video syncing "I think you should be the one to do the narration," Victoria said.

"Aw no, I don't want to. You should do it."

"Why? The real Copernicus was male."

"I don't like the sound of my voice," Larry admitted.

"Probably because you hear it in stereo from Barry," she said.

"If it's female, then we're affirming girls can grow up to be scientists and space travelers. We'd be promoting that whole Girl Power thing."

"A valid point. Fine, I'll do it," Victoria surrendered.

Paige walked over to watch until her attention span gave out, which wasn't very long. Her critique that she expected to see this kind of programing on PBS could have been taken as a compliment. Hard to tell, coming from Paige.

Victoria read sections of their script while Larry timed her with a stopwatch. Then he would slow down or speed up the video as needed. When they got to the part about Jupiter, Larry seemed distracted.

"Are you paying attention?" Victoria stopped reading.

"I am, keep reading. Start over at 'The fifth planet from the Sun.'" He looked down, concentration creased lines on his forehead.

"What are you doing?" she asked.

"I'll show you in a minute. Keep reading."

Victoria sighed and went back to the script. After completing a couple more sections Larry asked, "Are you ready for this?"

"Sure." Victoria rested her head in her hand.

Larry held up a matchstick sculpture of a spider. "Ta Da!" he proclaimed.

His creation was sort of cute.

"That's cool," she complimented.

Larry's smile grew broad. Even in the dimness of the computer camera in his basement room she saw him blush. "Do you know, they estimate there are quadrillion spiders on our planet? Mathematically it's like 3 million spiders for every human! And there's always one within six feet of you."

"I don't find that to be comforting." She shuddered.

"Most spiders have eight eyes, so they have a 360 view of what's around them. The odds are, one is watching you right now!"

"If I didn't have a fear of spiders before, I do now. You're creeping me out." She chuckled uncomfortably, looking around for eight legged, eight eyed creatures.

To her surprise, Larry contributed hours of his time that snow day and Victoria took advantage of every second. Their two minds produced a great collaboration. Late that night, long after Paige snuggled down in bed with the pillow over her head, just when Victoria and Larry were about to sign off, the shrill reverberations of a woman's voice yelling came through Victoria's speakers. "You little bastard, who the fuck do you think you are?"

"Is that your mother? Are you in trouble?" Victoria asked in a panic.

"No. I've gotta go!" Larry answered, vanishing in a flash. Stunned, Victoria climbed into bed next to Paige. She lay there, staring at the ceiling. Her brain imagining what might be happening at the Devlin house.

She knew the make-up of people who were abusive from textbooks. The foreign concept of a mother being cruel to her child didn't register with her own experience.

As far back as she could recall, her mother had never even raised her voice at her, let alone called her a curse word. The very idea Larry's mother would say that crawled up Victoria's spine.

Struggling with the question of responsibility she debated waking her parents, telling them about the yelling. Wanting to hide, she sunk deeper under the covers.

Larry hadn't asked for help. Did it matter who Mrs. Devlin was yelling at? Didn't both boys deserve protection?

Victoria agonized terribly over the scenario of her parents calling the police; she might be breaking some code of trust with Larry. She reminded herself if he wanted her help, he could've asked for it, he still could.

If he had, everything might have turned out very different for the Devlin twins.

4

FIRE !

The jingle of her cell phone at 4:00 in the morning woke Victoria. *Who'd call now?* She'd shared her phone number with several classmates but the only people who actually called were her parents and Paige. "Hello?" she answered, more asleep than awake.

"Victoria, it's Sean, Sean Weeden. The Devlin twins' house is on fire!"

"Sean? What are you talking about?" Victoria asked incoherently.

"Larry Devlin's house is on fire; my dad responded to it. I was sure you'd want me to call you," he said.

Entirely awake now, Victoria raced to her bedroom window. The sirens' distant blare and an eerie orange glow in the sky confirmed it. Victoria's phone slipped from her fingers and hit the floor. Without another thought she stepped into her slippers and plush bathrobe. Rushing down the hall, she banged on her parent's bedroom door, screaming, "Larry's house is on fire!"

Victoria flew down the stairs and out the front door. Running down the snow-drifted street she couldn't feel the stinging cold on her legs, her only thought was Larry. Her breath came out in a fog. She didn't even realize it wasn't snowing anymore.

Rounding the corner, two fire trucks with lights swirling dominated the scene. The street in front of the Devlin house had been blocked off with barriers.

Victoria pushed her way through the mob of curious onlookers to get as close as possible. She shimmied between people and ducked and weaved until she made it to the front of the crowd. A wooden barricade halted her.

Flames shot from the roof of the fully engulfed house. The windows on the second floor shattered from the intense heat. Black streaks stained the grey stones from the heat and the smoke. A team of firefighters were dowsing the house with water hoses.

Officer Weeden vigorously performed CPR on one of the twins on the front lawn. Startled, Victoria jolted when Sean suddenly appeared next to her.

"Thanks for calling me," she acknowledged absently.

"No problem. My dad lives his life tuned into the scanners," Sean said.

"Who's your dad working on?" she asked. Standing on her tiptoes, Victoria tried to get a better look.

"It's only been a few minutes; I'm not sure which twin that is." Dressed for the slopes, Sean looked ready to go cross-country skiing.

Just then, a fireman rushed into view behind a staggering second twin. The boy, alive and breathing, covered in soot, coughed until he gagged. His blonde hair looked black. He shivered severely, water droplets freezing on his skin. An ambulance arrived and the paramedics took over for Sargent Weeden.

Sean's father draped a blanket around the other twin who looked shellshocked but was still standing on his own two bare feet.

The warmth of a coat enveloped Victoria. She glanced up to see her father. He wrapped her in one of his own coats, fitting it over her bathrobe. He put a knit cap on her head and tugged it down over her ears.

"You're cold as ice," James Lawrence said. He took hold of his daughter's legs one at a time and removed her slippers, then pulled her snow boots on. He wrapped his arms around her and pulled her close to warm her up.

Even from a distance, Victoria could see the boy on the ground, covered in blood. Like a replay of Barry's failed science attempt, only this time it was real. The emergency responders swiftly moved him onto a gurney and loaded him into an ambulance which sped off with lights flashing and siren blaring

"Larry!" Victoria called. She wanted to be sure it was him. Was he wearing the same shirt she'd seen him in only hours before when they worked on the computer together? She tried to remember but couldn't. She wished she'd paid closer attention. Maybe it wasn't Larry. The boy didn't look up or give any response.

James whispered in his daughter's ear, "Honey, he can't hear you. The water from the fire hoses is too loud."

"He's in shock," Victoria surmised.

Suddenly, Larry collapsed on his knees and sobbed. Sargent Weeden put his arm around the boy, talking to him reassuringly. At the same time a second ambulance arrived whining and blinking in secession with the rest of the emergency vehicles. The EMTs blocked their view of Larry.

Victoria turned to Sean. "Have you seen their mother yet?"

"Not since I've been here. They could've got her out first."

"I hope so," Victoria and her father said in unison.

Shivering, she felt more numb than cold. The ambulance revved into motion and sped away.

"Sweetheart, you're shaking. There's nothing you can do here, let me take you home," her father said compassionately.

Victoria nodded. They walked a few steps away from the spectators, when her father stopped and simply picked her up in the cradle of his arms. He carried her home.

Lillian, in a long winter coat, paced the front porch. She came running when she saw them. "I've put the kettle on for tea, or I could make some hot chocolate," Lillian said desperately.

"Hot toddies would be better. I'm going to take her to our bed and put the electric blanket on low. We need to warm her up slowly," James said.

"I'm fine," Victoria protested.

"Don't even, little girl," Lillian placed a mothering hand on her head.

"Okay, Mom," she said, suddenly too cold and too tired to object.

Victoria woke in the morning snuggled warmly in the sweet-smelling sheets of her parents' bed. Her mother slept next to her. Her father snored softly, covered with a quilt, in the wingback chair. She loved them so much it brought tears to her eyes to see how unselfishly they cared for her. After all their fussing to warm her up, she slept dreamlessly in the safety of their love.

Now, remembering the horror of the fire and the images of her classmates in distress, she began to sob.

Little did she know, the Devlin twins and the events of the last six hours would cause her nightmares for years to come.

Part 2

Malice & Forethought

5

Foster "Care"

Had the experts known the whole truth, they would have said Larry and Barry Devlin didn't stand much of a chance after their father died when they were four years old. The final report of his death stated a spark igniting a gas can caused that deadly explosion in the garage. Fire officials deemed it a freak accident.

To the rest of the world, Mr. Devlin's untimely end was just one of those tragic things that happen sometimes. The twins were small, but they knew differently. They knew their mother made him go away. They grew up with the knowledge she could make them go away too, if she wanted.

If the medical community had evaluated their mother, she would have been diagnosed as a psychopath incapable of feeling empathy toward anyone, including her own flesh and blood. They would have recognized the danger she posed to herself and her boys.

If the neighbors had called the authorities to alert them to possible child abuse when they'd heard screaming and yelling coming from the Devlin house, maybe someone would have done something about the situation.

If someone, anyone, had intervened on their behalf, maybe things wouldn't have turned out so dreadful for the boys. But no one did and after the house fire, the Devlins and all the terrible things that happened within their home became the topic of gossip and speculation.

The coroner's autopsy of Mrs. Devlin confirmed what Sargent Weeden already knew; she didn't die as a result of the fire or smoke inhalation. The twenty-seven stab wounds Barry inflicted ended her life. No doubt remained: Barry had been the one who committed the murder. When the firefighters rescued him from the burning building, his clothes were covered with her blood.

Larry corroborated their theory during hours of interrogation in a claustrophobic interview room. Sean's father took Larry to the Evanston police station as soon as the doctors released the boy.

"They got into an argument," Larry said, picking at bandages on his arm. Aside from a few minor cuts and scrapes he'd received when he'd struggled to crawl to safety, Larry was fine and clear-headed enough to give them a detailed statement.

"What caused the argument?" Sargent Weeden asked. Leaning against the wall, he crossed his arms in front of his chest.

"I don't know. I was in my bedroom. It doesn't matter what they fought about. Mom and Barry argued all the time," the boy said.

"You didn't argue with her?" Officer Weeden felt he needed to probe a bit deeper, something seemed off.

Larry shook his head. "I just tried to stay out of her way when she got into one of her moods. I learned a long time ago fighting with her wasn't worth it."

"What do you mean?" a second officer asked.

"When she'd lose her temper she'd grab the first thing she found and start beating us with it. I stayed out of her way and didn't talk back. But Barry, well, he insisted on antagonizing her." The boy focused on a smudge on the table.

"So what was different about the other night?" Detective Jeffers chimed in. A seasoned detective, his skills at interrogation meant he sat in on most of the conversations that took place in this room.

"I don't know. I guess Barry just lost it. He went off on her. I heard them yelling and screaming, that wasn't anything new. They did it all the time. I didn't go upstairs until I smelled smoke."

Sargent Weeden paced the small interview room. He uncrossed his arms and turned back to Larry. "See, I have a problem with the idea Barry just went off on your mother. I think he planned the attack when he went after her with the eight-inch knife. Investigators were able to sift through the ashes of your house, they discovered jars containing internal organs once belonging to dogs in your brother's basement bedroom."

"My father did experiments for his inventions; squirrels, monkeys, that's what you found." The boy wiped some sweat from his forehead.

"No. these specimens were fresh kills," Detective Jeffers said.

"I swear, I don't know anything about jars with animal organs." The look of shock on Larry's face tugged at the officers, their hardened expressions softening with reluctant pity.

"We aren't accusing you of anything, son," Detective Miller assured him, taking his glasses off and rubbing his eyes. "We're telling you he practiced killing on the animals in the neighborhood with the intention of murdering your mother once he knew how to do it effectively. The forensic team has already closed the case on the pet mutilations in the area." They went over more things then Larry suddenly asked about his brother.

"Barry's in bad shape. The doctors aren't holding out much hope he's going to make it," Officer Weeden told him in a sympathetic tone.

Tears streamed down the boy's face. "I never even saw her. When I came up from my room the whole house was in flames. I tried to find them." He put his hands over his face.

"I know you did." The officers figured they'd never find out exactly what happened. Basically Barry's plan backfired, trapped by the flames he'd set to destroy the evidence of his crime, Barry almost died.

The doctors determined he'd suffered significant brain damage from blunt force trauma and lack of oxygen, which meant he would never be competent to stand trial if he even survived. Fortunately, Larry could fill in some of the blanks for the investigators. Because Barry's condition made it unlikely they'd even question him, they built their case on the facts which made sense.

For the next few hours they talked. Larry described the extensive abuse Barry had suffered at the hands of their mother. The police had their motive for the murder. Yet, Larry's claim that she took her frustrations out mainly on Barry didn't ring true with Sargent Weeden. With no way to prove otherwise, he stayed silent.

Larry was too embarrassed to tell the cops the sexual component to Mrs. Devlin's transgressions against her sons. Since he and his brother were the only living souls who knew this, he saw no benefit in broadcasting it to the world.

Divulging the severity of her beatings and the general cruelty already had the lawmen looking at him in a way that made him feel like a freak. The rest of the story, to his young mind, would only make it worse.

When the interview ended, Larry went to a special section of a youth services center. Meanwhile, in Evanston Hospital, hooked up to machines breathing for him, Barry fought for his life.

Sitting at a table in the community room, Larry picked at the peeling paint on the wall next to him. The carpet reeked of urine. Dark spots on the ceiling indicated a roof long overdue for repair.

He looked around at the twenty other boys who were in limbo while authorities tried to find next of kin or extended family who were willing to take them in. *What tragedy caused the separation from their parents? There were no girls. They must keep them someplace else,* he thought.

The TV blasted reruns of Full House. *Happy family, what a load of crap.* A boy came and sat down across the table. "I'm Nick," he turned to a teenager next to him.

"Todd," the other bored kid responded.

"How long have you been here?" Nick asked.

Larry didn't respond. He didn't intend to make any friends in this shithole.

"Five days, they're looking for my old man," Todd said.

Five days? Larry felt the air go out of his chest along with any hope he'd been hanging on to. Some kids challenged each other on the worn-out ping pong table. Others flipped the pages of dog-eared paperback novels Larry considered below his standards. *How long will I be here?*

At night he listened to the sniffling of the children around him as he lay on an uncomfortable cot. He didn't cry. He built an impenetrable wall around himself. He didn't let anyone in.

Yet, when he closed his eyes, he saw the fire, licking the ceiling like a dragon's tongue. Barry, clinging to their mother, sobbing, covered in her blood. His mother's face, an expression of terror, a knife sticking out of her chest. The gurgling noises her blood-filled throat made as she pleaded for mercy.

He dreamed of removing her topaz ring and putting it in his pocket. The one with the pointy setting that had cut him when she punched him during one of many tirades. He bolted upright when the overhead beam came down and hit his mother and Barry. In a cold sweat, he lay back down. Breathing deeply he tried to reclaim a grip on reality. *This was not supposed to happen. It's wrong, it's all wrong.*

On his third morning in the DCF facility, a custodian came in and called his name. He led the boy down the hall to a small office where a social worker put out her hand to shake his. He complied.

"I'm Yolanda Murphy. I'm assigned to your case." Dressed in an attractive suit, the woman motioned for him to take a seat. Her fake smile was obvious. "Let me first say I'm so sorry for your loss."

"How's Barry?"

"It's been touch and go. I won't lie to you. He's stabilized now and the doctors are hopeful," she answered.

"When can I see my brother?"

"We'll see. Right now, with the burns he suffered, infections are a concern and the doctors want to limit visitors. On a different subject, the house is a total loss. Your mother didn't carry any kind of insurance," she said.

Larry knew where this was going.

"I bet she didn't have life insurance either."

Mrs. Murphy, shook her head. "We've found nothing. Not even bank accounts."

"Mom didn't trust the banks. Any money she did have she locked in a closet in her bedroom," Larry said. *Paranoid, crazy bitch. If only I'd thought to grab it before the fire. Everything happened so fast.*

"I'm sorry, honey. The bank is foreclosing on the property." She looked him in the eyes with true empathy. "You told the investigators you don't know any family who can take you in—"

"No. Other than Barry, there's no one," he interrupted, hostilely.

"Well, there is positive news, I've found you a lovely family you'll be staying with. I'm working out the details and you'll be with your new foster family in a few days," she said, overly cheerful.

"What about my friends from school? Couldn't I stay with them for a while?" Larry clutched the topaz ring in his pocket.

"Sorry, by law, I have to follow certain procedures..." She went on and on. Treating him like a complete idiot.

He understood what she said: he was screwed.

6

Rat Trap

A week after they buried Mrs. Devlin, the overworked Evanston/Skokie Metropolitan Department of Children and Family Services determined the twins indeed had no family. Fourteen-year-old Larry Devlin went into foster care, Barry remained in Evanston Hospital, unconscious and attached to a respirator.

Mr. and Mrs. Kirkland, who'd taken Larry in, cared for seven other children from varying backgrounds. Located in a rundown neighborhood in Chicago, the house needed a coat of paint. Old and dilapidated, the floors slanted and the stairs groaned under Larry's feet. The place gave off the funk of old cheese.

The four girls shared a small pink bedroom equipped with two sets of bunkbeds. The woman escorted Larry to a blue bedroom with the same set up. More noticeable than the rest of the house, the bedroom reeked like a locker room.

Mrs. Kirkland pointed to the bottom bunk on the right side of the room. "This will be your bed," she explained, through narrow lips.

A thin woman, she looked under nourished. With dark hair striped by kinky white strands which stuck out at weird angles she reminded Larry of a witch. "Dinner is in an hour. I'll let you get settled in." She left him alone.

Larry dropped his backpack on the stained bedspread.

Settle in? He only owned three sets of clothes: used crap given to him by his social worker. He looked around the room and gave a sigh of disgust. Scarcely two feet of floor made up the space between the beds. It was absolutely claustrophobic. Although Larry couldn't honestly say he mourned their mother, the downside was this diminished life.

When his foster parents informed him he would be attending public school, the loss of his homeschool group and his cherished science fair project was a gut punch.

There was only one small positive thing. Starting over where none of the kids knew about his past deprived them of the ammunition to judge him. The realization of being completely alone in the world terrified him. His only option: survival mode.

The high school they sent him to was a joke. He'd already learned what they were teaching years ago. The teachers were so stressed all they focused on was making it through each day. Larry flat out refused to do remedial work. Instead, he checked books out of the school library and read about things he found interesting.

The way the other students looked at him unnerved Larry. He'd never experienced cultural and racial diversity and felt threatened as he walked the halls between classes. Keeping his head down and his mouth shut he hoped would shield him from the boys he suspected ran with gangs.

The switchblade pocketknife he'd stolen from one of the boys at the youth service center came in handy the second week when a group of tough looking kids crowded around him at his locker.

The tallest hulking kid, the one Larry assumed led the others, wore a red T-shirt under a black hoodie. His oversized jeans rode low on his hips. He had letter tattoos on his knuckles and an intricate barbed wire design inked on his neck.

"What's your story, you some kinda ass kisser?" their leader said in a menacing hiss. The other youth around him chuckled harassingly.

Larry's heart raced with a flush of adrenaline. He glared at his aggressor, then at the gang surrounding him. They weren't backing down. In one swift motion, he whipped out the knife, popped it open and tapped it on Black Hoodie's chest.

"Far from it," Larry snarled, the heat of rage crawled up his neck. "I know exactly where to stick this that will cause you to bleed out before you even hit the floor."

The hooded kid took a step back, drawing open his sweatshirt barely enough to reveal a gun in his waistband. "Better be watching your back, fool." Then he slapped his palm loudly on the adjacent locker, it echoed like a gun shot. Laughing, he and his entourage sauntered down the hallway as if nothing had happened.

Shaking, Larry let out a slow long sigh and warily returned the knife to his pocket. It didn't matter that the day was only half over. He'd had enough of this place. He grabbed his coat and backpack and headed outside. Walking with purpose, no one stopped him.

His first month in foster care passed so slowly it might as well have been a life sentence. Larry marginally tolerated the other foster children in the house and only spoke when it was essential. The do-gooder foster parents irritated him to the point he thought he might develop hives. The life he planned for himself hadn't included any of this shit.

Unbeknownst to his foster family, on the day of the science competition, he skipped school and rode several CTA buses to the McCormick Place Convention Center.

A misty rain fell from dense gray clouds. Skyscrapers disappeared into the thick fog. Larry's thoughts turned to Victoria. Their project should place. How would it feel to see her again? He shifted nervously in his seat.

He kept a stealthy profile to avoid contact with his former classmates. His overwhelming need to see how the projects scored won out over caution.

From across the exhibit hall, he saw her!

With a jolt to the heart he willed her not to look in his direction. She didn't. Dolled up in a dress with a flowing skirt which fit in all the right places, she smiled sweetly at the exhibit goers stopping at her table. The white with blue flowered pattern looked divine on her. She wore her dark brown hair pulled back at the sides, shining under the industrial lighting. She'd grown prettier than he remembered.

When the contestants were ushered into the ballroom for the awards ceremony, he approached the table. It pissed him off the solar system project was presented by Sean Weeden and Victoria Lawrence. They'd scrapped the circulatory system project entirely and taken credit for all his work.

He could only imagine how Sean must have wrangled his way into pairing up with Victoria. His blood boiled with hatred while he listened to Sean's voice narrate their adorable droid's imaginary trip through the solar system. In the end though, he smiled with smug satisfaction to see they'd only received an honorable mention.

As Larry descended the stairs to an exit door, the unmistakable nasal pitch of Sean Weeden's voice stopped him cold. Peeking around the corner, he observed Victoria and Sean standing by a pillar in the lobby. "It's too bad we didn't win," Sean said, as if he'd contributed half the work.

"It's all right. It's not the end of the world," Victoria consoled him.

"I see what you did there – solar system – end of the world," Sean said, snorting a laugh. Victoria crossed her arms and swayed. She gave Sean her sensational one dimpled smile.

Is she blushing? Is she flirting with Sean the weasel?

"What took you guys so long?" Victoria called to a handsome couple coming into view. They were holding hands. Larry recognized Victoria's mother from the times he'd seen them together at school. Behind them were Sean's parents. Larry slipped further into the shadows. He couldn't be seen by Officer Weeden.

"Who's up for Johnny Rockets?" Mr. Lawrence suggested.

"I'd rather go to Wienner and Still Champion. It's closer to home," Victoria countered.

"Sounds good to me; it's been a long day," Sean agreed.

Larry watched as his former classmates and their two sets of parents casually made their way toward the parking lot, talking and laughing as if everything was fine.

On the bus back to his foster house, the streetlights of the city came on. Chicagoans squeezed on at every stop. It smelled like gas fumes and wet hair. Larry ignored a woman whose expression implored him to give up his seat.

He seethed with anger.

"It's not the end of the world," Victoria's words bounced off the walls in his brain in an unstoppable echo. Not for her it wasn't, or Sean. Life had gone on for everyone as if the Devlin twins had never existed. No one cared. No one even seemed to remember. He shook with the thought that they'd been forgotten so fast.

Victoria's dismissal hurt him the most. Larry cared about her. Now she had buddied up with Sean Weasel, of all the crappy people! Condemned to oblivion, nothing more than a faded bad memory to the girl who'd acted like she cared, that's what he got. She'd put on one hell of a show. He'd actually believed her capable of enormous empathy. Victoria was right; involvement with her would only ruin everything. She had definitely been Larry's undoing.

He arrived at the foster home right as the residents were sitting down to dinner. At the moment, he couldn't look at them with anything less than loathing; all seven of the damaged, dysfunctional pseudo siblings made him sick. They sat around the table clamoring for food like greedy little beggars.

"Where have you been young man?" Mrs. Kirkland scolded.

"I had something to do," Larry answered, annoyed by the shrillness in her voice, she reminded him of his mother.

"What did you have to do that was more important than going to school, young man?" his foster mother kept up the badgering.

"Just something," he shot back.

"Now you listen here. We don't tolerate disrespectful attitudes in this house. I asked you a question and I expect a straight answer," she said in an authoritarian tone.

"None of your business!" he barked with the viciousness of a fighting Pitbull.

"Enough!" Mr. Kirkland intervened, pounding his fist on the table.

This pale, fuck of a man goes off to some meaningless office job every day. Then sits in front of the TV at night, yelling at everyone to keep down the noise so he can hear his stupid shows. I hate him.

Larry glared at his foster father. His hands clinched in fists ready to attack.

"Just for that, you can march yourself right up those stairs and go to bed without dinner. While you're up there, you need to think about your actions and how to respond differently in the future," Mr. Kirkland said.

Larry bolted from the room, taking the stairs two at a time, stomping with the intention to piss them off even more. He slammed the door of the little bedroom. He paced the floor; his heart rate drummed dangerously in his chest. He hated this place.

Shoving his hand under his mattress, he located wooden matchsticks he'd pilfered from Mrs. Kirkland's pantry the other day. Sitting on the bed, he carefully wound the matchsticks together with dental floss until he'd constructed a menacing looking cobra.

He thought about fire; its life-giving properties; its ability to purify. He flashed back to crawling on the floor, flames rolling across the ceiling and walls with a life of their own, devouring everything. He remembered how panic seized him as toxic smoke threatened to trap him in a hellish inferno.

He wondered what would happen if he struck a match and set his fancy little snake on fire.

Larry imagined how fast this rat trap of a house would go up in a blaze of orange.

7 Freedom

"Yolanda Murphy called earlier today," Mrs. Kirkland informed Larry with faux sympathy in her tone. "Your brother regained consciousness this morning and the doctors are hopeful they will be able to take him off the respirator so he can breathe on his own."

"I want to see him," Larry demanded without missing a beat.

"We'll see. I'll talk to Mrs. Murphy and see what she thinks," Mrs. Kirkland said.

A few days later, Mrs. Kirkland drove Larry to visit Barry. It surprised him to find Mrs. Murphy, parked in a chair outside his brother's room, scribbling notes on a form in an open file folder.

"Hi, Larry, it's good to see you again. How are things going?" she asked cheerfully as if her life consisted of nothing but flowers, sunshine and rainbows.

What a fake. "Splendidly peachy," Larry answered, sarcasm dripped heavy mixed with his bad attitude.

Yolanda Murphy's smile hardened into a straight firm line. "Before you go in, I need to talk to you about Barry."

Larry raised his eyebrows and offered an open-palmed gesture, which with his glare indicated: *So. Get on with it, bitch.*

She frowned but ignored the teen attitude. "Barry's not going to look like he used to. I want to warn you so it's not too much of a shock for you. The brain damage he suffered is causing seizures and is disrupting his motor functions. He may not even know who you are."

"Fine, can I see my brother now?" Larry asked impatiently.

Obviously disappointed he rebuffed her kindness; she ushered him into the hospital room and stood by the door as Larry approached the bed.

"Hi," Larry greeted his twin. Barry's blue eyes were unfocused and slightly crossed. The right side of his face drooped causing his mouth to sag as drool trickled a path to his chin. The fire singed off his eyebrows and patches of hair from his head, leaving disgusting burns in its place.

One of his arms bent in an unnatural pose and his fist balled tight, like a palsy patient. They no longer looked like twins.

Larry leaned in close to his side. "Hey, buddy, remember me?"

Barry's attention turned to the sound. With the eyes of a newborn lacking understanding, he curiously stared at Larry.

No recognition.

"He can't speak; he may never be able to."

"So, is he going to spend the rest of his life in a wheelchair, drooling, staring off into space?" Larry asked.

"He'll be moved to Bellview in a few days. They'll take marvelous care of him. He'll get physical therapy and who knows, he might exceed expectations. It's ultimately up to him from here on out," the social worker said.

"It would have been better if he died," Larry hissed, tears welling up in his eyes. He brushed past Mrs. Murphy and almost knocked Mrs. Kirkland over in the hallway in his effort to flee. For the first time both women witnessed a rare emotional reaction from the boy. As he turned the corner and punched the down button for the elevator, he heard Mrs. Kirkland say, "We're trying with him but I don't know?"

"He's been through a terrible trauma. Be patient. He just needs some time to adjust," Yolanda Murphy encouraged.

In the following months, Larry Devlin withdrew into himself even more. The loneliness and sense of abandonment chafed inside him like sand on sunburn. Convinced detachment would make life bearable, he formed a layer of hardness around his heart. He didn't need anyone.

Yet, in the back of his mind, Victoria Lawrence haunted him. He remembered every detail of how she looked, down to the dimple she got in her cheek when she found something amusing but wasn't about to let you know. And her eyes. Dark, intelligent, knowing eyes; he'd never forget those. He could almost smell her. Then he would scold himself, *Be careful, Larry, you're about to open up and someone will for sure take advantage.*

He despised Mr. & Mrs. Kirkland and their prayers at dinnertime, their condescending looks and their efforts to straighten him out. The gaggle of screwballs the couple fostered got on his last nerve. At least his twin brother always knew when to give him space. This bunch reminded him of pesky little gnats he'd just as soon squish than put up with.

In early September, the disappointing new school year already underway, he tiptoed to the kitchen for a late-night snack.

He didn't have a clue how Mrs. Kirkland really felt about him. He was about to be enlightened. Larry heard her talking on the phone.

"I know… I understand that, Yolanda, but he's clearly not fitting in here."

Standing in the shadows in the darkened dining room, he watched her go to the pantry for matches. Like everything else in the house, the ancient gas stove had a worn-out starter that needed to be lit manually. She ignited the burner and put the tea kettle on. She shuffled out of view again but was still within earshot.

"He's got some deep-seated issues and we can't seem to get through to him... Okay, for instance, he steals things... Yes, but I'm worried about the other children. He refuses to do schoolwork and contributes nothing to the chores around the house." She stepped up to the counter, placed a mug next to the stove, opened the cupboard and took down a tea bag.

Larry resented her telling Mrs. Murphy he stole. She lied. He'd only taken some matchsticks. The other missing things must have been taken by one of the other kleptomaniacs in the house.

"I assure you; I've been patient with him..." She wandered out of view again. "He hates it here. And let me tell you, if looks could kill, we'd all be six feet under." She broke off talking to listen. "Yolonda, I think he's dangerous. I don't want him in my house anymore." She paused again. "Months? Are you serious? ... Well, see what you can do. Okay, thanks."

Larry snuck back upstairs forgetting the snack. He fumed in anger and hurt.

Four months later, Mrs. Murphy arrived and helped him pack his meager belongings into a backpack. She explained the arrangements to move him to the home of a benevolent couple who were looking forward to having him.

While the women were distracted in a conversation, Larry snuck into the pantry and stole the remaining supply of wooden matches. *Take that, bitches.*

Fifteen minutes later, having lived there for almost a year, he was gone from their lives. Just another memory for them, he'd soon be forgotten.

The next foster home was worse than the last.

Mr. & Mrs. Bradford looked after nine little bastards and this couple really didn't give a shit. It didn't take Larry long to figure out free money from the state inspired this couple to take in the hardest-cases.

They slept four and five to a room, in beds that weren't fit for a dog. The food was deplorable and inadequate.

Hungry all the time, he started stealing in earnest then. On his way home from school, he'd look for unlocked cars. People were predictable; they left their loose change in the ash trays and in the cubbies of their consoles.

Then he'd hit the local food mart, carefully lifting lunchmeat packages or peanut butter, whatever appealed to him. He never drew attention to himself because with the change he'd pilfered, he always bought something, like a loaf of bread to go with the peanut butter in his pocket. He'd hide his bounty in the dingy basement at the foster home and sneak away when it was safe to eat like a rat in the dark. But his belly was full now. Plus he enjoyed the rush of getting away with it.

He lasted seven months in the Bradford home until the couple got a scathing evaluation from DCFS and they removed all of the children from their care. By this time Larry had graduated to breaking into neighbor's homes. Again, people were predictable; all you had to do was watch them for a while to figure out their patterns. It was simple as pie and tastier than cake.

Then he landed in the home of Mary Ellen Hobbs, a dotty old bitch who took in lost kids to keep her from being lonely. When he arrived, there were two others and to his delight he was given a room of his own. Situated in a dormer, the window overlooked her small backyard.

The room was painted light blue with plaid blue and green wallpaper on the bottom half of the walls. In the comfy twin-size bed he slept well every night, under a goose down comforter. It had to be the most splendid room he'd ever stayed in.

Another plus was that his foster mother was a fantastic cook. In the evenings she made lavish meals with succulent meats and elaborate side dishes. There were pancakes, cinnamon rolls, bacon and eggs in the mornings before school. She handed them filling sack lunches on their way out the door, which included homemade cookies. "Eat well," she'd tell them. "You can't study hard if your tummy is rumbling." Eat well they did.

The best part was Mary Ellen lived in her own happy little world where everyone was good. A chubby, white lady in her mid to late sixties, her hazel eyes sparkled when she smiled. She dressed in cotton dresses and wore her white hair in a neat bun at the back of her head. She naïvely trusted those around her and at almost sixteen, Larry came and went as he pleased.

Puttering around in her flower beds tending brightly colored zinnias, Mary Ellen hummed happily to herself. Mowing her lawn and carrying bags of mulch, Larry made himself indispensable to his foster mother. In exchange, when he told her he needed something, she'd give him money to buy it.

He carried an expensive cell phone and owned a laptop now. The gloves and black hoody from Sears came in handy for breaking into houses, as did the knife he borrowed for each 'adventure' from the kitchen. You never knew when you might need something like that. He thrived on the exhilaration of deviance and even though his current situation was rather cushy, his need for the rush of prowling was profound now. He couldn't bear to give it up.

Always be respectful to Mary Ellen, he often reminded himself. In this classier Chicago neighborhood, he attended a better school. He did all his homework and made straight As without studying. Relieved to be away from the thugs at the other public school, he thought the curriculum at the new school was still too easy.

He helped the younger children with their homework. Kaylee, who was seven, struggled with reading. Missing her two front teeth, she reminded him of a cute American Girl doll. Alex, who was in 5th grade, needed help with math. Larry worked with them patiently while Mary Ellen Hobbs looked on adoringly.

To his credit the younger children's grades improved. For once in his life Larry appeared to be part of a happy little family, even if only on the surface. He made sure Mary Ellen's opinion of him included her assurance to the social worker that sweetness ran in his veins.

Yolanda Murphy was satisfied when she did her routine checks. Both women were sure that he was over his acting out due to grief and was back on the right track.

Yes, life was great with good old batty Mary Ellen. It was too bad she keeled over in her flowerbed and died right after Larry turned seventeen. Bringing that sweet ride to an end.

He only lasted three days in the next place. Larry never even bothered to learn their names. He'd had enough of this shit. He didn't need anyone to tell him what to do or to take care of him. He could take care of himself.

That third night when everyone slept, he grabbed his backpack and crept from the house. The L-train took him to an area where trench coat entrepreneurs bought, traded and sold black market treasures. He sold the few pieces of Mary Ellen's jewelry he five-finger inherited when he'd packed up his belongings there. He traded his fancy phone for a burner and a wad of cash. It didn't make sense to hang onto a phone that would quit working once the bill went unpaid. He decided to keep the laptop, knowing he might have to sell it in the future; for now he didn't want to part with it.

Continuing to the next part of his plan, Larry stood on an overpass, a freight train yard in motion below. He looked around at the city of Chicago, sparkling like a chest of diamonds against the night sky. Even at this late hour, horns and an occasional siren punctuated the hum of the traffic. A subdued breeze came off Lake Michigan, its musty smell, the only air he'd ever known.

"Fuck you, Chicago," he said out loud. Then he slid down the embankment and jumped on a freight train.

Hiding in a box car full of canned food, he ate his fill from the ones with pop-tops and stashed some in his gear for later. Where this train was headed didn't matter. He intended to ride it to the end of the line. Wherever it ended up would be far away from Evanston, and Victoria Lawrence.

He wasn't sure what he'd do now.

Miss Rogers said the Devlin twins were gifted. He believed her assessment. He would adapt and overcome. He possessed the ability to be stealthy. Never having been caught for his crimes gave him a sense of superiority and reinforced the belief he had an extraordinary mind.

When the train stopped and he feared his car might be next to be unloaded, he slunk out the sliding door and vanished.

Larry Devlin disappeared off the face of the earth.

The police couldn't find him and the foster parents were clueless. The case worker didn't have time to look for him herself and even if she did, she wouldn't know where to start. The stack of files for kids who needed her help demanded her attention. If he turned up, he'd be among the stack again.

In the meantime, he took up an insignificant slot on her list of priorities. He'd undoubtably be another runaway she'd felt sorry for who'd soon become a distant memory.

8

Satisfaction

When Larry escaped from the train yard in Detroit, Michigan, he set off on an unknown adventure. For weeks he slept in abandoned buildings and stole what he needed to eat. On a moonlit night he crept through an overgrown back yard and jimmied the side door of an old boarded up house and slipped inside. He'd trained himself to listen for sounds of life. It was never smart to encroach on some other homeless guy's squat. Satisfied he was alone, he lit a match and looked around.

He stood in the kitchen which probably hadn't been remodeled since the 1930s. All the surfaces were covered with a thick layer of dust. Looking through the cabinets and drawers he found a discarded candle and lit it. A small rat squeaked and scurried across the floorboards, disappearing into some darkened hole.

Larry made his way through the dining room. A broken table leaned on three legs with a couple of sad chairs standing guard. In the living room he found a dilapidated sofa. He tested its sturdiness and pulled the cushions off to make sure there were no creatures living in it. Bone-weary, he pulled out a fleece throw blanket he nipped from a department store. Using his backpack for a pillow, he rolled himself into the coverlet like a burrito and settled into sleep on the sagging couch.

During the wee hours, a scraping noise awoke him. He sat up, bolt straight, and strained his ears to listen. Someone had come in the back door. Larry stuffed his blanket in his backpack and grabbed his knife. In the dim rays of the streetlights seeping in through the cracks of the boarded-up windows he made out the silhouette of a man coming toward him. Larry's heart quickened with each thump of the stranger's footsteps.

As quietly as doable, Larry clutched the straps of his backpack and stood up.

"Who's in here?" a gravelly deep voice asked.

"I've got a knife," Larry warned.

This didn't scare the trespasser; he lunged toward Larry, knocking him hard to the floor. The boy dropped his backpack. The intruder outweighed Larry by a notable eighty pounds and stank of body odor and cheap stale whisky. The bum pinned him to the floor. In a panic, Larry thrust the knife into his attacker's chest. The man groaned in agony; he rolled onto his back. In a frenzy Larry stabbed him repeatedly until the man lay motionless on the dirty floor.

Shaking, Larry collapsed backward and sat leaning against the wall until his heartbeat regulated and he breathed steady again. He summoned his courage to relight the candle. In the flickering glow, he noticed the blood splattered all over his own hands and clothes. He held the candle up to the homeless man he'd fought with. Judging by his fixed dilated eyes he was definitely dead. Larry leaned against the wall and laughed. *What is it about stabbing someone that gives me this kind of rush?*

Larry undressed and threw his bloody clothes on the sofa. He located the dingy bathroom and using a bottle of water and some soap from his backpack, he scrubbed the evidence of the murder from his skin and his special knife.

Dressed in clean clothes, Larry went back to the body and searched the dead man's pockets finding fifty dollars in wadded up bills. Larry's hands weren't trembling anymore.

"I guess you won't be needing this." He shoved the money in his pocket. "You should have listened to me when I told you I had a knife." Before leaving, Larry set fire to a matchstick lizard. He watched from the alley behind the house to make sure the flames did their job.

Unnerved by his close encounter with the dead hobo, Larry decided he needed to come up with a better way to survive. If he had been more deeply asleep, the vagabond might have been the one walking away. He pawned his beloved laptop.

In the years since his mother's death, he'd grown to look like a man. With a beard he kept neatly trimmed he'd pass as over twenty-one. Choosing crowded bars where hookers hung out he tried his hand at picking pockets and purses off the drunken patrons. Lightly bumping into distracted victims and with sleight of hand, he snatched their wallets. To his delight, he possessed a remarkable talent for this type of robbery. It was like picking flowers in a meadow.

Racking up big-time money, he laughed at the stupid assholes who commuted to menial jobs each day. He came away with more money in one night than they made in a paycheck. He started sleeping in pay-by-the-night hotels and actually paid for his meals, never eating at the same restaurant or fast-food place twice. He liked this.

Several months into his stay in Detroit, while prowling the red-light district, a prostitute approached him looking for a score. She looked a lot like Victoria, with classic dark hair and eyes. Her red droopy eye lids verified her drug use. Heroin or crack could be procured on every corner in this neighborhood. She came on to him, friendly and approachable and wasted.

"You want to party, handsome?" she asked, slurring her words. He flashed a wad of bills at her and she led him to a hotel room.

Once inside, she rummaged in her purse and pulled out a bottle of Jack Daniels. "Wanna' drink?"

"Sure." Nerves caused his voice to quiver. He snatched two plastic wrapped cups off the counter by the sink and let her pour. "How much?" His mouth was suddenly dry.

"Depends on what you want." She swayed her hips trying for sexy.

"I want to have sex with you," he muttered, unable to look her in the eyes. He envisioned Victoria. Imagined her life had gone to hell, she was a hooker now that she'd fallen from her lofty pedestal. The debasement of her aroused him.

"A wham, bam, thank you ma'am is fifty and you have to use a condom." The clone of the girl he lusted after lit a cigarette and waited.

He dug in his pocket and pulled out the bills. She snatched them up and squirreled them away somewhere he didn't see. She handed him a wrapped condom.

"Take off your pants and underwear," the hooker said.

He did. She picked his clothes up, deposited them in the bathroom and shut the door. She knew the ropes and didn't make stupid mistakes. If this got weird, she'd be closer to the door than his clothes were and most Johns weren't going to chase you down the street naked.

Larry breathed fast when she knelt down in front of him and asked, "How do you want it, baby? Do you want it hard and rough or sweet and slow?"

"Sweet and slow, I think. I want you to act like you love me," Larry said.

"Oh, you want the girlfriend experience; I can do that," she assured, in a confident tone. For the next half hour he fantasized he was with Victoria while he had sex with a hooker.

When they finished, the naked prostitute retrieved a cigarette from the pack on the bedside table. "That was actually kinda' nice for a change." Flipping the red button on her disposable lighter; the flint refused to spark.

Climbing off the bed, Larry produced a box of wooden matches from his backpack. Just as he'd done thousands of times for his mother, he struck the match on the strip on the side of the box and held the flame to the end of her cigarette.

"Was it good for you, sweetheart?" the woman asked, taking a drag.

Staring at the still burning end of the match, Larry knew exactly what he needed to do. He blew out the match and placed it in the ash tray. He answered, "Not bad."

Turning his back as if he planned to get dressed, he reached into his gear bag and grasped the handle of the kitchen knife. He wheeled back around and plunged it into her vocal cords. Her eyes were wide with sheer terror. She managed a gurgling sound as a plea for help.

"Yeah, it was good for me, but this is going to be even better." He stabbed her again and again. The adrenaline rush was like free falling and soaring at the same time. When he finally stopped, out of breath, his bare body tingled with exhilaration and dripped with blood. Calmly, he stepped into the shower and washed the splatter off the weapon and himself. He dried off, dressed and collected all his belongings.

Larry dumped her purse, pocketing the three hundred dollars she'd been paid that night for selling her body. Then he emptied her liquor bottle all over the bloody blankets on the bed. He removed the battery from the smoke alarm and disabled the fire sprinkler on the ceiling. Just before leaving the room, he constructed a matchstick butterfly. Impressed with the beauty of his creation, he used the crappy camera feature on his burner phone to take a picture. The image of the sculpture was adequate, in the blurry background was the murdered prostitute. He struck a match and lit the butterfly throwing it on the bed.

Larry stood in a thicket of trees behind the hotel and stayed long enough to watch the room become fully enveloped. As the flames ate their way through the roof and the fire department arrived, he walked in the opposite direction and once again disappeared.

Bound for the West Coast, he covertly hitched a ride in the back of a moving van with a broken lock. Settling in for the long haul, he borrowed some of the homeowner's bedding and made himself a little nest amongst the boxes. The ride in the dark gave him plenty of time to consider the crime he'd impulsively committed.

People would talk about the murder and fire for a short while, at least until they found a more interesting topic. But just like the Devlin twins, that poor hooker probably didn't have anyone who gave a shit about her and before long she'd be forgotten.

The endless hum of truck tires made it easy for his mind to drift back to Victoria. She'd be sixteen now, almost seventeen. Sweet sixteen and never been kissed; but she had been, once. He wondered if she'd let

Sean the Weasel kiss her after he'd left. The possibility made him sick.

For a month, Larry roamed around Spokane, scavenging from unsuspecting strangers. Boredom with picking pockets made him numb and lethargic. Sitting in a booth at an all-night diner, he considered ways to get more excitement into his life.

Doing another hooker crossed his mind. That first one gave him an intense high. Because of the viciousness of the crime, if he didn't want to get caught, he would have to leave Washington State immediately afterward and he didn't want to move on just yet.

Sipping his coffee, Larry tuned into a conversation between two friends in the booth next to him. "Yeah, I gotta take Peggy to wine country day after tomorrow," one man complained.

"Wine country? Why the hell do you want to go to wine country?" his male counterpart scoffed.

"I don't want to go but if I don't take my wife on this trip, she won't let me go on the fishing trip with you," he explained.

"Bring me back an expensive bottle of chardonnay," his friend said with a chuckle.

"I told her we gotta be back Sunday. I got ta watch the ball game on my big TV at home, not on some tiny set in a dainty bed and breakfast."

"I hear ya, man."

Just then Larry was hit with a magnificent idea. People were so stupid; they never paid any attention to who might be listening in on their idle chatter. When the man got up to leave, Larry followed him, nabbing his wallet on his way out the door.

At a gas station across the street he bought a map and found the street on the man's driver's license. Only three blocks away, Larry hiked over to the house and dropped the wallet in the driveway. He didn't want to put any kinks in the couple's plans for their trip and a lost wallet had the potential to derail this scheme. He concealed himself in the bushes and waited… until twenty minutes later, when the man came out of the house. "Maybe I left it in the car," he was saying. "Oh, never mind, here it is on the driveway."

"You need to be a little more careful, George," a woman's voice called from the doorway.

Larry spied on the house for two days until, sure enough, exactly like George told his friend, the couple put suitcases in their car and drove off for their romantic getaway. Larry learned people are predictable; they tended to leave emergency house keys outside in one of those fake rocks or other obvious hiding places. In less than fifteen seconds he'd gained access to the inside of George's house.

The house wasn't anything special; only a three-bedroom ranch with dated décor. The family pictures displayed two grown sons who had children of their own. *Happy family; I wonder what dark secrets these people guard. Everyone's a liar.*

Apparently, Peggy hadn't learned to cook for just the two of them yet because the freezer was full of plastic containers of leftovers from homemade meals neatly labeled with the contents and dated. Larry selected beef stroganoff and popped it in the microwave. While he waited for it to heat through he explored the rest of the rooms.

The huge flat screen TV was right in front of a recliner with the remote control.

George's house wasn't anything fancy but it beat the hell out of the foster homes Larry lived in, so he spent the next six days eating George's food, sleeping in George's bed and watching the man's big screen TV.

Larry also spent time on George's computer, looking up helpful websites about hot wiring cars, disarming security alarms, surveillance equipment and other useful techniques. He surfed social media sites for potential future house-sitting opportunities.

He never understood why some morons posted comments like, "21 days until Bermuda and 2 weeks away from my asshole boss; can't wait!" *Stupid people deserve what they get. They might as well have posted a sign in their front yard advertising:* **I'm gone for two weeks, come and steal my shit.** *I think I will,* Larry decided.

Before dawn on Sunday morning, Larry Devlin fixed himself one last extravagant breakfast from Peggy's refrigerator. He pocketed the cash he'd found in the house, packed up his gear, along with a few small trinkets George would never even know were missing and lit a praying mantis on his way out the door. He took a picture of his matchstick bug first. This allowed him to keep his artwork while also using it for its destructive purpose.

He did this several more times in the Spokane area before deciding the time had come to move on.

That meant he could indulge himself. He finally got to repeat his performance with a hooker before jumping a train to Portland.

9
Finding Her

Larry made his way down the coast, stopping in cities for two to four months to take advantage of people he considered were asking for it. He committed the same crimes, falling into a habit. However, murdering prostitutes didn't give him the incredible rush anymore. He didn't understand what was happening. He craved that euphoric feeling again. He must be doing something wrong but he couldn't figure out what.

When he ultimately arrived in Los Angeles, he'd been gone from the Midwest for over a year. In southern California he developed a preference for multimillion dollar homes to squat in while the owners were off on globe-trotting vacations. He had the gadgets now to scramble electronic feeds and reprogram alarm systems. Rich people owned cool, pawnable toys. In just a month his nest egg exceeded several grand.

He'd thought this luxury living would get Victoria out of his mind but he was more obsessed with her than ever. At this stage, she'd be scouting out universities and making decisions about her future. Her rich daddy would surely send her to a fancy Ivy League school. *Which school will she end up in?*

When Larry was "house sitting," he would Google **Victoria Lawrence.** He always found something new; National Honor society this and Outstanding Academic achievement that. Sometimes he even found photographs featuring her participating in a charity event. There were a few pictures showing she'd paired up on some project with Natalie Perry from their homeschool class. The best schools required philanthropy on college applications.

One night when he made himself at home in a fifteen-million-dollar house with canyon views, he stared at a photograph of Victoria and some other overachievers presenting books to kids in foster homes. "Don't make me sick," Larry said in disgust.

His mind took off: Trim and happy and beautiful, described this older Victoria. Life went on. How could he have seen her as wholesome, pure even? She had turned into someone calculating, so hurtful, like his mother; or had she been this way the whole time? Oh, Victoria gave off the impression she cared about people, when really, she only cared about herself. *Manipulative bitch.*

Larry left the computer and walked to the wall of windows. It was like an IMAX movie of a breath-taking sunset. "Little Miss Goodie Two-Shoes," he uttered out loud to the universe, silence answered. *Everyone who seems altruistic has ulterior motives.*

All at once it hit him! The reason for his dissatisfaction with the murders of the prostitutes: they were *bad* people who no one cared about. Victoria presented herself as a good person, surrounded by people who cherished her and believed her lies. *That's it! I've been targeting the wrong sluts!* A sudden elation came over him; he knew what would restore the intense high he craved.

Going after girls of Victoria's caliber would take planning and stalking; he'd improved his skills on researching the homes he planned to break into. All he'd had to do to get alone with a hooker was flash some money at her, not difficult. Larry loved a new challenge and stalking a girl who had so much going for her validated his intelligence and excited him.

He parked his ass in the chair in front of the computer, barely sleeping or eating, cyber-hunting his next Victoria look-alike victim. Scouring Facebook for students from UCLA, he narrowed down the field by Googling them and perusing their social media pages. Many of their sites were open entirely to the world.

He hacked into the UCLA student database and found their class schedules, addresses, financial files. The information he gleaned on the five girls who fit his criteria he transferred to a USB drive. He realized it was the night before the homeowners were due back; he'd lost all track of time. He'd stayed too long with a fuzzy brain, then focused too hard on getting new targets.

Rummaging through their elegant house, he looked for cash and small things easily pawned on the street. This time, he did something he'd never done before; he took their laptop. He'd need technology to keep an eye on these college girls.

His last act was torching the place with an elephant to destroy the evidence. He'd heard somewhere an elephant never forgets. He hadn't been able to forget Victoria, so an elephant was appropriate and soothed his nerves as he created it. He was now in the habit of always preserving his art in a photograph.

He walked down the hill to join the throngs of humans in LA and became just another nameless, faceless person in a crowd. He honed his talent for being in a place but not being seen or remembered when police interviewed neighbors or witnesses. It wasn't simply a talent; he possessed a gift.

That same night, Larry stole his first car. He'd never driven before but being endowed with above average intelligence, he figured it out quickly. By the time he got on I-5 heading toward San Diego, he'd gotten the hang of it. He enjoyed the rush of fresh air through the windows and the glimmer of the taillights in front of him.

In the past he'd considered grand theft auto too risky but at this stage of the game, it would make following college girls much easier. Plus, this type of surveillance meant accumulating too much stuff to haul around in a backpack anymore; he needed a place to keep his loot. It seemed like a wise idea to have a mobile base of operations.

When he reached San Diego, he took Proctor Valley Road to an out of the way canyon road where he ignited a matchstick fox and lit the car on fire. Then he walked back into town and the next morning he scouted an office complex parking lot for a new vehicle.

Figuring the car wouldn't be missed until the end of the workday and by then he'd be back in LA, he selected an innocuous blue soccer-mom minivan. The tinted windows and dashboard GPS appealed to him.

Next he drove to an auto body shop with unattended cars parked around back and stole license plates, lessening the odds he'd be pulled over after the car was reported stolen. Always hyper vigilant, Larry made sure to use his scrambler for any security cameras in both parking lots.

Happy with the success of this enterprise, he drove back to Los Angeles to begin the surveillance of Ashley French, the first new target he'd chosen because of her striking resemblance to Victoria Lawrence and her foolish disregard for cyber security.

At an electronic and spy shop the sales guy steered him to a package deal which included micro mini cameras hidden in real smoke detectors and functioning electrical wall outlets. Larry chose equipment designed to be used with wi fi.

They would give him the ability to watch as well as listen in real time from anywhere in the world. It set Larry back nearly a grand but the advantage in the game would be worth it. *What good is money if I don't spend it on things that bring me joy?*

"Your girlfriend cheating on you?" the clerk asked, while he rang up the purchase.

"What? No, it's for home security." Larry's tone was full of false rebuke, as if spying on someone in this manner was grossly offensive. He paid cash, snatched up his bags and hurried out the door.

His next stop was at a uniform outlet where he purchased a pair of khaki pants, a cotton shirt and baseball style hat to match. When the sales lady was assisting another customer he stole a Building Maintenance iron on patch and another with the name Chuck for the space above the pocket of the shirt.

Afterward, he shopped at a hardware store where he picked up duct tape. He changed clothes and his hair style. At a different big box hardware store he bought a canvas tool bag finishing with a few hand tools for the outside pockets to make his handyman costume look legitimate. He picked up cotton clothesline rope and zip ties. He used the self-checkout. Three blocks away, in a cheap hotel room, he warmed up the iron provided for guests and doctored up his new disguise.

Later, he parked in the lot of a restaurant facing the back of Ashley's apartment building on Wilshire Boulevard. Dressed as casual and nondescript as other pedestrians, he cased the property and calculated the building had over a hundred units. With shops and restaurants at street level, it would be easy for him to hang around without calling attention to himself. He walked into the underground parking garage, spotted a security camera, and zapped it.

For the next few days, he followed Ashley to learn her routine. She went to classes each week day, which kept her away from her apartment most of the day. Once satisfied he'd have plenty of time to deploy his cameras, he dressed in his maintenance man uniform and waited until her car left the ground level parking lot.

Lowering his chin and adjusting his cap to hide his face, he scrambled the camera feed, then waited by the elevator which was card key activated. Within minutes, a resident stepped off the elevator talking on his cell. Distracted, he never saw Larry slip into the elevator and gain access to the building.

Getting off on the third floor, he located Ashley's door: 310. A corner unit. He felt an erection start and laughed to himself. *Yes, this is exactly what I needed.* He put on medical gloves and knocked firmly, calling, "Maintenance."

To his relief no one answered. Picking the lock, he entered her one-bedroom home and set to work immediately. He installed his new electrical sockets in the living room, bedroom and bathroom enabling him to see throughout the apartment. He swapped the original smoke detectors with his. Activating the system, he placed the control box, out of sight, behind the heating and cooling unit in the hallway closet.

Then he searched her drawers and closets, being very careful nothing appeared to have been disturbed. He located an extra door key and a card key for the building's elevator and parking garage and stuck them in his pocket. He found her UCLA schedule of classes; it matched his hack into the UCLA database. Confident that as long as she didn't skip any classes today, he'd have another three hours to snoop around in her life, he explored her apartment.

If she did happen to come home while he was there, he'd practiced his excuse. "Oh I'm sorry ma'am. Didn't the leasing office contact you? They should have. The upstairs tenant has a leaky dishwasher. They sent me over to check for water damage in your apartment. We apologize for the inconvenience."

He read her love letters from the boyfriend she dumped last month. In them, her ex apologized for being a jerk with a bad temper. Larry hacked into her desktop computer. Her Facebook relationship status was still unattached, which was good, because it meant he wouldn't have a boyfriend to contend with and her ex would probably be the prime suspect when she turned up dead.

Looking at her credit card statements and bank records he determined how she spent her money, which was haphazard. Other records showed evidence of parents residing in Palm Beach who paid her bills.

Snooping in her closet he counted the number of shoes she owned; forty-two pairs. An investigation of her medicine chest revealed she took birth control pills. He even checked her refrigerator and pantry to evaluate what kind of a diet she had: yogurt and beer. By the time he ducked out in late afternoon sunshine, he knew a considerable amount about Ashley French and the prospect of stalking her excited him once again: physically and mentally.

That night, Larry camped out in the minivan, his stolen laptop tuned into Ashley's home to see a show as soon as she got home. At 7:30, while gabbing on her cell, she walked into camera view. "Yeah, I'm game... What time do you want me to meet you? ... Okay, I'll see you then."

She went to the refrigerator and grabbed a beer, then stripped naked and stepped into the shower. *This is great!* For the next hour and a half he played with himself as he watched her primp for her night out. This was a whole new release for him, he felt powerful. He controlled her life and her death. He was nearly raw by the time she headed out the door.

When she drove out of the underground parking lot, he followed her flashy, red Fiat which she drove like a maniac. He could barely keep up with her and hoped she wouldn't kill herself before he got the chance to do it.

She finally pulled into the parking lot of a club and went in. He was glad she'd chosen such a place. His cash depleted since his major purchase of surveillance toys, he would work this trendy spot, picking the pockets of the easiest targets while discretely keeping an eye on her.

Ashley sat at a table with three other college girls and for the next few hours drank like a fish, refusing any invitations to dance. The thumping beat of the music and the strobe lighting gave Larry a headache.

Watching his prey until the wee hours of the morning exhausted him. When she finally decided to drive herself home, he followed at a safe distance. She maintained remarkable control of her car considering the tremendous quantity of alcohol she'd consumed.

In the weeks that followed, Larry shadowed Ashley to school, restaurants, and everywhere else. When she was in her apartment, he knew every tiny detail of her life. From the tap he'd installed on her phone, he knew she and her ex-boyfriend were still in the fighting stages of their breakup. A lot of hateful text messages flew between them.

Her study habits were non-existent. *Is she so smart she doesn't need to study? Like me? Or does she just not give a shit about the investment her parents are making in her education?*

Eventually, he discovered her grades were average and so was she. The time had come to put an end to this game.

On a Wednesday afternoon, with his hands gloved, he slipped back into her apartment and removed all of his spy gadgets, stashing them in his tool case. He replaced the original smoke detectors... just without their batteries. This building wasn't equipped with a sprinkler system, which meant the fire inside the apartment would have time to destroy the evidence before a connected unit's detectors went off and the fire trucks arrived.

Larry then hid in her bedroom closet. When she'd gone into the bathroom to take a shower, which was her habit every evening, he would wait to attack her until she entered her bedroom wrapped in a towel. He leaned against the wall so he would be behind her as she walked out of the bathroom. His heart pounded, yet his breath was slow and steady. Every sense was sharp and feeding his brain.

The water turned off.

He grabbed her from behind and gagged her mouth with a scarf. In minutes he had her tied to the bed, duct tape layered over the scarf in her mouth to keep her from being heard. Stripping naked he put his clothes in a plastic bag.

Watching the fear in her eyes aroused him.

Larry laughed and stretched out beside her. He didn't have to be in a hurry; this was his reward for months of hard work. As an afterthought, he went to his gear and retrieved his mother's topaz ring and slipped it on her left ring finger. To his surprise, it excited him so much he felt he was ready for the next phase of his crime. He grabbed her by the hair and forced her to look at him. Her muffled sounds of pain were just what he needed. He raped her hard and long making himself last. While she lay there in shock and crying; he walked naked to his backpack and held up the knife for her to see.

Then Larry brutally stabbed her to death.

Using her shower to clean up, he dressed again in his maintenance man disguise. Before he gripped his gear bag he lit his scorpion creature, setting yet another purifying fire. He'd read somewhere the name scorpion meant "to cut" and they were classified as predators. *That's who I am, a predator who cuts.*

The rush was even more intense than his first murder of the prostitute in Detroit. Creating a building aura of fear to terror, a magician, before stabbing his prey had been exquisite. This kill had satisfied all his hungers. *Oh yes, this is what I was born for!*

Clutching his surveillance gear, he left the apartment building unnoticed precisely as the fire alarm went off down the hall. Later that night, in a pay-by-the-day hotel, he watched the story on the local news about a fire in an apartment building and the vicious murder of a college student. As he suspected, the ex-boyfriend with a bad temper was being held as a person of interest in the case.

Larry smiled with satisfaction.

He'd done all of it intentionally and attained the desired outcome. He didn't get caught and his enjoyment was maximized beyond his wildest imagination.

10

Spider Awakes

Larry drove to Fresno, stole a little SUV hatchback, transferred his belongings then changed the license plates. He burned the blue van with a chimpanzee match sculpture. Chimpanzees were considered the smartest animals on the planet. He was now feeling the magic of creation in his matchstick avatars; they were feeding his strength and focus. He felt strong. He felt assured.

With a clear head and adrenaline pumping, he returned to the Los Angeles area. After a month, what Larry considered an appropriate cooling off period, he began his observation of Susan Powell, his second target from UCLA. He repeated his pattern of stalking; and when he knew her routines, then grew bored with her, he raped and killed her the same way he'd done with Ashley.

By the end of the spring semester, four dark-haired female co-eds from UCLA had been heinously murdered. Forensics at the scenes were muddled each time by arson. Clearly, the college had a serial killer in their midst. The FBI joined the LA taskforce. Fear fueled outrage from parents and students at the university's inability to keep its students safe. The school administration blamed the police and the police accused the FBI.

It was a tangled, hot mess.

Larry, pleased by the havoc he had created, had a warm smile and a deep chuckle while watching news stories about his work. The next day his humor soured when the news reported a witness came forward and stated they'd seen a white delivery van in the vicinity of the last murder. That was his current mode of transportation.

His mouth went dry when a penciled composite drawing of his own face flashed up on the screen. Not perfect, but close enough to be dangerous.

"Authorities are asking anyone who might have additional information to please contact the FBI," the newscaster said, with sincerity. "That number is at the bottom of our screen."

Panic rushed through him in waves.

He'd never made any mistakes before, but this time he had. Without thinking twice, sweat dripping off his forehead, he packed up his backpack. He transferred all the stalking files on the computer to USB memory sticks. He hated to destroy the laptop, but it would take up too much space in his pack.

Out in the desert, he pulled over in a secluded spot that was an hour's hike from a rail yard, the time was well after midnight to ensure no one was close enough to see the flames. Larry set fire to the van using a chicken. This avatar matched his feeling of defeat and low energy. There was still a rage boiling deep, but the surface of his thoughts were self-castigating, blame and cowardice.

He watched as flames came to life to devour the upholstery in ripples of curling faux leather. The vehicle hissed a dying song, destroying any evidence capable of linking him to the murders. Then he set out across the loose sand and pebbles toward the tracks.

That very morning he boarded a freight train heading back east. His murderous run in California abruptly at an end. He felt lost. He didn't know what to do now. He thought about his brother. *Should I visit him?* He quickly decided against sentimentality. He couldn't bear to think about the last time he'd seen Barry.

This is all Victoria's fault. If he'd never met her, none of this would have happened. If she hadn't made the impression on him that she did, he never would have killed those young women. Anger and hatred for her grew from the ever-present ember to an ignited flare up; loathing burned like fire inside his heart and he knew the only way he would ever be able to extinguish it would be to make Victoria pay for her callous toying with his emotions. Forever giving him false hope in a world full of useless people.

A new plan formulated in his mind and while he imagined what he would do next, he lovingly created matchstick spiders. It gave him his focus back. "Welcome to my parlor, said the spider to the fly," he whispered sinisterly remembering a delicious shudder that Victoria had not been able to hide once long ago, once when he talked to her about spiders.

In a Kansas City hotel room, Larry cut his hair short. Using a store box of hair color, he dyed his blonde hair dark brown. He'd also bought a pair of vanity contact lenses and changed his eyes from blue to brown. Looking in the mirror, even he didn't recognize himself. He was sure Victoria wouldn't either. The next day he stole another car and drove to downtown Chicago with a plan to once and for all put an end to his torment.

For the first time since the night of his mother's murder, he drove by the site of his childhood home. He knew from maps on Google Earth a new home had been built on the lot. They'd built a grand place with fancy stonework proclaiming, **people who matter live here.** What a far cry from the Devlin twins' home which had been large but deteriorating, somber and plain.

The fading sunset streaked the sky with purplish pink. He looped over to Victoria's street and drove slowly past her house. Cicadas buzzed an intermittent song on the warm August evening. A subdued light shown out from the living room window. Deeper into the residence, the flickering blue glow of a television in a family room played off the walls. He evaluated the neighbors for activity or dogs. In this community, a strange car parked on the street would be noticed. He'd have to come back on foot after dark.

When the streetlights came on, he waited two more hours. One by one the residents of the quiet neighborhood extinguished their lights and settled in for the night, signaling it was safe to return to the Lawerance house. Cutting down the alley, he avoided the homes with dogs and crept silently to Victoria's yard.

A cooling breeze from the lake was kicking in. The lights of the city gave the sky an eerie grayish orange glow.

It felt evil. Larry smiled.

It felt like it was welcoming him home.

He jumped the fence next to the garage. Camouflaged by the shrubs which separated the yards, he made his way to the screened-in back porch where he kneeled on the ground, behind a bush.

Muffled voices and footsteps of the Lawrence family, living their happy little lives, let him know they were still awake. He bolted to the shadows and crouched low as the backdoor opened and a woman's voice said, "Yumm, the air off the lake is so refreshing after how hot it got today."

"I'm looking forward to the ocean breezes," a man's voice said.

"Oh, that reminds me, I've got all your clothes packed, but you need to make sure you have what you want for your shaving kit."

"I'll check. What time's the flight tomorrow?" the man asked.

"Noon so we should leave here by 8:15 because of the lines."

"Then we'd better head to bed," the man suggested. A moment later the couple went back in and Larry heard the lock thrown.

They're going on a trip tomorrow! Chicago is welcoming me back. This is perfect but... He wondered if Victoria was going with them. Surely she'd go along; with only a few weeks until college started, this trip signified the end of her childhood. Mr. Lawrence said he looked forward to the ocean breeze. Perhaps he could find out what beach they were going to. *What a stroke of luck!*

Larry examined the lattice work concealing the underside of the screened-in porch. With just a pop of his knife, he quietly loosened one nail at a time, freeing the end panel, making enough room to squeeze inside. He really didn't like spiders either, and fortunately, the moisture barrier helped with the yuckiness. He pushed the decorative underpinning back into place. Squinting in the diffused light of his new surroundings, he caught sight of a basement window.

The screened porch was an addition to the original design and it added great privacy since it was covering that little window at ground level. Larry crawled over, peeked in… the muted glow of the streetlight came through an opposite window, casting shadows it showed a typical unfinished cellar found in traditional centuries-old homes. Not chancing making noise by trying to break in now which might alert the family to his presence, he curled up to a light sleep, biding his time until the family left for their vacation.

In the morning, he woke to the sound of the Lawrences stirring. At 8:20 the back door opened and their footfalls overhead made his heart beat wildly. The family descended the steps and headed down the path to the garage.

"Oh wait! I forgot to water my plants!" Mrs. Lawrence said.

"Don't worry about it, Lillian. We're going to miss our flight," her husband urged.

"I'll text Paige and have her do it when she comes to check the house on Wednesday," Victoria offered.

The sound of her voice sent electric shocks through Larry's body. His pulse hammered in his ears. His groin instantly reacted, throbbing so hard it hurt. He nearly rushed out of his burrow to tackle her; stab her right there! Shaking, he could barely force himself to stay crouched down and watching. He thought of a scorpion, stinger up, slowly circling its prey. He poured his urges into that image and was able to control himself.

Finally, the car pulled out into the alley and drove away.

Waiting another ten minutes, on the outside chance Mr. Lawrence might return for something else his wife forgot, Larry used his knife to unlatch the old lock on the hidden basement window. He slid it open with ease. He squiggled in, past the frame and dropped to the floor next to the hot water heater, relieved they hadn't installed alarm sensors on the forgotten window.

Tiptoeing up the stairs, he soundlessly eased the basement door open and scoped out the spacious, beautifully appointed kitchen. The gleaming clean granite counter tops reflected soft morning light. No motion detector guarded the inside rooms. He quickly walked to the front and back doors and disarmed the burglar alarm.

Moving past the dining room, Larry entered the living room glancing at the tweed sofa and cream-colored, button-tufted accent chairs. On the fireplace mantel photographs of their cherished daughter proclaimed her importance in their lives. He imagined them sitting in this room, engrossed in conversation, giving the girl their undivided attention.

A life I could never have. A life taunting me about my family's failure. If I can't have it, no one can have it. I'll burn every damn happy family in the world. I'll be laughing as the whole fucking world goes up in flames. Realizing he was about to rip things off the mantle and smash them, he reached out to his mental scorpion guide and danced with it in his imagination until he settled down enough to keep going.

He made his way into the den. *Where does Victoria like to sit when they watch TV as a family?* Plopping down on the middle cushion of a soft leather sofa, he pictured her there. Taking a deep breath, Larry felt almost tingly; he couldn't believe he was in Victoria's house.

This had been astonishingly easy!

11

Dear Diary

Exploring Victoria's bedroom and private bath aroused him, much like he knew stealing a glimpse of her naked would. He smelled her pillow and buzzed with her heavenly sweet scent. He ran his hand over the pink flowered bedspread, envisioning her body sleeping under the covers.

In her bathroom he discovered the regular assortment of feminine hygiene products. He didn't find any birth control in her medicine cabinets, leaving him smugly satisfied she wasn't sexually active.

I'll be her first.

And her last.

After a moment of consideration, it occurred to him that if she did have birth control she would have taken it with her on vacation. This notion made him scowl.

Larry opened her walk-in closet and spun around as if it were a mirrored room in a fun house. Like many older homes, it had twelve-foot ceilings, providing ample space for storage above the rods. A convenient step stool on gliders rested in the corner. A green striped deco style chair gave it a cohesive dressing room vibe.

On one shelf he spotted a collection of journals, the cloth covered kind, expensive and well-made, all lined up neatly. He moved the stool over and climbed up to inspect the first one on the very left. Like a special present, he opened it to the first page; her slanted, very neat for a nine-year-old's handwriting, seemed to flash out at him from the page. *Mom, Dad, Paige and I went putt-putt golfing tonight; it was a blast. Dad won but only by one point and I was second.*

He slid the fabric-bound pink book back into its hiding place, exactly where he'd found it. Skipping two books he read: *Dad and I took down the nursery today. We took all the baby stuff to Catholic charities. I heard mom crying last night, she said she was done. My heart hurt, Mom is so sad and I'll never get to be a big sister.*

Five books later, he pulled out one with white and blue polka dots. Her writing was more defined, she was surer of herself. *Dad asked me what I wanted for my birthday this year and I told him I didn't need anything.*

He said he wasn't going to let my 12th birthday go by without magic and joy. He asked me if he was a fairy and could grant me a wish, what would it be?

I responded, 'I'd wish I could be a fairy and grant a wish.'

He said it was an interesting idea and he'd think about it. This morning, on my birthday, I found fairy wings and a magic wand in my bedroom! Now I have to decide what I will do. Gillson Park is having a neighborhood planting day; maybe I can donate a bunch of trees and bulbs. Or I could donate some books to Paige's school library. I'll have to think about it. This should be fun to be a good fairy at least once before I get too old for it...

Larry placed the diary back in its original space thinking, *You hadn't even met me yet. Too bad, I'd like to give you a wish to grant.* Five more down, he found the one that really sparked his interest. Settling into the cushiony chair still in the cozy closet, he opened a green and pink plaid book and read and read, hearing her every thought and impression.

Mother and Dad are sending me to a home-school group next week. He poured over her words. Fifty pages later he found, *First day of class with an interesting group of kids. Sean Weeden's father is a police officer... Blah Blah Blah,* he thought as he soaked up her insights into their classmates.

His heart pounded faster when he came to, *I'm most intrigued by the Devlin twins.* Portions stuck onto his brain like an insect to a fly trap.

Can't tell them apart, but I will learn.

Being around the identical Devlin twins reminds me of when I was little and pretended my reflection in the mirror was my identical twin. It was a silly thing to do but it helped me feel less lonely.

Larry is my new partner for our science project, and I'm glad.

Larry made me laugh today with one of his quips...

She also described in detail Miss Rogers' contributions to her students and how she inspired them as individuals. Victoria wrote about doing the project over the internet and her impressions of the Devlin's home, *It looks like Larry lives in a cave...I don't understand why Mrs. Devlin is so against Larry coming to my house to work on our project.*

Mrs. Devlin strikes me as a strange woman. She never comes into the school. She always sits in her car, smoking cigarettes...

Mom told me Mrs. Devlin is a widow. Mr. Devlin was an inventor of medical gadgets and died in a freak accident...

Working with Larry is unsettling. When he is close to me my nerves seem to tingle. He gives off this sent. . . I don't know. Am I attracted to him?

Then he came to it!

His whole world froze for a second as he gathered the courage to read on ...

Larry Devlin kissed me today... He read as if his life flickered in her words like a movie ***The Devlin Twins star in the Truman Show.***

As much as I rejected him I enjoyed his lips on mine. I can't stop thinking about it! He poured over her conflicted feelings and stung at the words *Involvement at our age could only ruin everything.*

The journal came to an end, he snapped it shut and bolted from the chair. Involvement with her *had* ruined everything.

He paced for a few minutes then put the book back and grabbed the next one. Settling into the striped chair again he buried himself in her account of the night of the fire and the aftermath.

I'm devastated by what has happened to those boys...

I wish they would tell me where Larry has been sent. I wish I knew if he is all right...

I thought their mother might be abusing them but I didn't tell anyone. I should have...

Now I know why his room was so dark. She locked the twins in the basement...

Sean tells me things about the investigation, I'm sure he's not supposed to...

Larry spent the night in the closet reading all the journals catching up on the last four and a half years of her life. The final journal stopped about a month before the present day. Searching her room he deduced she'd taken the current notebook with her to Aruba where they'd gone on vacation; he'd seen the notation on her desk calendar.

Now he knew all her thoughts and feelings; he knew about her childhood imaginary twin. She'd never let another boy kiss her and he found out that she and Sean Weeden were just friends, good friends, but only friends.

Was he wrong about his private allegations regarding Victoria's mendaciousness? Did she try to have a caring heart and do her best to live a life with purpose? *No, she just wants people to think she is virtuous! Her charity work is a cover for her own ambition.* Larry convinced himself it was a false face she wore. She was a tease! *She played with my feelings while we worked on our science project and then made me feel guilty for suspecting she felt the same way. What a bitch!*

Her diary spoke of the countless times she'd thought of the Devlin twins and her compassion for their circumstances; he was nearing the end of this last journal when his blood ran cold.

What struck an acute chord of fear in him was this entry:

I find myself thinking about Larry Devlin. It's like a gut feeling that he is in trouble. He'd be eighteen by now and out of the foster care system. I think I should try to find him...

All the times she'd thought of them had been sent to him like a message from the universe. She'd poisoned him. If she came looking for him, she would expose him for the killer he was. The scorpion totem forced itself into his mind.

He had to circle all threats and sting them with death.

He had to survive.

The words from her last pages indicated she was ready to search for him now that she was college-aged, and worse, that she was determined to find him to put things right.

He had to stop her.

Her interest in him had the potential to ruin everything, ruin every bit of pleasure he had found a way to squeeze out of his days. Ruin the only life he knew; display the skills he had worked so hard to develop to the judgment of others. He'd have to think this through very carefully.

The fire must look like an accident.

With Sean Weeden still in the picture, if he used his usual methods, the connection to the Devlin fire would be made since that was only a block away.

He wouldn't be able to murder the whole family with a knife, which he preferred when attacking one on one. How could he do this without anyone getting out of the house? He'd have to find a way to subdue them. A way to make it look like just a fire. No stabbing.

All this made his mind spin. He would need to know more about them to pull this off. The small voice that tried to push the image of him kissing her faded immediately to a strutting scorpion. *She's a fake, a liar, a tease. Just like all the girls I attacked. Like them, she needs to be taught a lesson!*

Larry spent the entire day looking through the house, gathering as much information as available about Victoria and her parents. Late at night, when the quiet Evanston streets eased into slumber, he left the house unnoticed and disappeared. He left no trace he'd been there. He hadn't slept in their beds or eaten their food. He didn't take any trinkets with him or steal their cash. Every cell in his hands had twitched to reach out and take earrings and loose cash.

This behavior was foreign to him; and instead of his normal happy excitement, this time while planning a murder, his overwhelming sensation was fear.

Part 3

Cat & Mouse

12

Bad Dreams

The trip to Aruba had been precisely what the Lawerance family needed. They'd enjoyed snorkeling and deep-sea fishing. They'd relaxed on the beach, indulged in fine dining and been spoiled at the luxury resort. It marked a major and bittersweet milestone: Victoria was now a college student. An adult.

Everything was about to change.

When they returned home, life became a whirlwind of activity. Lillian made a long list of things to be ready for Victoria's first week of college at Northwestern. A dozen prestigious schools had courted Victoria to choose them, stroking the pride Lillian had in her daughter. Further stoking her pride, Victoria chose to stay close to home. Lillian was feeling an easing of the tightness from those premonitions of doom about her daughter, memories of those feelings which had come to her again not long after her miscarriage. Though she had tried to put them off as tied in with all the other emotions, they were too real. Too specific about Victoria (not just a daughter) never reaching adulthood. Her balance of keeping this secret and protecting her daughter while encouraging Victoria to grow and flourish had exhausted her. But Victoria was about to enter the adult world. Because of her intelligence, Victoria was starting university at seventeen. Lillian's anxiety was less than it would have been had Victoria chosen a college far from Evanston. Attending Northwestern meant she would continue to live at home. It was the other first steps that made her nervous. Perhaps she had changed the future; perhaps Victoria would make it now.

The two of them shopped for a new laptop and a large cross body to carry it and other class supplies. Then Lillian talked her into clothes shopping. "Your clothes give professors an impression of you, so what do you want your image to be?"

Victoria looked down at her blue jeans and T-shirt printed with: **I'm**

not weird, I'm a limited edition. "Well, right now my image says that I have no fashion sense what-so-ever."

They both laughed.

Lillian said, "Oh, you have fashion sense; it's just not a good fashion sense." Then they both roared in laughter. Her mother pulled a sweater from the rack and held it up to Victoria.

Suddenly, the hairs on the back of Victoria's neck and arms stood up as if she'd been jolted by static electricity. A numbness came across her head and her heart began to race.

"Victoria, are you all right?" Her mother's voice sounded like it traveled through water into her ears and came in slow motion.

"I don't feel right," the girl whispered.

This ended the shopping spree. That also ended the relaxed few hours Lillian had about the future. She rushed Victoria to the nearest emergency room before the girl could object. Victoria was admitted and put through tests, scans and blood work. The following evening their family doctor arrived to join them for dinner and give them the results. He assured them it was a panic attack, most likely due to the pressure of starting college.

"I strongly disagree with your diagnosis," Victoria protested. "I'm not at all stressed about starting at Northwestern. Trust me, I'm excited about starting my classes. I don't understand this. I've never had a panic attack in my whole life."

The doctor dismissed her objections. He gave her parents a prescription bottle with anti-anxiety pills. The adults carried on the conversation for the rest of the evening.

When Lillian presented her one at bedtime, Victoria begrudgingly but dutifully took the pill.

The medication seemed to make things worse and gave her strange dreams. In one of her nightmares, she was looking for Larry in a thick fog, catching sight of him, then losing him again. The fog turned to smoke. She coughed, still pressing on, calling his name. A hallway, choked with a heavy noxious haze, led to a room filled with matchstick spiders. Suddenly the room burst into flames.

Victoria lurched straight up in bed, shaking and covered in sweat. She breathed in the sweet, safe air of her bedroom, relieved those frightening visions were fading like other bad dreams. She went to her bathroom sink and splashed her face with cold water. In the blue glow of the night light she examined her reflection in the mirror. She told her imaginary twin, "You'd better pull it together; you can't afford to flake out."

On the first day at Northwestern University, Sean Weeden was waiting for her by the math classroom door. When they'd made their schedules, they'd intentionally taken several classes together.

They planned for lunch when the ninety-minute class ended. The two followed a sea of students out the main doors of Lunt Building into the glorious autumn sunshine. The trees on campus were slightly touched with the promised fall colors. Turning onto the path toward Swift Hall, Sean asked, "What are you doing for lunch?"

"Brought mine." Victoria pulled a brown paper sack from her satchel as evidence. "What about you?"

Sean laughed. "Brought mine too. We can skip the crowded food court."

"God, we are such creatures of habit," she said with mock disgust. "There's a pleasant little garden over here. I was hoping we could sit in the sun and eat lunch."

"Maybe it's good we're creatures of habit. I've eaten lunch with you every school day for the last five years; I don't see any reason to change it now."

"I don't either." She smiled at him knowing he had a mild case of obsessive-compulsive disorder.

The pair strolled down the sidewalk; all around them other students filled the pathways, chatting, laughing and hurrying to their next class or lunch or back to their dorm for a crash nap. A few freshmen appeared to be lost, backtracking with odd looks on their faces.

The air smelled woodsy, warm and heavenly. They settled on a bench which overlooked the manicured shrubbery and classical Greek sculptures arranged in a formal garden setting. "Reminds me of Versailles, on a much smaller scale of course," Victoria said, with a chuckle.

"I've never been there," Sean remarked as he unwrapped a tuna salad sandwich.

"My parents took me there when I was fifteen. It's truly over-the-top."

They ate in silence for a while, taking in the surroundings. Victoria stared into space thinking about Larry Devlin and her latest nightmare. After a while, Sean asked, "Are you feeling okay; you seem kind of out of it?"

"It's probably these." She handed him her new prescription and took a bite of her peanut butter and grape jelly sandwich.

"Prozac! Why the hell are you on Prozac?" he asked.

Victoria covered her lips with her hand and spoke with her mouth full. "My family doctor thinks I had a panic attack last week."

"You're the last person to have an anxiety disorder."

Victoria took a swig of Snapple tea. "That's exactly what I told them. I did have some kind of episode though. It was the weirdest feeling." She explained about the doctor's diagnosis and blood tests that were still out. The side effects concerned her more than another panic attack. "I'm drowsy half the time, which can be one of the side effects, so is agitation and insomnia. When I do sleep, I have disturbing dreams."

"What kind of dreams?"

"The Devlin twins."

Sean hung his head in sorrow. He'd lived it. He still experienced the occasional nightmare himself. After all, his dog's heart had been found in the twins' burned-out basement; his dad's buddies in forensics confirmed it.

Seeing his distress she said, "I'm sorry. You asked me and I'm not going to lie to you."

"You're a shitty liar, anyway. I'd see right through you," he told her.

Victoria took a deep breath, nodded and then spilled her guts. "I can't stop thinking about Larry, dreaming about him. What happened to him? Where is he now? I've got an odd feeling he's in trouble. I've looked on the internet for him but I can't find anything."

She went into detail about her nightmares and matchstick spiders. Then she explained she surfed the internet and spent a half hour that morning on dream analysis sites. "Keep in mind, my time was limited so I didn't get to apply Miss Rogers' rule: find three sources that say the same thing. I looked for dream interpretation."

Since Sean seemed interested and wasn't making fun of her, she continued, "Fire can symbolize destruction, passion, purification, illumination, passage into something new with the destruction of the old. Basically, fire is about change. Spiders, conversely, freaked me out a little more because I found references to feeling trapped and unable to escape. That's exactly how I felt in the dream. I'm not sure if my subconscious is trying to tell me something or it's these stupid pills and their side effects."

Sean's face paled. Whatever the root cause, this was serious. "Your dad always tells you to trust your gut. What does your instinct tell you?"

"That I'm not going crazy. I believe, wherever Larry is right now, he's calling out to me for help. I feel like if I don't respond, we'll both go off the edge."

Sean gave a heavy sigh, like he knew what was coming next.

Victoria spoke slowly, "Your dad was on the scene that night. He must have some information about where Larry went. He could help me find him. If he'd at least let me have the name of his social worker, it would help immensely."

"I'll see what I can get out of casual conversation with him," Sean agreed. "But I can tell you, even though I know my dad loves me very much, he always viewed our home school group as a bizarre cluster of weirdoes. The Devlin twins only reinforced his opinion."

"We're not weird, we're special," Victoria said, with a dimpled smile.

13
The Next Fire

During one of their lunch breaks the following week, Sean gave Victoria a piece of paper with Larry's case worker's name. "My dad was none too happy about my bringing up the Devlin twins. It's a memory he'd like us all to forget. He wouldn't give me any information, but he keeps notebooks at home about his cases. He says he's thinking about writing a book, someday."

Victoria sighed and looked him in the eyes. "So you got this without him knowing about it?"

Sean nodded.

"I'm sorry I asked, now."

"I have to agree with my dad, I wish you'd forget all about those two. It's bad, Victoria. Mrs. Devlin was murdered, stabbed to death, a bunch of times. They were being abused, beaten and my dad suspects sexually as well, but Larry didn't admit to any incest."

"I thought that might be the case," Victoria hung her head. Tears burned behind her eyes; she blinked them away. "Even more reason for me to find Larry."

"You're not listening to me! When Mr. Devlin had his alleged accident, my dad headed up that investigation too. The twins were almost five, they saw the garage blow up! Dad thinks Mrs. Devlin killed him, but there wasn't even circumstantial evidence that pointed at her. They had no choice but to classify it as a terrible accident. You need to let this go," Sean advised. "The whole family was messed up. There's no helping them."

"You know I can't. I have no control over my dreams. I have to find Larry, at least look for him. I have to at least try to help my friend."

Sean shook his head. "You didn't find him in your dream. It led you into a fire. It might be an omen, or something..."

"What if he got adopted and he's going to Loyola? Wouldn't you want to know too? If a family adopted him, his name would be changed and that's why I can't find him," she reasoned.

"People who are running from something also change their names," Sean said.

"Just because their mother was a psychopath doesn't mean they are." She stared at the information, written in Sean's precision printing.

"It runs in families. Let it go!" he pleaded. "Victoria, Barry, is locked up in Bellview, a drooling retard that stabbed his murdering mother, and Larry's probably out there trying to forget about his former life."

"I know, you're right. I'll think about it. Thanks for this though." She held up the paper with Yolanda Murphy's name on it. She folded it and put it in her backpack.

The leaves went from frost kissed to full blown blazing color during the weeks while Victoria thought it over. She tried to look at it from every angle; everyone involved, the pros and cons. Convinced Mrs. Murphy would tell her Larry had been adopted by a wonderful family and was doing great, she called her office.

All she needed was for the social worker to tell her he was happy, then she'd have closure. Then she could just let it drop and imagine Larry having a decent life.

Victoria called Children and Family Services numerous times and always landed in Yolanda Murphy's voicemail. The social worker didn't bother to return her calls. *Odd, is she unprofessional? Busy? Hiding something?*

Finally, in late October, Victoria just showed up at DCFS. Mrs. Murphy was on the phone when Victoria reached her cubicle. Stacks of folders covered every surface of her workspace. Thumbtacked to her partitioned walls she displayed pictures of smiling children. Yolanda dabbed at a coffee stain on the front of her white blouse, evidence of a not so stellar day.

"No. I understand, putting stuff up his nose isn't normal behavior... Yes, take him to the emergency room… don't worry, the state will cover the cost and call me back after you get home... Okay, thanks. I'll talk to you later." The woman hung up the phone and sized up the professional looking college student standing there.

"I'm Victoria Lawrence. I've left you several messages looking for information about Larry Devlin. You haven't returned my calls. He is eighteen by now."

"I'm sorry Miss ..." the social worker acted like she couldn't remember her name.

"Lawrence."

"Miss Lawrence, I did receive your messages but as you can see, I can barely keep up with the kids currently in my charge; I don't have time to worry about one who has aged out of the system."

"I understand you have a very difficult job, Mrs. Murphy. But I was wondering if you'd be so kind as to grant me a precious second of your time and tell me if you remember anything about Larry Devlin. There was a house fire and…"

"Yes, I remember Larry. He bounced around from foster home to foster home. They all do." This conversation irritated Mrs. Murphy and Victoria sensed she wasn't going to get any straight information from her.

Victoria tried another tact. "He was a real sweet kid. I know you're probably not allowed to give out information but if you could give him my name and phone number, so he knows how to get in touch with me. I was the closest thing to a best friend Larry had. I can't imagine what it must have been like for him to have his whole world ripped away."

After a long pause, wistfully, Yolanda Murphy said, "He managed. I think he was even happy in his last foster home. But that woman passed away and Larry took off. We never found him. After a year, he turned eighteen. Not under our authority anymore so…"

"So his case got filed and forgotten?" Victoria asked with an appalled tone. Yolanda nodded. "If you don't mind me asking, how did his foster mom pass away?"

"She suffered a heart attack, she was elderly. Sweet woman, she thought Larry hung the moon," Mrs. Murphy said.

"Thank you for your time, Mrs. Murphy. I'll let you get back to work." Victoria left feeling worse than after her nightmare. Although relieved to know the foster mom didn't die in a fire or from being stabbed, she felt a punch of pity squeeze her heart. She was also surprised with this feeling of relief, she hadn't realized she had suppressed the thought that Larry might have turned into an arsonist or murderer from his environment, from the sudden change in his life.

Larry disappeared and was forgotten by the people who were supposed to look out for him. She would fix this.

When she arrived home Paige was in the kitchen talking with Lillian.

"Mom and I got into a hassle, so I'm spending the night here. I can't take any more of her bullshit tonight," Paige informed her. Not much had changed between her cousin and her aunt over the years. Paige still defied her mother at every juncture and Aunt Lisa still overreacted to her daughter's attitude and brought too many new boyfriends home to get back at her ex-husband.

Paige's phone rang, walking out of the room, she answered, "Yo!"

Victoria shot a look at her mom who rolled her eyes. "What's the deal this time?"

"Lisa can't afford to send Paige to cosmetology school and insists Roland should cough up the money. You'd think by now she'd have learned he won't step up to support his daughter," Lillian answered wiping down the counter.

"Couldn't you and Dad pay for it? I mean..." Victoria whispered.

"Of course we could. I've offered. But my sister says we do too much for Paige already. I even suggested we make it a loan Paige is responsible for paying back. She won't hear of it," Lillian said.

"That makes no sense," Victoria said.

"I agree. But there's some lines I can't cross and this is one of them. The crazy thing is, if the roles were reversed and you needed help, Lisa would move heaven and earth to give you what you needed," Lillian speculated.

Victoria nodded and changed the subject. "Smells good in here, what's cooking?" Victoria lifted the lid of the crock pot.

"White chili; it's been cooking all afternoon and it's making me hungry," Lillian answered. She gave the meal a stir.

"Another one for that cookbook you're going to write someday?"

Lillian laughed. "Perhaps. Dad's going to be a little late. If you girls are hungry, you can eat without him."

"No, we'll wait."

Victoria treasured time with her father over their evening meals. It gave them the chance to connect as a family.

After dinner, the family settled in the den to watch a rerun of Myth Busters. Sooner than normal, Victoria began to feel sleepy.

"I'm beat tonight. I think I'm going to turn in," she announced, yawning.

Paige echoed that and they headed upstairs.

It didn't take two minutes for Victoria to fall asleep after climbing into bed. Paige pulled the pillow over her head and snuggled in next to her cousin. She was out just as fast.

It had been a long time since the deep rest her body required came this fast for Victoria.

In the middle of the night, Victoria woke herself coughing. There was smoke. Her eyes fluttered and she saw flames climbing up her curtains.

Then she spotted it; a matchstick spider displayed on her desk next to her computer. She wanted to run but her feet wouldn't move; she was trapped.

"Oh no, not another one of those dreams," she muttered. Rolling over, she shook Paige. "Wake me up I'm having a bad dream."

Her cousin didn't move.

Panic swept through Victoria at being unable to escape from this nightmare. She'd always been able to wake up from bad dreams before. Why was this one so different?

All of a sudden a wet blanket wrapped around her and someone picked her up and carried her safely into another dream where she shivered in the cold.

Then unconsciousness closed in again.

She didn't realize she'd heroically been rescued from a very real fire and her true nightmare had just begun.

14

Wrongness

When Victoria came to, she didn't know where she was. The walls were white, the florescent lights overhead gave a cold institutional glow to everything. Pulling at the oxygen mask strapped over her nose and mouth, she strained to hear a muffled conversation.

"Some one's got to tell her," one voice said.

"It will be too overwhelming. A shock..." a man with a deep voice disagreed.

"No, Dad. You're wrong; she's too smart for avoidance. By not telling her, you're telling her."

Victoria recognized this one as Sean's voice.

"Tell me what, Sean?" Victoria meant to sound stern, but only managed to whisper. Her throat was as sore as after tonsil surgery. In a blink, Sean was by her side. Victoria's eyes focused on him and then on Officer Weeden.

"What do you remember?" Officer Weeden asked.

"Remember? About what? Where am I?" Victoria asked.

"There was a fire, Victoria. You're in the hospital," Sean's father told her.

"No. That was a dream. Where's Paige? Where are my parents? I want my parents." Her voice came out in tortured raspy breaths.

Sean shook his head sadly. "They didn't make it out."

Victoria's chest went tight, as if a two-hundred-pound wrecking ball had dropped on her. She closed her eyes, wanting to shut out the horrible truth. It demanded attention. She sobbed. "It was a dream; I saw a matchstick spider. If the fire was real, it was like when Barry Devlin killed his mother," she managed to utter.

Officer Weeden's concerned expression, deepened the lines in his forehead. "Barry Devlin is doing life in Bellview. He can't even feed himself; it's impossible he started the fire."

"Then it's Larry! No one even knows where he is," Victoria hissed trying for volume and failing.

"Accidental fires happen all the time," Sean tried to explain.

"The fire marshal found a frayed lamp cord which sparked some drapes," Officer Weeden clarified.

Victoria shook her head; she didn't believe it. That spider, it brought back memories. It let suppressed suspicions come forward.

She wished Paige would wake her up and stop this madness. But the dream wouldn't end and reality set in gradually as the days passed. The hospital treated her for smoke inhalation. Aunt Lisa took her back to her Portage Park apartment when the hospital released her. Lisa became the girl's guardian until she turned eighteen.

It was hard to say who was taking care of whom as the two of them numbly planned their loved ones' funerals. Lisa Jensen's face was like a frozen mask. Victoria often got frustrated when her aunt ignored questions. At this moment, Victoria needed her to answer the one question she couldn't answer for herself, "How did I make it out alive?"

Lisa looked at her niece sorrowfully, hesitated, then said, "They think your dad carried you out. They found you on the front lawn and the front door was wide open. He must have gone back in for Lillian and Paige." Her voice cracked with emotion and a tear raced down her cheek before she continued. "They found his... him downstairs. He tried to save them; I know he did."

Victoria buried her face in her aunt's shoulder and wept. She didn't know how they were going to make it through their lives, much less the funerals.

Across town in a seedy hotel on Chicago's south side, Larry Devlin listened to the midday broadcast of WGN news and prepared to consume the barely eaten foot-long sub he'd scavenged from the trash can in front of Subway. He hated wasteful people.

Then he laughed. If the thriftless moron hadn't pitched it, he'd still be looking for something to eat. Wasteful and careless people were what he lived on. He took a bite of the turkey club, satisfied with the presumption that in general people were idiots.

He wondered what his next move should be. Now that he'd disposed of Victoria, he felt unfocused. Burning down the Lawrence home hadn't given him the rush he'd expected, hoped for. But then again, he didn't rape or stab her or her mother.

I should have raped Victoria and stabbed all three of them after, I could have tied up them all while I did it. Maybe they wouldn't have connected it to Mom's stabbing. Maybe. No, I did this right, no stabbing so this looks accidental.

He'd considered kidnapping Victoria and torturing her for a few days before killing her, but the complications of such a plan also seemed too risky.

All the bodies had to be in the fire.

Besides, Mrs. Lawrence made his job easy by whipping-up dinner in the crock pot, then running out to do shopping. She'd left him the perfect delivery system and ample opportunity to carry out his plan. He'd even nipped some of Victoria's journals, the ones mentioning him.

He'd never burned up three people at the same time before so it worried him they might escape if he didn't drug them. He was able to dissolve some pills in the chili. It was brilliant.

He wondered what Victoria would have become had she lived. A doctor or professor. She could have been anything she wanted. She was smart enough.

In a way, he was sorry she never got the chance to be a wife and mother. She might have made a good mom. Maybe one of the few good ones in the whole world. But it was too late to save the world, people were all idiots or selfish or evil like he was, there was no saving humanity; only immediate survival. He'd sacrificed a virgin to the heartless crazy gods controlling his urges. Instead of feeling cosmic euphoria, he'd been left with a dismal emptiness and the cruel realization that the chase was over. He'd won, but at the same time, he'd lost the object of his madness and the reason for his life.

A huge nothingness stretched ahead of him. The thought of killing another college student that looked like Victoria felt like dry ashes on his tongue. Somehow, there was no energy in his thoughts anymore.

Larry's attention went from his sandwich to the co-anchor on WGN:

> And now an update on a story we reported last week. Fire officials have ruled out arson in the house fire in Evanston last Tuesday. They believe faulty wiring was responsible for the blaze which took the lives of three people.

I got away with it. Larry sneered. He'd made sure to stage the fire to look like an accident and it worked like a charm.

"Funerals for James and Lillian Lawrence are scheduled for noon tomorrow at Thompson's Funeral Home, and the service for the couples' niece, Paige Peterson, will be held Friday at noon at Thompson's as well," the anchor-man reported.

The couples' niece? Paige?

"Such a sad story," his female co-anchor affirmed, oozing sympathy. **"In other news, commuters from the western suburbs can expect more traffic headaches as a proposal was approved today to widen the stretch of road between..."**

Larry switched off the TV trembling. *Victoria didn't die! I didn't even know Paige was in the house!* He couldn't believe it; he'd somehow screwed up. Victoria Lawrence was still alive. Suddenly he was infused with energy.

Plans! Redemption! Survival!

Perhaps he would have a different way to sacrifice this virgin and quiet the gods and demons in his head. She was still alive and that must be the reason everything felt wrong and still before. Everything was moving and alive now!

He called Thompson's funeral home. The solemn man gave Larry the location of the Lawrence's grave site.

Larry didn't sleep at all that night. Like a pulsating ball of energy, he bounced from one side of the bed to the other. Victoria was still alive. The emptiness had subsided. But he needed to be sure; he must see for himself.

Larry staked out Calvary Cemetery. He dressed in groundskeeper clothes and a cap to shield his face. He'd gotten to the cemetery at lunch time and located the two freshly dug graves.

Fall leaves drifted off the trees leaving a carpet of color. Squirrels scampered in the tree above him. Reverent Peace should have been the name of the cemetery. He picked up a rake to look like he belonged there and waited.

Shortly after 4:00pm, two hearses navigated the gothic stone archway entrance, followed by a long line of cars making up the funeral procession. Hiding in plain sight, Larry looked on as the caskets were settled and those in attendance made their way across the grass to the graveside.

That's when he spotted her.

The wind was teasing her shiny dark hair. Her smart black pants suit made her look older. Victoria's pale skin and downcast eyes were like a victory lap for him. He'd beaten her. He'd taken her life and turned it upside down. This was more delicious than when he thought she was dead.

He hadn't foreseen this delectable bonus.

He figured the woman next to Victoria crying uncontrollably must be her aunt. The bereaved spectators listened reverently as the minister offered up final prayers for the couple, then filed past family members extending condolences.

"Ashes to ashes, dust to dust, bitch," Larry said under his breath as the people strolled slowly back to their cars and their lives. He tensed when he saw Sean Weeden place his arm around Victoria and lead her back to the funeral home's limousine.

Before sliding back into the black sedan, Victoria suddenly straightened her shoulders as if someone karate chopped her in the middle of the back. Whirling around she frantically searched the landscape. Larry ducked behind a monument before her eyes reached his area.

When he got brave enough to peek at her again, Sean was bent over, talking into the back seat of the car, nodding. After a moment he closed the door and joined his own family. All the cars departed leaving the cemetery as peaceful and serene as earlier in the day.

Larry didn't know where Victoria would end up living; he assumed it would be with the aunt, at least for a little while or possibly she would move into a dorm at the university.

Right now he contented himself with the knowledge he was a cat with a mouse to chase and toy with for as long as he wanted to extend this game. The very idea made him giddy.

He never paused to wonder how his love for her had turned to vicious hate. Or the warm feelings he'd once had for her morphed into hard survival mode.

He never questioned his intelligence; he never questioned his mental health.

15

Changes

Victoria barricaded herself in her aunt's tiny, two-bedroom apartment. It was cramped, airless. The emptiness of loss penetrated every pore of her body. She'd never considered her parents might die before she was old. They were supposed to always be there. She couldn't concentrate. She withdrew from Northwestern. Important aspects of life seemed meaningless now.

Overwhelmed by grief, she went from feeling physical pain to profound numbness. She'd cry heaving sobs for hours, then float somewhere disconnected.

Nothing mattered.

Sean and friends from their homeschool group called, she let it all go to voicemail and didn't listen to their messages. She didn't want to talk to anyone. She couldn't deal with their pity and placating sentiments.

Staring out her aunt's front window at grey clouds, her heart ached. A cold November rain ran in rivulets down the glass. Her finger traced the path of one.

She saw Officer Weeden's unmarked police car pull into a parking spot in front of their building. Sean got out at the same time as his father. She buzzed them in.

"I hope we're not intruding," Officer Weeden said as his only greeting. They exchanged small talk pleasantries in which everyone claimed to be doing fine. Victoria appeared far from fine. She hadn't showered in days and her oily hair hung limp around her face. Dressed in sweatpants and a Northwestern T-shirt, she didn't care how she looked. The clothes hung on her, indicating she'd lost weight.

She invited them to sit. Richard Weeden remained standing. Sean took a place next to her on the loveseat. He leaned in, putting his hand on her back, and asked, "Have you eaten today?"

Victoria nodded. "Yeah, I warmed up some tomato soup for lunch.

Aunt Lisa is napping now."

"It's important you eat," he said softly.

"I know that, Sean! I'm trying." Her words came out sharper than she meant them to. She shrugged off his touch. Then softer, she said, "Sorry. We have a ton of food in the freezer, casseroles from neighbors. We'll be fine."

Sean repositioned himself, out of Victoria's personal space and put his hands in his lap. Officer Weeden took a place on the couch and got down to the reason for their visit. "Victoria, do you want to go over to the house to see if there's anything to salvage?"

Victoria found it hard to breathe, the room closed in, airless. "I... I don't..." she caught her breath. "I can't. I've seen the pictures... I just..." Tears streamed down her face.

Sean instinctively took hold of her hand. "It's alright, Victoria," her friend whispered.

"We were able to recover something you might want to have. Your mom's laptop was in the trunk of the Lexis and survived what the front half of the car did not. It boots up." Officer Weeden placed the computer on the coffee table. Victoria smiled through tears.

She put a trembling hand to her mouth and gulped for air. "Oh my God, thank you!" She immediately opened the display and logged in. More tears broke loose. With a little laugh she nodded. "I'm good. Thank you for this. You have no idea how much having her laptop means to me."

They said hollow goodbyes.

Days turned into weeks as Victoria lost herself in her mother's life on the precious laptop. Lillian's photo files had sync'd every picture, from before Victoria was born up to the picture she'd taken for her recipe for white chili the night of the fire. Their whole life was chronicled in those pictures.

All Lillian's recipes, assembled over the decades, were filed under course designations, as if she'd begun to work on her cookbook. Victoria was beyond grateful. These types of mementos were most often lost forever after a fire.

Aunt Lisa wasn't doing as well as her niece. For a time, she didn't have the stamina to get dressed most days. The woman's despondency over the loss of her daughter seemed insurmountable and her guilt over their last angry words to each other dominated every thought. Drinking and smoking too much, she self-medicated to dull her pain. Unable to cope with her preoccupation with loss, Lisa lost her job. She rarely got out of bed before noon.

Thanksgiving and Christmas passed without celebration.

Sean came by a few times a week and brought them food. Victoria forced herself to eat, even though she had no appetite. She coaxed Lisa to eat as well.

On one such visit, Sean looked Victoria deep in the eyes and said, "I know I can't possibly understand what you're going through. People talk about the five stages of grief..."

"I'm aware of the five stages of grief. Trust me I've gone through all of them and back again." Victoria looked down at her hands picking at a nail.

Sean took a piece of paper from his pocket holding it tight in his hands. "My mom said she'd be happy to refer you to her therapist. He's helped her a lot over the years, you know, because she worries about my dad on the job. I looked up some grief support groups in the area, if you're interested in joining one."

He reached out and offered her his notes.

She took it without reading and said, "Thank you, Sean." She didn't confirm she'd consider the help he offered.

A small sad smile was all she could give him to acknowledge his efforts.

Intellectually, she knew, she had no choice but to deal with the aftermath of this tragedy. Lawyers were calling and decisions needed to be made. Out of necessity, because Lisa wasn't capable, Victoria took the lead in the family. With the insurance and investments her parents made, Victoria was set for life.

Yet there was still the matter of the house.

The insurance company declared it a total loss and wanted to know if she intended to rebuild.

She couldn't make herself go back there and see the burned-out shell of her previous life.

Victoria got her lawyers to demolish it and sell the lot.

After the monument company called to inform her they'd set her parents' headstone, Victoria mustered the strength to tearfully write a letter to her parents.

Dear Mom and Dad,

I wake up, every morning and for a brief moment, everything is fine. Then it hits me. You're gone. I still can't believe it. I never knew something could hurt this bad. I miss you so much, every second of every day. I've felt so lost without you that I don't even know who I am anymore. Nothing could have prepared me for a life without you in it.

The thing is, I know, deep down, you would not want me to continue to wallow in my grief. You would want me to move forward and chase my goals. It's felt impossible to do that, but I'm certain if you could talk to me now, you would tell me it's time. So, as frightening as this feels, I'm going to try to put one foot in front of the other and step back into the life you helped me plan for myself.

I can't thank you enough for the financial security you set up for me with your estate. It means so much to me that even now you are taking care of me. Without your support, I don't know how I would manage. I plan to use it to help Aunt Lisa get back on her feet too. She's a wreck right now. Another good reason for me to pull myself together. She needs me.

I still struggle with the fact I'm the only survivor from the fire. I view my life is a precious gift and I vow to honor your sacrifice by becoming the woman you believed I would be. My hope is, wherever you are, you're able to guide me with your love beyond death. I will strive to contribute meaningfully to this world and make you proud.

I will love and miss you always,

Victoria

Drying her eyes, she sealed the envelope and borrowed her aunt's Toyota to visit the cemetery for the first time since the funeral. On this freezing January morning, the wind off the lake was brutal. Stinging ice pellets pricked her exposed skin like a thousand tiny needles. The wind blew flurries around and lifted snow already covering the ground.

She'd planned to leave her heartfelt letter at the base of their headstone. As she approached the graves, she stopped. Shocked into stillness at the sight of something placed on the top of their marker. A matchstick sculpture of a spider perched menacingly as if prepared to strike. Her heart raced and she experienced the same symptoms she did in the store when she'd had her so-called panic attack.

Somehow, she found her legs and sprinted back to the car where she'd left her phone. She tapped Sean's number from her recent calls list. He didn't even get out a hello.

"He was here. He left a matchstick spider on my parents' grave marker!" she blurted.

"Slow down, what are you talking about?"

"I'm going to take a picture of it and send it right now!" In three steps she realized the spider was gone. "What the hell?"

"What's wrong?"

"It's gone. I swear to God, it was there. I saw it with my own two eyes," Victoria said, breathlessly.

Sean sounded patronizing. "Did you take your medication this morning?"

"No. But this has nothing to do with those stupid pills. I'm not losing my mind; there was a matchstick spider here a second ago." She visually scanned the area. She'd sensed the same feeling the day of her parents' funeral, as if someone was watching her. But she didn't see another soul. She was all alone in a field of gravestones.

"Victoria?" Sean called; she didn't answer. "Victoria!" he shouted urgently.

"I'm here," she finally answered.

"You've been through a terrible tragedy; it's only natural you might start seeing things." Again patronizing to try to calm her.

"I'm not crazy. I know what I saw! I'll talk to you later." She disconnected and jumped into the car. Maybe the wind knocked it behind their gravestone. Yet the chill gripping her spine was so tight, she couldn't bring herself to go check. Her fight or flight instinct kicked into high.

She revved the car and sped off toward her aunt's apartment. She considered all of the possibilities; first, and blaringly obvious, Larry Devlin, so deeply traumatized by his mother's murder, had suffered a psychotic break.

If Larry had gone off the deep end, why now? It was almost five years since Mrs. Devlin's murder. It didn't make sense he'd waited this long. But who else possibly knew about the matchstick animals he used to make?

The next possibility didn't sit well: *I'm losing my mind.* Mental illness often showed up in the late teens and early twenties. She'd read about it. What about the spider disappearing so fast?

There was no way I hallucinated this. It was there! Panic attacks be damned, I know I saw it. This sensation is from an intense rush of adrenaline created by a sense of danger. The probability the stalker watched her and her mother in the store the day of her first episode made sense; even though she didn't realize it back then, her subconscious had been alerting her to his presence.

He's toying with me!

She could've proved it if she'd taken pictures at the cemetery. She could still go back. If it snowed tonight, as predicted, it would cover any evidence there might be by morning. The thought of exposing herself made her stomach hurt as if she'd swallowed rocks. She was disappointed in herself for being such a coward. But she was unequipped to deal with this fresh terror.

Tickling her unconscious was the feeling that he might have started the fire in their home, right now that was too far for her conscious mind to go. It was pushed down, pushed away intentionally in order to survive in the present.

Yet the Spidy-senses warnings of danger picked up everything hidden and sent chills of fear up her spine.

The only sensible thing to do was run.

If Larry Devlin had been able to disappear, she could do the same. He had been stalking her for months, probably closer to a year. She was behind in this sick game. To escape would take some careful strategy on her part and she needed plausible answers for Aunt Lisa to go along with this new plan.

After several days of mulling it over she came to her aunt, who was exactly the way she'd found her most days, dressed in flannel pajamas, wrapped in a fleece blanket with her thumb on the television remote control. As if she might find the answer that was going to make this okay, she flipped the channels like a zombie.

Evaluating Lisa's condition, it was obvious she couldn't tell her the whole truth. If she shared her suspicions about a stalker, Lisa would most likely treat her the way everyone else did, as if she were a few slices short of a full loaf of bread.

"Aunt Lisa, we need to make some decisions," Victoria began. "Aunt Lisa," Victoria repeated firmly. The woman kept flipping the television channels as if she hadn't heard. "Aunt Lisa!" Victoria snatched the remote from her aunt's grip and hit the button killing the power.

Lisa furrowed her brow, which Victoria ignored. "We've got to stop this. Mom, Dad and Paige would want us to move on."

"They would." Lisa nodded. "I don't know about Paige though." A small smile played on her lips. "She liked to punish me."

Victoria nodded. "I think you've done a pretty good job of punishing yourself. It's just you and me now and I need you." She didn't want to be judgmental, but watching her aunt slowly killing herself was heartbreaking.

Lisa's eyes filled with tears. "I'm so sorry. I'm struggling. I can't get it together."

"I'll help. We need a change of scenery. I think we should move. Staying here, we're tripping over memories everywhere we go. Look at this apartment; it's like a tomb! Grief is holding us prisoners. Living somewhere else could make all the difference in the world."

"Where do you want to move?" Lisa asked.

"We can look at options. I want to start back to school. But I don't want to do it here."

"I thought you wanted to go to Northwestern?"

"I can go to school anywhere. I want to start over where no one knows us." Victoria got up and paced the room. "What do you want to do? You could go back to school too; do something you love. My parents provided enough money to take care of both of us."

Lisa shook her head. "I wouldn't want to go back to college. I used to love to paint, though. Some critics said I showed promise."

"Perfect! You can paint and I'll go to college. Let's make a plan!"

The older woman nodded in agreement; the way they'd been living wasn't working. It had been months since Lisa felt like a human. Victoria came back to the couch and pulled her into a hug. "Thank you. There's one more thing, I want to change my name to Darcy Jensen."

"Why do you want to change your name? You have a beautiful name and why use my maiden name?"

"Because it will give us a fresh start. Everything is different now and I'm not that girl anymore. Remember when you changed your name from Peterson back to Jensen? If I change my last name to Jensen, people won't question our relationship and I won't have to answer questions about Mom and Dad."

To her surprise, it didn't take much to convince her aunt to relocate and start over. She contacted her lawyers. They facilitated her name change. Then all the estate business was handled. She informed Sean about her plans to move away and told him not to worry.

When he pressed her about where she was going, she evaded his questions by saying they were going to be spontaneous and land where it felt right. This struck Sean as very out of character for the girl who typically wanted an outlined plan for every aspect of her life. She promised to keep in touch. She didn't tell him she'd changed her name to protect him as well as herself.

Her mother's intuition was correct: Victoria Lawrence never made it to full adulthood. Lillian's sweet, confident child ceased to exist due to the trauma of loss. She was replaced by a determined young woman whose major goal was survival.

Five months after the fire, the Jensens traveled south of Chicago to the rural college town of Champaign Urbana. Victoria Lawrence, now known as Darcy Jensen, cut her hair much shorter and enrolled in the University of Illinois. They rented an old farmhouse on the outskirts of town on South Rising Road.

The house was cute and fairly large. It had two bedrooms separated by a full bath on the first level along with the living room, kitchen and formal dining room. A staircase led to the second floor with a second bathroom and two more bedrooms that had slanted ceilings and cute little windows. The landlords who updated it focused on the trendy farmhouse charm vibe. Not high-end, but adequate for a rental in a college town. Lisa called it their Shabby Chic farmhouse. Darcy intentionally chose the place for its lack of shrubs or outbuildings where stalkers might hide. Every angle on the property allowed her to see if anyone or anything was there.

She and Aunt Lisa slept in freshly painted bedrooms on the first floor; it would be easier to escape a fire from the ground floor. With Darcy's encouragement, Lisa set up an art studio upstairs and followed her passion to paint again. At first, her work was dark and brooding: sullen portraits of Paige, abandoned farmhouses, ominous paintings of storms overtaking farm fields.

Then Lisa bought a camera and went in search of inspiration. She tacked up photographs of covered bridges and light playing off water in creeks. Her work began to change and evolve.

Still uneasy, Darcy didn't sleep much. She woke with each creak the old house made or any car passing on the road. Darcy started the summer semester with a full course load to catch up. She'd missed out on what should have been her freshman year and imagined she'd fallen way behind everyone her age.

Lisa took a job in a local craft store giving painting lessons and they slowly developed a new normal to their routine.

Lisa seemed to relax and became more of a caregiver. She checked on Darcy when she studied, bringing her water or coffee and making sure she took breaks to eat. Every day Lisa asked her niece if she'd taken her medication. Darcy would lie and report she did.

Lisa also planted a herb garden in containers right outside the back door. The rabbits ate the tomato plants she tried to grow, so she gave up on homegrown fresh vegetables and supported the local farmers market instead. She had started to think of the future—of their health in the long run and that was a very good sign Lisa was pulling past the debilitating part of grief.

Lisa cooked the majority of their meals and kept the house clean. On occasion, she'd cooked one of Lillian's specialties from the recipes preserved on her sister's computer. One midsummer evening, they sat down to Lillian's smothered chicken. Dusky light played on the wind-ruffled corn fields seen through their dining room window.

Lisa asked Darcy, "How is it?"

Darcy finished the bite in her mouth. Holding her hand up in a pledge she said, "God's honest truth, it's as good as Mom's."

"I was thinking. Would it be alright with you if I worked at putting Lillian's cookbook together, see if I can get it published?"

"I love that idea."

"Yeah?" Lisa said with a growing smile.

"Yes, do it!" Darcy said, thrilled to see Lisa taking an interest in a new project. Her aunt seemed better and better as the days went by.

Back in Evanston, Larry Devlin strolled past the site of the Lawrences' home. The house had been torn down and the rubble hauled away. The real estate sign in the yard showed SOLD. Frustrated that in his effort to prolong the chase, he'd inadvertently lost track of Victoria, the warm tingle that preceded a rage flowed through is body.

After the funeral, he had staked out the cemetery in different cars and at different times. It was his bait to figure out where she was staying and start to plan his next move against her. He'd almost been able to follow her the day she showed up at the cemetery and saw his well-placed warning. But she'd taken off so fast by the time he got his stolen car started and out the gates, he lost sight of her. Finding her again turned out to be quite a challenge.

Victoria hadn't returned to Northwestern. He staked out the campus. When she didn't turn up for the second semester, he began to worry he'd lost her for good. He'd remembered from Paige Peterson's obituary that her mother's name was Lisa. However, the woman's phone number didn't show up in the Chicago telephone directories. He'd searched them all. Perhaps she only used a cell. Whatever the reason, he couldn't find Lisa Peterson.

He would need to get online to do research. He decided against using public computers at the library. There were always cameras in those places and easy to track histories of searches. This meant he would have to plan another break-in to steal a new laptop. Such a job took planning.

May came around by the time he finally got his hands on a stolen computer. He'd been so excited when he'd found the aunt's address on one of those people search sites, listed to a Roland and Lisa Peterson. Only to be completely let down when he went to the building and saw the For Rent sign in the living room window.

A man was digging holes in the flowerbed next to the front steps, seeing Larry he asked, "Can I help you, son?"

"That apartment is for rent?"

"Yeah, I'm the super. You wanna see it?" asked the pudgy guy with a strong Chicago accent.

Normally, Larry wouldn't have spoken to a stranger; he never left anyone alive to remember him. But he needed to find some clues. "Sure."

"You're in luck, pal; it wasn't due for a new lease for another three months but the tenant and the kid just up and moved out one night, no forwarding address or nothin'. They did leave the last months of rent they owed me, so I can't complain."

"Just took everything and split, imagine that," Larry said as a probe, hoping to keep the guy talking.

"Not everything, they left furniture. They took all the personal stuff though. I'm not sure if I'll rent it as a furnished apartment or not. Depends on who leases it."

"Does that happen a lot, tenants moving out without notice?" Larry feigned interest as he followed the man up the front stairs of the apartment building.

"Not as much as you might think. Usually it's a character several months behind in the rent or who's in some kinda' trouble, if you get my drift." Once inside, they took the stairs leading to the third floor. "I wouldn't have thought this chick to be the type and I'm a real good judge of character. People can fool you sometimes." He continued to talk about rental agreements and utilities arrangements. When they reached the apartment door, the middle-aged man was breathing hard. *Must be a smoker*, Larry thought feeling superior.

The superintendent ushered him into the living room. The scent of her dangled in the air; it was intoxicating.

"So what's your story? You a student or somethin'?"

"Northwestern," Larry lied.

"Really? I would have pegged you as a Loyola man."

A jolt of panic punched Larry in the chest. Loyola was the school he'd wanted to go to. It was his father's alma mater. *How does this guy know that? This is a bad idea. No, he is just talking, he doesn't know anything.*

They continued the tour.

Larry caught a glimpse of himself in the full-length mirror on a closet door and relaxed. He'd kept up with coloring his hair and using brown contacts. He'd grown a beard, which he wore close shaven and colored. He looked nothing like the Larry Devlin Victoria knew. He resembled a typical college student.

As they came to the end of the tour, Larry asked, "How much is the rent?"

"Nine fifty a month."

"Oh, that's way out of my price range." Larry used that as a way to start ending this encounter, it had gone on too long.

"It's got two bedrooms, get cha' a roommate and split the cost," the super said hopefully.

"I don't know anyone I'd want to live with," Larry joked, then made a hasty departure. His senses were still filled with the tingle of having been where Victoria once lived, but it was also mingled with the unrelenting anxiety that he'd lost her again.

As the days passed, his anger grew stronger and so did his evil urges. He needed relief. He spent hours remembering his first hooker in Detroit in order to masturbate and attain some relief so he could think. It helped at first, then his cravings grew again until they became unbearable. When he couldn't take it anymore, he drove to Milwaukee and found a prostitute who looked like Victoria, he didn't bother with a hotel room. He walked with her in an alley, paid her for sex, came nearly immediately, then he stabbed her forty-seven times. He stole all her money before hoisting her into a dumpster he lit on fire with a matchstick bird.

A phoenix to rise his mind out of the ashes.

He headed for Iowa, putting distance between him and his last crime. Along the drive, he had to admit he felt better. Killing that bitch cleared his head so he'd be able to concentrate on his real objective, finding Victoria Lawrence.

16

New Normal

On a warm evening in late July, Darcy Jensen skipped down the stairs of the university library and breathed in deep. A light breeze chased away the oppressive heat of earlier in the day. It felt good to be back at school. She excelled in her classes. She'd quit taking the sense-dulling Prozac altogether. If the stalker was around, she didn't want to miss the signals.

Taking the path through the south quad she watched groups of students sitting on the grass. Four guys in T-shirts and shorts were playing Frisbee in an open area. She blushed when one of them smiled and winked at her. Darcy held her books a little tighter to her chest and continued to the parking lot.

She beeped open the doors of her late model, black Honda, a purchase she made when Lisa started working at the craft store. The decent price at the used car lot sealed the deal. She preferred the red Ford Mustang parked next to it, but she didn't need a car so flashy. The last thing she wanted to do was draw attention to herself. The Honda didn't scream **look at me** and it got better gas mileage. She smiled thinking how proud her dad would be of her for being so practical.

Glancing back at the campus as she turned toward home, she wished she were in the position to make friends. Getting close to people other than her family had always been difficult. She missed the friends she'd made in high school, especially Sean. They still communicated via her old e-mail address.

She craved the normalcy of hanging out with someone her own age. Part of her didn't want to get close to anyone. It hurt too much when you lost them. The other part of her needed human connection. Still, getting a degree was her goal. Eager to start on her major, which she decided would be Psychology, she reminded herself she didn't have time for these foolish longings.

She'd been enjoying the wind through the car windows when the farmhouse came into view. There was a strange car in the driveway, a black Mercedes sedan. Parking behind it, she recorded the license with a snap shot from her cell and went in the back door, into the kitchen.

"I'm home," Darcy called in a loud voice. Passing through to the dining room she put her backpack and loose books on the table. A man's suit jacket was draped over the back of a dining chair. That's when she heard muffled voices and laughter coming from upstairs.

"Aunt Lisa?" she called again.

"Up here, Darcy," Lisa's voice came from the stairwell. "Come up to my studio, I'd like to introduce you to someone."

In her aunt's creative domain, she found a man with salt and pepper hair. He stood about 6'1", dressed in suit pants and a white shirt with a tie. He had a friendly smile and warm brown eyes. He reached out to shake her hand. "I'm Howard Atkins. I'm the owner of Impressions, the art gallery downtown."

"Nice to meet you, I'm Darcy." She shook his hand, then looked at her aunt for an explanation.

"Mr. Atkins has come into the hobby store a few times and we've talked about art—" Lisa began.

"Please, call me Howard," he interrupted.

"Howard asked to see my work." Lisa smiled. "He wants to put some of my pieces in his gallery and see how they sell."

"You've got solid talent. I love your landscapes, especially this one with the light on the corn fields and the contrast of the red barn with the storm clouds behind it... it's stunning. I'm amazed by your ability to go from realism to impressionism, to Americana."

"I've been telling you how fabulous they are." Darcy beamed.

Lisa blushed with pleasure. "Well, I hope you aren't disappointed, but I don't dabble at all in Futurism."

"Not at all. Your work is unique. Let me start with three." Mr. Atkins took the one he'd been gushing over and then went to the pieces leaning against the wall, studying them. He picked up another landscape of a farm with cattle dotting the fields. He paused at a painting of Paige, wearing a melancholy expression, looking out a curtained window.

"That one's not for sale," Lisa said quickly in a defensive tone.

Howard gave her a surprised look but didn't press for an explanation. Instead, he chose a still life of a vase of sunflowers.

"I've got a ham and mushroom quiche ready to go into the oven if you would like to stay for dinner, Howard?" Lisa asked, her hand fidgeting nervously at her side.

"Sounds great, I'd love to join you for dinner." He smiled. Darcy believed his best feature was that smile. It brimmed with honesty. She liked him from the moment they met.

Lisa's paintings sold quickly at Impressions. Howard then planned on a dedicated exhibit of thirty of her pieces. Which meant she needed to create twelve more on a short deadline. Lisa texted the good news to Darcy.

Arriving home from school, Darcy took the stairs two at a time to Lisa's studio room. Her aunt wore a thigh length short sleeve man's shirt splattered with several colors of paint. "I guess your mom's cookbook is going to have to go to the back burner again," Lisa said by way of an apology. She used a fine brush to create whisper eyelashes on her current work in progress. A sleeping child with a rag doll.

"It'll still be there when you have the time," Darcy reassured her. "Besides, you're about to be a featured artist! That's pretty cool." She looked closer at the painting. The technique Lisa deployed created an effect so lifelike it resembled a photograph.

"It is pretty cool, isn't it?" Lisa clapped.

Darcy marveled at this happy version of her aunt. "So, you've been spending a lot of time with Howard lately. How's he doing?"

"Howard's wonderful. He's sweet. He is so totally not the type of man I've been... um... friends with, before."

"And are you *friends?"* Darcy raised her eyebrows.

"Not yet. But it's not out of the realm of possibilities. Do you think it's a bad idea? Please tell me if Howard is a bad idea." Lisa's face wrinkled with worry. She wiped off her brush, then selected a slightly larger one, dipping it in pale pink paint.

"Are you seeing any red flags? Do you feel a weird vibe?"

"God, you sound like a recording of your mother," Lisa gasped. "I swear, sometimes your mom was psychic. She'd get a gut instinct about something and sure enough, it would happen."

Darcy believed it and Lillian passed at least some of this premonition ability on to Darcy. Instead of saying this out loud, she asked, "Is he giving you signals he wants to take it to the *friendship* level?"

"Yes, yes he is." Lisa touched the brush to the canvas, giving a youthful glow to the child's cheek.

"Well, red flags?" Darcy pulled up a chair, taking in both the painting and her aunt's facial expressions.

"Not one, and no weird vibes, other than spending time with a sincerely decent guy is weird for ***me.*** I like him. He's funny. God he makes me laugh. When I opened up to him about Paige and you know, everything, he was so compassionate. He's such a good listener. He's not at all judgmental."

Darcy smiled. "I like Howard. He's good for you. The thing I want most for you is happiness, and if Howard Adkins makes you happy, then don't over think it."

Soon, Howard became a regular fixture at their house. Darcy enjoyed having him around but it also made her miss her father in the worst way. He was smart and witty, gentle and strong at the same time, like her dad.

During the fall semester Darcy once again took a full load of classes. Howard was spending most evenings with Lisa which Darcy appreciated since she basically only came home to eat and sleep. The three of them spent Thanksgiving and Christmas together like a family.

Over time, she learned Howard's life story. He cared for his first wife throughout her treatments for ovarian cancer. She passed four years ago. They weren't able to have children. He talked about her with the open vulnerability of a man who lost someone he loved very much. Darcy wasn't surprised when Howard proposed marriage to Lisa on the following Valentine's Day.

"I know this is quick but I'm thirty-seven; my biological clock is ticking. I want to have more children. Maybe this time, with Howard, I can get it right." Lisa thought she might have to justify her decision to remarry.

"The two of you are happy together, don't worry if marrying him seems fast. I trust him."

"He wants me to move into his place in town after the wedding; are you okay with that?" Lisa asked, afraid of Darcy's reaction.

"Absolutely."

What Darcy appreciated the most was how Howard sought her out later to make sure the changes were okay with her. He did this over lunch. As they sat in a booth at a quaint little deli close to campus Darcy marveled that this distinguished man seemed nervous.

"So, do I have your blessing to marry Lisa?" he asked, rolling and unrolling the paper from the straw in his soft drink.

"Of course you do. She loves you very much. I don't think I have ever seen her happier. Are you going to let me call you Uncle Howard?" Darcy asked.

"I'm comfortable with that, I guess." He laughed. Then he became somber. "Your aunt told me what happened in the past and I'm so sorry,"

"I'm glad she told you." Darcy held his gaze.

"I love her dearly and I want you to feel like you can always count on me as well as Lisa." Howard leaned forward and took her hand.

"You're sweet. I wish you both all the happiness in the world." After a beat, Darcy slid her hand away, her eyes cast on the chicken sandwich on the plate in front of her.

"But?" Howard asked. He sat up straight as if waiting for a punch, it was hanging in the air... something was wrong.

"Am I that obvious? Okay. I'll feel better if I know you're capable of keeping her safe." Darcy went on to explain about the matchstick sculptures and her suspicions about a stalker. "Everyone I've told about this thinks I've got a screw lose. I know I don't. I can't explain it; it's just a gut feeling I have. The hairs on the back of my neck stand up."

"I don't think you're crazy. Some people have a gift. It's possible we all have the ability, but over time our senses become numb from not using them. I've rarely met individuals as smart and perceptive as you are. If you have a gut feeling you should trust it. I can also say that creative people seem to use their senses differently and I have heard stories from my artists about their own gut feelings that have turned out to be true."

"My parents taught me to always trust my instincts." She looked him in the eyes again, relieved he hadn't dismissed the theory.

"I'm glad you told me. I also expect you to tell me if you feel this... Spidey-sense of yours again," Howard said.

Darcy smirked.

"Yes, for lack of a better word, let's call it that. I know you keep things from Lisa. I thought it was to not upset her, now I see it is that and more: you're protecting her too. You're an extremely gifted young woman. Now that I know what to look out for, believe me, I'll do my best to keep Lisa safe," he said.

"With her last name changed to Atkins it will make her harder to find. I've always worried that her living with me put her in danger. I'm sure I'd lose my sanity if there was another fire and anything happened to her," Darcy said.

"I won't let any harm come to her, I swear," Howard assured her.

Darcy hoped, with all her heart, this was a promise he'd be able to keep.

The couple married in late April under an arch of cherry blossoms in the small backyard of Howard's century-old home right in town. The gallery occupied the first-floor storefront; the upper two floors contained a modern apartment with an art deco motif.

They'd tried to convince Darcy to move in with them but she

refused, insisting she'd be fine right where she was. She wanted them to have a normal honeymoon period without someone cramping their style. Plus, with Aunt Lisa living under a different roof she was safer. Something was telling Darcy danger was still coming.

The farmhouse had too much space for one person and it was quiet without Lisa. Never having lived alone, she quickly came to the conclusion she didn't like it. Darcy compensated by turning on the television for background noise, usually to the Investigation ID channel or some other true crime program. She listened to them on the periphery of her attention while she sat at the dining room table and worked on assignments or studied.

Most nights she went to the newlyweds' house for dinner and was sent home with leftovers to put in her freezer for the nights she didn't come over. Darcy derived a peaceful joy being around the two of them. It spurred memories of being around her parents again. It mirrored a warm and loving life.

When at the farmhouse, alone, she functioned on high alert, waiting for signs of her earlier episodes, but there was nothing. She hoped this sense of security would continue, that the vague unease was just residual feelings.

The couple announced in July they were expecting a baby. Darcy couldn't have been happier for them.

Then it happened.

Right at the end of the summer Darcy felt that unwelcomed prickly sensation, the hairs on the back of her neck stood up. She knew he must be close. She confided in Howard. In no uncertain terms, the time had come for her to leave.

"Where will you go?" Howard asked.

"I'm thinking about the University of Texas in Austin. They have a marvelous program at the Center of Social Work Research," Darcy said.

"So you've decided to become a social worker?" Howard asked.

"I'm more interested in the research end of psychology. Social work involves getting in the middle of problems with real people, face to face, and I don't know how comfortable I'd be in those situations. I'd interact with people while doing research, but that's more about data and less about fixing. Human behavior fascinates me, strange but true." Darcy shrugged; she realized it sounded like rationalizing. "I'll let you know where I am but you can't have my address on paper or tell anyone where I've gone."

"I understand," her new uncle told her. "I'll smooth it over with Lisa. You need to do what you think you should. I'll back you anyway I can."

"I'm so glad you came along." Darcy hugged him gratefully.

17
Psychology

Darcy moved into a small white house on the corner of East 13th and Waller Streets in Austin, Texas. Staying in a dorm or an apartment building might put someone else in danger. Plus it would be easier for someone to blend into a crowd to watch the entrance. The plan was to travel light; be ready to move again if needed.

The house wasn't much, *nothing like the home my parents raised me in,* she thought as she carried in her meager belongings from the car. She chose it because it came furnished. The decor looked like leftovers from a hotel remodeling sale.

In the one bedroom she had a queen bed with a black lacquer headboard along with a nightstand and dresser to match. No linens. Good thing she'd brought one set. She liked the open floor plan for the kitchen, dining and living rooms, the space worked for one person.

It was generic. Neutral colored. Too quiet. She turned on the TV for white noise. To Darcy it felt as claustrophobic as Lisa's apartment in Chicago.

Walking through, she checked out the small backyard that lacked the privacy fences bordering most neighboring lots. She didn't like the idea of someone being able to lurk around behind a fence where she couldn't see them coming. It had been one of the selling points for her, though most would have considered it a negative point.

When she came back into the kitchen a hairy grass spider skittered across the floor in front of her. With a loud thwack she crushed it under the toe of her boot.

"I hate fucking spiders," she said as a warning to any other arachnids hiding nearby. Using a tissue, she removed the gore from the bottom of her shoe. "Ugh, disgusting." She flushed it down the toilet.

The first pang of homesickness hit. This was college life. She needed to put on her big girl panties and deal with it. Everyone went through some level of this angst.

She logged into her new student portal. She'd earned enough credits to start pursuing her major in Psychology. The problem was, she didn't know what discipline she wanted to declare as her focus.

There were so many to choose from. Her interests were criminal, cognitive, developmental and personality psychology. She made a plan to take classes in each area, then choose.

She hoped this move would throw the stalker off her tracks and she'd earn her bachelor's degree here. Having spent her life in the Midwest with long cold winters, Darcy enjoyed the heat.

When snow fell that winter in Chicago, the sun shone brightly and the daytime temperature hit sixty-eight degrees in Austin. She bought a bicycle and on pleasant weather days, she'd ride along the bike paths in the medical district and pass through Waterloo Park to her classes. She loved the wind blowing through her hair and the surge of energy pumping her heart as she pedaled.

Her classes were in a 1950s era building with variegated tan-colored bricks.

The student ratio to professor was high which supplied an ample crowd for her to blend into. She mainly kept to herself, not wanting to make friends who might come to harm because of her. To save off loneliness she called Sean every few weeks but wouldn't tell him where she'd moved. She always blocked her phone number.

"You're so paranoid," he told her one night.

She sat on her front stoop, crickets singing in the background. She missed him and his offbeat sense of humor. *That's okay, paranoid is better than dead.* "I choose to think of it as overly protective," she quipped back.

Sean let it go. "You'll never believe who's getting married!"

"Not you?" Darcy said in jest, as she nabbed a lightening bug who flew close to her. She opened her hand and the insect blinked on and off, climbing around her fingers.

"No, the only girl I even want to hang out with moved away," he said joking, but not joking. "Natalie Perry. I ran into her at the bank, she came home for a funeral or something. Anyway, she met some guy at Yale and they're engaged. He's going for a law degree."

"If I know Natalie, she has their entire lives planned, from graduating to fabulous legal careers to three and half kids and a summer cottage in the Hamptons." She couldn't imagine being that certain of life-decisions right now.

"You know it," Sean laughed.

"Well, if anyone can pull it off, it's Natalie. If you see her again, give her my best."

Darcy cherished her chats with Sean. It didn't take him long to quit asking probing questions about her whereabouts.

Communications with Aunt Lisa were handled differently. They made an agreement she would call every Sunday evening at 5:00 with the premise that if they didn't hear from her, they'd know she was in trouble. She faithfully called. Starved for connection, those calls usually lasted over an hour.

UT Austin quickly became the bright spot in Darcy's new life. She thoroughly enjoyed the field of psychology and insightful mentors.

Her interest piqued one day when the discussion turned to theories of nature or nurture in a propensity towards violence. Identical twins were brought up as great subjects for this topic.

"Identical twins aren't as identical as you might think. Even though they come from a single egg, environment plays a significant part in who they become," Professor Nelson elaborated. "For instance, they don't have the same fingerprints."

"How can that be if they have identical DNA?" a male student asked.

"How indeed? DNA isn't solely responsible for the formation of one's fingerprints. Even with the same environment in the womb, the amount of nutrients and other key elements passed from the mother to the babies can vary and it also may have more to do with something as simple as the length of the umbilical cord," the professor explained.

"What if they're separated at birth?" another student asked.

"Those studies have been done too. During the post World War II years, also known as the Baby Scoop Era, there were twins born in homes for unwed mothers who were split up and adopted by different families. Undisclosed to them, they and their adopted children were tracked. Most happy parents didn't think anything about the adoption agency checking in once a year on the child. Even though the method used to collect that data would be considered unethical today, it offered up some really fascinating information. The scale tips in favor of the environment they were raised in," the professor said.

"So evil doesn't run in a family?" a young man asked from the back of the room.

"That's still up for debate. Take cases like Ronald and Reginald Kray who received life in prison for murder in England in 1969. Their older brother, Charles, was locked up also. Back then there were a lot of people who claimed evil resided in their genes. Bad seed, if you will. Of course, they didn't have the sophisticated DNA tests we do today. And that field of science will become more definitive as technology improves," Dr. Nelson answered.

"There's so much research on DNA taking place right now. They're making new discoveries every day. Carl Bruder, at the University of Alabama, has investigated what he calls the copy number of variants."

She turned to the whiteboard and drew small rectangles to illustrate genomes showing two copies of genes. "There are some regions in the genome where the two-copy rule doesn't hold true and you can have anywhere from zero to fourteen copies of a gene. He found even in identical twins, these can vary. Plus, there are environmental differences even when children are raised in the same home. Preferences for the type of food or physical activity can change the gene make-up. The genes we are born with are not the genes we have when we get old."

As the discussion continued Darcy's thoughts turned to the Devlin twins for the rest of the class. She'd seen firsthand how different they were. Larry had been the calmer one, whereas Barry had a quick temper. Neither nature nor nurture explained their situation. Then there were their parents, the mother was obviously mentally unstable, but had the father been also? In his own way? She didn't have much information about their dad.

Larry almost caught up to Victoria in Champaign Urbana by tracking down her aunt on the internet. For months he looked for Lisa Peterson, assuming she shared the same last name with her daughter. As a last resort, he looked up Paige Peterson's obituary again and found the discrepancy. The mother had a different last name! Jensen was a common name, there were over 4,500 women with that name in the United States. The exasperating search was like looking for a matchstick in a field of haystacks.

By the time he got to the farmhouse they'd lived in, they were long gone. He'd been so angry he kicked in the back door of the empty house and destroyed everything that would give under the force of his fury. His vandalism caused thousands of dollars in damage but this time he didn't have the desire to burn the place to the ground. His mind was already solving how to track her movements. He got in his stolen car and headed for St. Louis.

Again, she'd ostensibly dropped off the face of the earth. He'd been positive he would have found information about her academic successes on the internet. Nothing showed up. Perhaps the death of her parents so destroyed her that she'd lost the drive to continue with her education. It was a possibility, yet improbable, since she and her aunt relocated to a college town. A student like Victoria didn't fly below the radar.

He continued to look for them as he moved from city to town. He decided since he had a new guiding mission, he could indulge in sex and stabbing when he left each town. For each sweet and bloody good bye, he ended it with a glorious house fire.

When winter hit, he settled in Mississippi. On the Gulf Coast he made a comfortable living picking the pockets of unsuspecting tourists. He'd raked in staggering amounts of cash in Biloxi from the casinos and drunken gamblers. He liked it there, except for the security cameras everywhere. He avoided the fancy casinos and mainly worked the restaurants and dive bars.

Larry planned on staying there for a while but one night he saw a dark-haired girl walking alone on the beach and his impulses went berserk. *How foolish to take a stroll after midnight without another soul in sight.*

The mighty crashing of the waves on the shore obliterated all other sound. He followed her, thinking he might jump her under the pier. But then, she turned and headed for a parking lot where a solitary car occupied a space under a streetlight. Larry skulked in the shadows of a boarded-up vender kiosk.

Almost to the curb, the young woman reached into her purse and pulled out her phone. She was texting. Distracted, she punched the button on her car key-fob and the lights of the vehicle flashed as the locks tumbled open. *Here's my chance!* He pulled a long knife from his backpack and vaulted toward her.

Without an inkling of danger, she didn't see the attack coming. The blade sliced a superficial flesh wound on her throat. Larry slapped a piece of duct tape over her mouth. He pushed her into the backseat, bound her wrists and ankles with zip ties then muscled her to the floor.

He retrieved the phone and keys she'd dropped, then jumped into the driver's seat and sped off down I-90 out of the city. He hadn't planned this, nor what to do with her; the impulse spiked with a crack like lightning. *This is all so spontaneous. What a high!* He cleared his head enough to check the text message she'd been engrossed in moments before.

"Oh, did you and your boyfriend have a lover's quarrel?" he asked in mock sympathy. Her muffled plea came from the floorboard behind him. The phone chimed with a new message. "He's a persistent little fucker, isn't he? I'll take care of this for you." Larry typed a response and told her what she'd sent, "Fuck off, asshole. I never want to see you again. I'm blocking your number." The girl thrashed like a fish on a dock. Her throaty screams sounded angry rather than panicked.

"What? No, no. ***This*** is how you handle guys like him." Larry laughed sadistically. Then he powered the phone down completely so it couldn't be traced. On a whim, he followed signs to the Big Lake region where he found a secluded, wooded area. The perfect remote spot. He picked a tree on a small raised area of ground. Dragging her to the trunk, he rummaged in her car, coming back with a hoodie that he sat on to fight the moisture. Sneering at her knowing the swampy ground must be siphoning off all her body heat, he started to create a lizard.

Lizard brain. Yes, this is the avatar to guide me tonight, all impulse and instinct.

Larry didn't have enough matchsticks to finish his lizard. He improvised using twisted pine needles and twigs.

Making the sculpture had cooled his craving. He usually stalked and planned every killing taking days if not weeks to build up the delicious energy wave for the final night. Part of the planning was the choice of animal he would create to end the session with fire: fire that was the only thing that took care of him. That wiped out evidence.

When he made his animals, the creative process calmed him. Allowed him to get a good night's sleep before the main event. He glanced over at her shaking body. *Cold or fear? Well, I have to get this party started, so I'll make sure it is fear.*

He took out his knife. HIS knife. The one he took many years ago, the same knife. Just holding it brought some of his energy back. She was watching him with wide eyes. *Good, good.* "Look what I have for you." She moaned. He felt power rushing through him.

After he'd had his way with her and carved her up to a bloody mess, he pulled needles and leaves all around her. Just now realizing there wasn't enough flammable material around her for a decent cleansing fire. Soon she was buried in fluffy debris.

He lit the matchstick lizard and walked off.

Driving off along the back road, he soon spotted a cabin nestled in the woods. He checked the rearview mirror and there was no sight of the small bonfire he had started, so he thought he should be safe from cops or firefighters here. He pulled off the drive in a spot where bushes hid the car and gave the cabin a good inspection. He decided some guy used it as a fishing retreat; it appeared deserted. Feeling unbelievably clear-headed, he slipped on the gloves good old Mary Ellen bought him and located the extra key above the door frame. *People are so stupid.*

Once inside, he stripped off his blood-soaked clothes and burned them in the stone fireplace. Ordinarily, he would have left them to burn when he torched a place. However, logic prevailed and two fires so close together would have the authorities focused and diligent to find the culprit, so he didn't plan to burn this whole place down when he left.

After a long, hot shower, he rummaged through the closets and found clean jeans and a shirt that fit him perfectly. In another stroke of luck, he caught sight of the keys to a boat hanging from a peg next to the back door. He grabbed some crackers from a shelf; indulging in carnal appetites made his body hungry. He snickered. Once he had some fuel in his stomach, Larry took all he might need from the car and drove it toward a hilly area that dropped down into the lake. Larry rolled out the door just as the car started to tip downward. That would cover the car and keep any cops looking at all the cabin owners in the area in connection to the burned body. Sadly, it was a sure thing they would find the body intact enough to figure she had been stabbed before being set on fire.

Gathering his gear, including his precious knife and gloves that had been with him the entire journey into power, and locking the cabin behind him, he strode down a gravel path to the water's edge where he found a Sportsman fishing boat docked by a rotting pier.

Feeling quite at ease since he hadn't heard fire trucks or emergency vehicles, Larry cruised slowly through the waterway. It was quiet, no other boats on the water. The sky was clear and full of stars.

By noon, he'd ditched the boat in Crossroads and stolen a black Nissan. In Gulfport, he stopped at a roadside diner for proper food and kept an eye on the news which was on in the corner, on mute with subtitles. Mid-way through his burger, the reporting turned to the gruesome murder of a waitress in Biloxi. Her boyfriend's photo flashed on the screen. He'd been arrested and charged with murder. The judge denied bail. His criminal record included assault, drug distribution, domestic abuse, the list went on.

Larry grinned. He hadn't intentionally set out to stir up trouble for this guy but, hey, he'd performed a public service by getting that piece of shit off the streets. *Live by the sword, die by the sword, motherfucker. Take the wrap for me you idiot. I'm not only smart, I'm lucky. I know I have to have a spirit watching out for me.*

He doubted the police found any clues linking him to the crime since fire burned the surfaces and in the cabin he wore gloves and wiped things down, plus he had let the shower run forever when he was done to flush anything down the drain that may have been there. Still, he thought it better not to take any chances. The boyfriend might come up with an alibi. So, in the afternoon, he headed to New Orleans where he would easily get lost in the crowd. He knew he could score big-time in the French Quarter and feeling considerably full of himself at the moment, he sang along with a classic rock station. He tapped his palm in time with the beat.

A few weeks before the start of Darcy's spring break, Howard called to give her news concerning her new baby cousin. "It's a girl! Lisa and the baby are just fine."

"You sound quite fine too, Uncle Howard," she said, laughing at the elation in his voice.

"I am. Here, Lisa wants to talk to you."

"Victoria?" Lisa's voice called.

"It's Darcy now, remember?"

"Sorry, I don't think I'll ever get used to calling you Darcy," her aunt said.

"Congratulations on the baby. How are you feeling?"

"I'm wonderful! Oh honey, I wish you were here to see her. She's so beautiful," the longing in her aunt's voice gave Darcy a sudden prick of homesickness.

"I wish I was there too," Darcy said.

"Why don't you come home for spring break so you can meet your new cousin?" Lisa suggested.

"I hadn't really thought about it." They talked for a few more minutes and then her uncle got back on the phone.

"Hey Darcy, we would seriously like you to come home on your break. There are some things I want to talk to you about and I don't want to do it over the phone."

"That sounds dire," Darcy said.

"Not dire; very important. I'm vehement you come home for a visit. I've walked out of the room so Lisa can't hear me. Your Spidey-senses haven't been going off, have they?" he asked.

"No. Not since I moved here." Now Darcy felt nervous. She felt a pull to rush to her aunt's home.

"I'll book a ticket tonight."

18
Austin to Dallas

Holding the new baby settled a calming peace over Darcy. This tiny person, pink and sweet with puckered rosebud lips, solidified her connection to this group as her family. The instant unbreakable bond Darcy formed with this helpless infant staggered her.

Lisa hadn't exaggerated when she described her daughter as beautiful. She had the softest pink skin and bluest eyes. Darcy thought she was perfect and well on her way to being royally spoiled by all three of them.

All of her calls to her family going forward would be done via skype so she'd be able to watch her sweet baby cousin grow up and interact with her. It would be hard to leave them after spring break.

"We've named her Lillian, we're calling her Lilly," Lisa told Darcy, worried the name may not sit well with Darcy.

"Aww, Mom would be so happy. Thank you for honoring her." Darcy felt a lump of emotion tighten in her throat, grateful for the gesture.

"She's a good baby," Howard bragged.

"She should be, the two of you never put her down," Darcy teased.

"That's not true. I have to lay her down to change her diaper," Lisa defended in jest. "Which, she's about due for. Give her here."

Darcy gently handed Lilly back and Lisa glided out of the room whispering loving secrets to her daughter.

Then the mood went suddenly sober.

"While we have a few minutes, I need to talk to you," Howard said in a hushed voice as he led her into the den. Without hesitation he began, "When you go back to Texas, I want you to buy a gun."

He retrieved a shiny revolver with a wooden hand grip from the desk drawer. He popped open the cylinder to show her it wasn't loaded. "First rule of the gun: always assume it's loaded; in this case you can be sure it's not. This is a .38 caliber; I want you to purchase the same make and model. I'm going to take you to the shooting range later today to teach you how to use it."

Darcy's eyes grew wide. "You're scaring me. Has something happened?"

"Right after Thanksgiving, someone went into the farmhouse you'd moved out of and trashed the place. The police blamed the wreckage on some fraternity prank but I talked to the owner and got to see the damage for myself. Whoever did it smashed light fixtures, mirrors, windows; ripped the cabinet doors off; punched holes..."

Darcy held up her hand, feeling dizzy. "I get the picture."

"If this is the guy who's stalking you, he was furious to not catch you there. He's dangerous," Howard stated in a no-nonsense manner.

Later that afternoon the two of them were at an outdoor shooting range standing under a long wooden pavilion. Several other marksmen were taking turns blasting at targets. At first the reverberations of gunfire made her jump. "Here put on these goggles. You'll want to buy some goggles and ear protecters too. If you don't wear these your ears will ring for a week." He handed her some clear safety glasses. He donned his safety gear. His voice was muffled but she could still hear him.

Howard loaded the revolver and announced, "We're hot." Then he handed the gun to Darcy.

"Now what?" she asked, holding the gun haphazardly. If it fired, it would have grazed her uncle's shoulder. With two fingers, Howard pointed the barrel toward the targets downrange.

"Second rule of the gun: never point it at someone you don't intend to kill," he instructed.

"Sorry," she said, concentrating on the barrel's direction.

"Here, take a comfortable stance. Point the gun at the target. Look down the barrel through the sight. Take aim. How does that feel?"

Darcy nodded.

"Good. Next you want to breathe in slowly and when you exhale, pull the trigger," Howard said.

She followed his instructions but the force of the gun and the bang of the explosion caused her to shoot off-target and stumble backward.

"It's all right, try again. Lock your elbows a little and lean just a little forward; you'll get used to it," he encouraged.

After a while and an entire box of ammunition, Darcy got the hang of it and was hitting the target's kill zone consistently. Howard said, "I'm pleased at the results of your first lesson. It's smart for a young woman on her own to know how to protect herself. The dude who busted up that house isn't the only danger out there. The world is full of crazy people."

"Thanks for teaching me. I wasn't sure about having a gun in the beginning, but now I like the power it gives me. I'll join a gun range. I'll bet there's several close to me, it is Texas after all."

"Good! Hey, third rule of the gun: if that nut job comes at you, don't miss." He smiled and patted her on the cheek like a proud father. "If anything happens to Lisa and me, we're going to need you to raise Lilly."

"I won't miss. But just remember, you promised to protect Aunt Lisa and now the baby."

"Believe me, ever since you told me about your premonitions, I've learned to sleep with one eye open. I'll protect them with my life." Her uncle was deadly earnest.

Darcy gave him a sad smile and a nod. Her father tried to save them but he only managed to rescue one, her. Howard reminded her so much of him, she found the comparison both endearing and frightening at the same time.

She took his advice and went to a gun store when she returned to Austin. She breezed through the background check, obtained a permit to carry and purchased a Smith and Wesson .38 snub-nose with a wooden handle, just like the one her uncle trained her with.

At the target range she honed her marksmanship skills weekly. As a precaution, she looked into other types of pistols and revolvers. Over time, she purchased a Ruger LCP .380 semi-automatic pistol which she kept in her car, a Ruger GP100 Magnum revolver she hid next to her bed and a Smith and Wesson .40 semi-automatic pistol she stowed in the kitchen. She carried her .38 on her all the time.

It surprised Darcy what a stress reliever and confidence builder that learning to fire a gun accurately was for her. Eventually, she got proficient enough to make a smiley face on her target, like Mel Gibson did in one of his movies. Maybe hers was a little cockeyed and the mouth sneered rather than smiled. Still, if she ever needed to use a gun to protect herself, she'd be ready.

Every city has its own flavor and vibe. New Orleans with its iron balconies, vivid colors and walled courtyards, pulsed with the type of energy in tune with the beat of Larry's heart.

Springtime was here, that meant Mardi Gras.

Tits everywhere.

He planned to stay until a solid lead on Victoria surfaced. The getting's were good in the Big Easy and the strip clubs held enough excitement to release his energy; to keep his urges at bay. His last kill, with the girl in her own car, was a favorite memory; he relived it often; that also served to keep the deeper cravings from taking over. Sometimes he pictured taking Victoria the same way, pine needles in her hair, shivering with fear.

He lived comfortably in that city. When checking into hotels he used IDs he'd pick-pocketed from out of state tourists when the true owner matched his height and build. Wearing a ball cap and sunglasses and paying cash made every check-in safer.

He enjoyed a good life for well over a year, never missing the chance to look for Victoria over someone else's wi-fi whenever available. One night, in a four-star hotel, when he'd been systematically searching the dean's list from random colleges and belting down vodka he'd stolen from a liquor store, he came across the name Darcy Jensen.

His heart skipped a beat. *Darcy, that's her make-believe twin's name and Jensen… that's her aunt's last name. She's changed her name! That bitch is at the University of Texas. Austin here I come!* A thrill coursed wildly through his body. He'd found her!

Toward the end of Darcy's fourth semester, the hairs on the back of her neck started to twitch. She didn't question it this time. She immediately began packing and researching her next location. Thank God for professors who gave complete syllabuses for their classes. Darcy always worked ahead and completed projects in advance of deadlines. She didn't have any trouble convincing her professors to let her take her final exams early, allowing her to leave for a family crisis.

As she left Austin in the dust, transcripts in hand, she called Howard. Being a Tuesday night, her calling put him on high alert.

"You okay?" he whispered a greeting. "I don't want Lisa to hear us; what's wrong?"

"For the moment I'm fine; I got an unsettling freaky feeling a week ago and tied up loose ends here. I'm headed to Dallas."

"Yes, you've got to trust your gut," Howard said

"I don't want to leave Texas. I love it here. I'll let you know when I find a place to stay," she told him.

"Be careful. I love you," Howard breathed.

"I love you too." Darcy disconnected; the pain of homesickness made her eyes tear up. She did love them and his sincere words underscored their concern for her. She couldn't help being afraid for them as well as for herself. A wiggling doubt teased across her mind. *I can't do this all my life. I have to find a way to put a stop to this.*

The next morning, while she brushed her teeth and listened to the news in a Dallas, Hampton Inn, she heard something about UT Austin. Walking to the TV she stood in shock while the reporter said, **"... tragically, Professor Amanda Nelson from UT Austin, died in a fiery car crash."**

Her heart sank to her stomach; *is this a warning?* Because she'd run, had he'd killed someone she cared about? Every instinct confirmed it. She rushed to the toilet and threw up. Crawling to the bed, she cried to the stage of exhaustion.

How could she tell the authorities in Austin what she knew?

How had he found her?

What had she done to single herself out?

Who is this person chasing her? Was all of this some wacked-out delusion on her part? Or was it really the Devlin twin?

Howard's words replayed in her mind: *'I believe you; has your Spidey-sense gone off; if the nut job comes at you, don't miss.' Boy, are my Spidey-senses going off now!*

Darcy tried to think of what she would say to the police to convince them. She spent hours going over different scenarios in her mind. The next day she showered, dressed and packed up her things all the while pacing and rehearsing the right words she'd say to the detectives. She felt pulled in eight different directions.

Finally, she sat down on the bed. Using the hotel phone, she dialed the Austin non-emergency number. A female voice identified she'd reached the police. Darcy said, "I'd like to talk to someone about the car accident that killed Professor Nelson."

She picked at a loose thread on the bedspread while she waited on hold for what felt like forever. When a gravelly voice picked up, she said, "I think the car wreck may not have been an accident." She rambled on, doing her best to not reveal her name but still put them onto the right path to catch the killer and end her nightmare.

"Uh huh," the detective said, obviously bored. She told him what she knew about the Devlin twins. The more she talked, the more she realized he didn't believe her.

"I know this sounds crazy," she pleaded, "please, you have to believe me, or just look into this and then you'll believe me."

She heard him typing away on a keyboard. Then he said, "If Larry Devlin is real, he's off the grid. I can't find him in any database. I checked on this Barry Devlin, he's locked up in Bellview. No hall pass coming in the near future for that dude." Muffled conversation clued her in due to her excellent hearing, he'd slid his hand over the mouthpiece and told someone, "I think this one's a candidate for a psych consult."

"Listen," she realized this could bring some very bad attention to her so she backtracked, "I'm sorry to have wasted your time. You obviously don't believe me and you aren't interested in following up on what I've told you, so—" A familiar sense of dread washed over Darcy; once again, they ignored what she said and this try that had been a possible solution had just puffed away like smoke.

"Miss, we follow up on any credible lead," he said defensively.

"Well, good luck with this case then." She hung up and let out a groan. Obviously, he didn't consider her lead credible.

Thunder rolled overhead. The sky outside her window grew dark and angry. When heavy rain drops sounded against the building, she dialed Howard and filled him in about what happened in the last thirty-six hours. "They won't listen to me; they think I'm crazy," she choaked back a sob. "Whoever the stalker is, he did this to my teacher as a warning; I know it in my bones. He's found me but I don't know how."

"Darcy, listen to me, breathe deep and calm down," Howard said.

She inhaled and exhaled several cleansing breaths and asked, "Okay, what now?"

"You're probably safe in Dallas for the time being. Enroll in classes. Be hyper-vigilant. At least you know Barry Devlin is still incarcerated at Bellview."

"That leaves Larry or some other psychopath as the prime suspect. I'm beginning to wonder if it's someone who was released from Bellview and knew Barry."

"Hard to say. It could be anyone. Be careful, girl. You've got your guns, don't be afraid to use one if you're threatened. At least you're in the great state of Texas where they understand self-defense and using guns as tools," Howard told her.

"Ain't that the truth!"

She promised to be extra careful as they ended the call.

19
Dean's List

No matter how she did the math, she couldn't reconcile that the Devlin twins were not at the center of her terrifying dilemma. Darcy's mind whirled while her intuition worked a late shift. Half the time she thought she should agree with the police in Austin and Sean and Officer Weeden: that she was losing her mind. Then her gut told her it was all solid as a rock and she better keep making plans to find an end to this before Lilly, Lisa or Howard were killed as this madman tried everything to find her. She had to be smart about this or she would end up in Bellview, right next to Barry.

In her new city, Darcy rented a one-bedroom furnished house with a lumpy bed and thrift store furniture. This place didn't come with a TV so she purchased a small flat screen. The kitchen was small but functional with a built-in microwave. On the go like this, Darcy rarely did any cooking, just heating and eating.

She spent the majority of her time at the oversized dining room table where she spread out her work. Nuked meals she ate on the couch in front of the TV. The semester hit the halfway mark without her fight or flight alarm going off. Another heavy course load at the University of Texas at Dallas kept her from obsessing so much. But one persistent question still bothered her, how was the stalker tracking her? He was far enough away that he was never directly following her when she moved, but within months he seemed to pick up her trail and close back in.

Just days into her second semester, one of her professors hit on a possible answer to her nagging question during a lecture. "In this day and age of social media and the internet, it's very simple for criminals to find easy marks for their crimes. If you haven't Googled yourself, you should; you're bound to be amazed at the information that's out there about you. God forbid any of you married students decide to cheat on your spouse because, with the sophisticated spy equipment available, phone tracking, GPS on your cars... you're likely to get caught. Keeping tabs on someone is easier than ever and relatively cheap."

Right after class, Darcy took her teacher's advice and Googled herself. Victoria Lawrence was all over the place, ending with her parents' obituaries. When she entered Darcy Jensen, she felt sick to her stomach. There she was, large as life: **Darcy Jensen, Dean's list University of Texas, Austin.** He had somehow figured out she'd changed her name. *Now, that sounds insane! How could he know? But that explains why he wasn't following me right away; it took him a while to figure it out.*

Panic rushed through her. She wondered how long it might be before he came after her again. *What if he's already tracked me down here?* Now her paranoia kicked into overdrive. "Get hold of yourself," she muttered as the room started to spin.

She had to outsmart him.

She Googled Larry and Barry Devlin and found the story about their mother's murder and the fire. Plus one article about Barry being unfit to stand trial and his incarceration at Bellview. Nothing else. The same things she'd seen years ago when she'd first tried to look for Larry.

Darcy remembered her professor's words about surveillance cameras and proceeded to tear apart the house she'd rented looking for bugs. After an hour she'd found nothing. But then again, she didn't know exactly what she should look for.

To educate herself she got back on the internet. The legality of buying some of the electronics available shocked her. She found a plethora of anti-spy and other things needed for home security. She went to a local electronics shop and purchased a bug sweeper and camera of her own.

A cute clerk with attention grabbing green hair demonstrated by flipping the power button on the sweeper and pointing it at the store's video surveillance. Darcy told her to ring it up.

A buzzer sounded at the door. Darcy paid and hurried on, eager to get all her errands done and get out of the open.

I wish I could dye my hair or dress like this, no, I wish even to be friends with someone so positive like her.

Next Darcy went to a super store where a tech guru (this one not colorful and in a dark blue uniform) set her up with everything else she needed to monitor her space.

At her rented cottage she turned off the power at the fuse box and swept the whole building. She found nothing. On the one hand this gave her a sense of relief. However, she felt a little foolish. *Am I overreacting?*

The only way to be sure would be to set up surveillance. Going through the directions, she positioned the cameras, installed window and door alarms and tied it all to her phone in real time.

She still couldn't shake the feeling he was going to find her again very soon. For the first time in her life, she intentionally got a C in one of her classes and that ploy kept her name from showing up on the Dean's list. She would have to become invisible again.

Fearful, knowing this new vigilance wouldn't cover all her tracks for more than a few months at best, she made a quick decision for the next semester and transferred to the Arlington campus of the university, located between Dallas and Fort Worth.

This would be her 5th campus in three years. It wouldn't look good on a resume unless she claimed to be a military brat who moved around with her family. She groaned when she thought of it. She hated lying.

To make herself harder to find, she didn't rent a place to live; she moved around using hotels and vacation rentals, never staying in one more than a month.

Life revolved around classes and her need to stay one step ahead of the psycho looking for her. Every night she used her little bug detector to make sure no one spied on her. Each time she moved she had to take down her security cameras and window locks and re-install them; resetting and testing it all on her phone. Already trained to function on very little sleep, her body let her keep going well past her previous point of endurance.

Occasionally she woke from nightmares. The one she hated the most involved a matchstick spider with Larry's head attached to it. The spider in her dream was the size of an SUV, no way to step on that one and kill it.

Pacing the kitchen in the bungalow she'd rented for the month, she faced some hard truths: she hated this game of cat and mouse. Her mind had slowly been pushing her about the choice of continuously moving, running as a way of life felt not only exhausting but empty. She was now accepting that this tactic wouldn't work past her graduating. Walking into the living room she paced some more. Moving constantly didn't work anymore; she was so miserable she ached. The loneliness, worry and fear *What's it all for? I'm studying for a job; I can't hold a job if I run. I need to start to create my life, find friends again.*

Exhausted, she sat in the living room until the emerging dusk closed in. It pissed her off she had to resort to downscaling her grade point average to maintain invisibility. *Why am I letting that son-of-a-bitch rob me of the life I should be enjoying?*

There had to be a way to make this stop. It would be so much easier if she found him before he located her again. But how do you find a phantom in the mist or, more accurately, a phantom in the smoke?

She went to her laptop and looked up Bellview. If she could talk to Barry or maybe someone there might share information about his brother, find out if he ever visited. After compiling a long list of questions she wanted to ask, she dialed the mental institution.

The woman cited privacy issues. Nothing could be shared.

"Can I visit him? I'm a friend of his from high school." Darcy tapped a pen on the page containing her questions.

"His statis is maximum security. Unless you're family, a clinician or law enforcement, all visitation is denied."

"Even if it's a matter of life and death?" Darcy asked, irritated at the lack of success with this fact-finding mission.

"I'm sure it isn't as serious as you're imagining. I'm sorry I couldn't be more help to you."

"No, you're not," Darcy snapped as she disconnected the call. She paced the floor trying to think of a way to find him. How did the FBI locate their suspects when they didn't know names?

Then it hit her; they looked at the crime pattern and linked together similar murders. Serial killers tended to repeat the same actions; the same signature appeared within their crimes.

This particular psychopath used arson as his modus operandi.

She needed proof. Sitting at her laptop, the screen's light glowing off her face in the dark house, she began a new investigation. She looked in online newspaper archives, searching in the places she'd lived for stories on arson fires. She needed to compile a list of this killer's crimes.

Larry was furious when he located a Darcy Jensen in Austin at the University of Texas, only to have her slip through his fingers again. He had to give her credit; changing her name was brilliant. He would have missed it too if he hadn't read her journals and learned about her make-believe twin.

Professor Nelson was the perfect surrogate for his rage. She'd been a popular psychology professor; Darcy took some of her classes and got perfect grades with this teacher. He remembered the interest Victoria showed in psychology.

Professor Nelson had been easy prey too, one of those stupid people who talked on their cells while walking to their cars. Distracted idiots don't pay attention to who is around them and, therefore, deserve the wake-up call they get.

He'd been surprised the media called her death an accident. They'd withheld details of her murder from the general public. Maybe the cops were complete morons and didn't find out she'd been stabbed. No matter, he knew the truth and he'd enjoyed repeating the crime like the one in Biloxi.

It took him another six months to locate Darcy Jensen's name on some psychology study she'd worked on in Dallas. Again, she evaded him. That time he took his frustrations out on a barmaid who was walking home alone after her shift at 3:00 in the morning. What a foolish thing to do and she paid for it.

She went up in another dumpster fire.

After Dallas, Darcy Jensen fell off his map. He couldn't find her anywhere.

Bored with not discovering anything new to go on, he made the decision to head back to New Orleans and the life he enjoyed there. He'd entertain himself until she surfaced; she'd turn up again, in time.

She always did.

20

Patterns

When Darcy transferred to UT Arlington, she'd planned to finish her degree there, assuming the serial stalker didn't catch up with her first. That objective changed the day she found out she'd been researching the wrong crime. For months she'd been looking into arson cases from around the country, trying to make a connection. It proved to be no small job, considering there were roughly 30,000 intentionally set fires every year.

Darcy's shocking discovery came quite by accident when her teacher used the unsolved murders of four UCLA students as an example of the hysteria which ensues when brutal crimes are aimed at a specific group, such as female college students. He played a recording of a news conference.

A chill ran up Darcy's spine when the pictures of four young women were displayed, all dark haired and dark eyed, and overall resembling her. Her heart beat wildly as the police chief described the heinous rape, stabbing, then arson committed by a monster who must be stopped. **"We are asking anyone who might have additional information to please contact the FBI,"** the police chief said. **"That number is at the bottom of your screen. We have a sketch of the suspect."** The camera zoomed in on a face she recognized, it looked remarkably like a Devlin twin. She gasped. The audio of the news conference, warbled as if coming a great distance through a tunnel. **"If you see this man, do not approach him. He's armed and dangerous."**

The girl sitting next to Darcy leaned over and whispered, "They had a crime eerily similar at UT Austin. A friend of mine's dad was one of the investigators. They left it out of the papers, but the professor had been raped, stabbed over a dozen times and then her car set on fire."

"Are you talking about Amanda Nelson?" Darcy whispered back.

"Yes. I guess they kept it hush-hush so as not to freak out the students," she answered. Darcy nodded absently. Stabbed and set on fire, just like Mrs. Devlin. A loud buzz clouded her hearing.

As soon as she returned to the cottage of the month, she looked up the murders of the girls at UCLA. Scanning the sites, including the full news conference she'd seen in class, she compiled all the information into a file on her computer. When she came across a composite sketch of the suspect again, she couldn't breathe.

One of the Devlin twins stared back at her.

She switched her focus from the thousands of arson deaths and narrowed her search to rape and stabbings, followed by fire. Astounded when the web search came up with pages upon pages of results, Darcy let out an exasperated sigh. She narrowed it again by searching for those types of crimes committed within the last three years. That search returned 600 possibilities. Paying for crime data sites, she eliminated the ones with male victims and those in which the killer had been caught. Then she looked for young women victims with her features and coloring. There were still over a hundred and they'd occurred all over the country.

A recent crime caught her eye. A young woman who'd worked in a bar in Dallas. The murder occurred one week after Darcy moved to Arlington. She couldn't prove it. Intuitively, she knew her stalker was responsible. She added it to the growing file.

She listed the pictures, names, city and date of death for each incident that could be a Devlin murder. Starting with her parents and Paige. As she went through the cases, more and more girls and women who looked like her were added to her file.

She created a map of where the murders occurred and pinned the locations. She stared at the faces and the map. The pain in her chest made it hard to breathe.

There were so many.

Over a dozen and she'd scarcely begun the search.

She only had two semesters left until graduation. What if she made the bold decision to transfer to UCLA? It would be a smart move, taking into consideration that UCLA was ranked 3rd in the nation for its psychology program. Would the psychopath follow her out there? What if she once again made the Dean's list? *He'll find it irresistible. It will be sure to bring him right to me, then what?*

It would be dangerous for him to be in a place where he'd come close to getting caught. If he struck again, the police in Los Angeles might be more willing to believe what she'd been saying about this guy. She sighed, so weary of hiding from him. He had too much power over her life. If this was ever going to end, she would have to draw him out, using herself as bait.

During spring break Darcy flew to Los Angeles and toured UCLA. Satisfied the school was a proper fit for how she would live her life if this hellish nightmare had never happened, she filled out all the transfer forms and applied for their honors program.

She was going to claim her life back one way or another.

Then she flew back to Texas to finish the spring semester. To her surprise the school quickly accepted her to the year-long-honors program. It would require her to start the third week in June with a faculty mentor: Rachel Morris. That gave her a month to settle in California after classes ended in Arlington.

Darcy rented a little house close to the campus in Los Angeles with a rock garden instead of a lawn. A sad, small palm tree was in the center of the front yard. No matter how much she watered it, it remained sickly.

The house was unfurnished so she bought the bare minimum from a thrift store and used a folding table for a desk. She outfitted it with a home security system and then made sure her stalker knew where she lived. She signed up on Facebook and began to live her life exposed, hoping it would bring him right to her.

Feeling prepared, Darcy headed to Pritzker Hall, an eleven story, 1960s era building. She marveled at the concrete grid system around the 144 windows on each side. In the bright California sun, it gave off a bronze tone. Entering the two-story lobby, she regarded the modern space in awe.

"Pretty impressive what a multi-million modernization will do, isn't it?" Professor Morris was walking toward her. She reached out her hand and they shook.

"It's beautiful," Darcy agreed. She followed her new mentor to the elevators. Rachel Morris looked to be in her early forties and was dressed in blue jeans and a sleeveless T-shirt. Tan and fit, her brown hair was highlighted with blonde streaks. They got off on the 6th floor and walked into a very neat and organized office.

Situating herself behind the desk, Professor Morris began, "So, tell me, why did you want to be part of our honors program?"

"I'm looking ahead to graduate school and I need the experience in research," Darcy answered.

"Do you think you'll want to continue here for your graduate degree?"

"I'm not sure yet."

"Well, you have plenty of time for such decisions. I'm excited about your research proposal on the impact of social media on adolescents. I can tell you, as a parent of two teenage girls, social media is often the bane of my existence. We have an adequate size pool of test subjects already in place, so you won't have to worry about recruiting. Most of them are participating in the neuroscience research studies."

"I'm happy to hear that."

"You'll be required to attend a weekly seminar but those won't start until the fall quarter. I recommend 196A. So be sure to sign up for it when you pick your classes." The woman continued on about the requirements necessary for the program.

Darcy nodded while note-taking. UCLA operated by quarters not semesters, so that would take her some getting used to. After an hour and a tour of the research facilities, they parted with Professor Morris making her feel very welcome.

The first earthquake Darcy experienced was two weeks into summer classes. Sitting in a study area on the mezzanine above the lobby, the building began to roll. Overhead lights swayed with the motion. A guy who was sitting at the end of her table started looking at his watch.

Should I stand in a doorway? Run outside? The rolling continued. She didn't like this at all. No one around her seemed concerned. When it finally stopped the guy said, "Thirty seconds."

"You're kidding? It felt like five minutes," Darcy objected.

"Your first earthquake?" he asked.

She nodded. "How often do they occur? And why are you so calm?"

He smiled. "They happen all the time. That one was nothing, a magnitude three, at best. Some are so weak you don't feel it. You'll get used to them."

"I doubt it." She took a deep breath, hoping to quiet her nerves.

"Well, even if it had been a four or better, you're in one of the safest buildings around. During the remodel they shored this place up for seismic resiliency. I'm Kurt, by the way."

"Darcy."

They talked a while longer and she learned that he majored in neuroscience. He'd lived his whole life in southern California. A few years older than she was, he'd done a stint in the marines and was going to school on the GI bill. Kurt's sun-streaked blonde hair fell close to his vibrant blue eyes, much longer than a military cut, yet not enough to be called long. He exuded a cute, boyish charm.

"Would you like to go over to Bruin Buzz, grab a cup of coffee?"

She wanted to say yes very badly. "Oh, sorry, I can't."

He studied her for a minute. "You already have a boyfriend. A lady as beautiful as you, of course you do. Can't blame a guy for trying," he said smiling, as he put his books in his backpack. "Maybe I'll see you around."

Darcy didn't correct him. Regret knotted her stomach as she watched him walk away. He'd be just the type of person she'd want to get to know better. *What would it be like to date him? What kind of a boyfriend would he make?*

After he left, Darcy rested her head in her hands. This solitary life was tiring. She couldn't imagine what her serial stalker would do to someone she was dating. Kurt said he served in the marine corps. If anyone could defeat the stalker, it'd be someone like him. Even though she'd been sensation free since Dallas, she wouldn't be taking any chances with other peoples' lives. No, she didn't want to gamble with Kurt's safety.

All her hope rested on putting an end to this soon to live a more normal life. She'd go it alone until she knew for sure no one else would be in harm's way.

Whenever earthquakes occurred, Darcy adapted Kurt's technique and kept an eye on the seconds on her watch. She was amazed how slowly time moved when the ground under her shook. He was wrong though; earthquakes were not something she would ever get used to.

21 All's Quiet

Summer flew by. With classes and preparing for the research project Darcy had very few hours left in the day. She ate out more and took selfies every time, then posted them randomly, never where she'd actually eaten that day. She lived looking over her shoulder and waiting for the tingle of her stalker's presence to be felt.

Nothing happened.

She joined more social media sites and tried to post something once a day. She resented the time it sucked from essential tasks and wondered why people were so invested in such meaningless endeavors. She double checked the privacy settings were set to public and accepted every friend and follower request she got. In no time she connected with hundreds of people. She wondered, hoped and feared that her stalker might be one of them.

August 17th she went down to one of the trendy clubs to celebrate her birthday. The loud music thumping and the packed crowds were so oppressive she understood why lots of people experienced panic attacks. She was on a mission, so she pushed forward. Hanging spotlights moved over the throng of people dancing, giving a strobe effect to the dance floor.

She made her way to the bar and ordered a shot of tequila and a Sprite. She needed some liquid courage to pull this off. She hated these places. She downed the liquor, shaking her head with disgust, then chased it with the sweet soda. She'd done it before with Paige just to try to understand what her cousin saw in drinking.

She ordered another, called an Uber and chose the one five minutes out. Then she made her way to the middle of a sizeable crowd. She wore a little black dress and had gone to the trouble of putting on makeup.

Raising the shot glass in the air, she shouted, "Hey, everybody, it's my 21st birthday!" She shot a selfie with everyone looking at her and raising their drinks in a toast. This made it seem as though she partied with a bunch of friends on her special day. She took another selfie of her slamming back the drink. *This is college life, right?*

A guy who looked to be in his thirties approached her. "Can I buy you a drink, birthday girl?" He slurred his words, clearly too far gone already.

"I'm sorry, no. I have to run. My boyfriend and a whole slew of people are waiting outside for me. They're throwing me a surprise party they think I don't know about." Her mention of a boyfriend put him off and he walked away.

She met her Uber and went home to post the pictures. Actually, she just turned 23, the 5th birthday without her parents, it filled her with a profound melancholy. Birthday's felt so hollow without them.

She continued to take pictures of herself in crowded places, as if surrounded by friends, and adding in close ups of glasses filled with colorful drinks. The online staging represented an overblown imitation of what she wanted.

Every night, while eating a microwaved dinner, she'd scroll through the video captured by the house cameras, even if the app hadn't pinged her. No one tried to break in. Nothing happened. The pings were an occasional cat or the guy delivering groceries both to her house and to other homes nearby; something she could see since she had picked a house with no bushes to block the view. She made the Dean's list her first quarter and figured if the killer planned to come after her, he'd do it soon.

Again, nothing happened.

She set up a meeting with Rachel Morris when the fall quarter began to present the research she designed.

"This looks good," Morris said. "You've got an adequate number of subjects signed up. Plus you've got a vast range of cultures for diversity as well as a balanced male to female ratio. Your questionnaire is thorough. Be sure to stress to these kids that none of this will be shared with their parents and guardians so it's vital they are completely honest with their answers."

"Yes. I will. They need to understand if they don't tell the truth none of this will be accurate," Darcy agreed. "So, am I approved to start?"

"Yes! Good luck. I'm looking forward to seeing the findings," Professor Morris answered.

Driving home, Darcy looked to the east and saw a massive column of thick black smoke rising beyond the hills. ***Fire.*** It had been a hot, dry summer, the area was a tinder box.

This was another thing she hated about California. Wildfires frightened her even more than earthquakes. She'd grown up fully immersed in the history of the great Chicago Fire of 1871; it only burned a little over three square miles. Here, fires burned thousands of acres, sometimes complete towns. For days she stayed tuned to the news and watched helicopters fly overhead with loads of water heading to the burn zone. A fleet of Cal Fire large aircrafts routinely dropped a pink colored fire retardant called Phos-Chek in advance of the blaze in hopes of halting the spread.

The smell of the smoke brought back memories of that terrible night her family died. The haze it created affected the lungs of even healthy people. More than once it made her question her decision to live in this area of the country.

She thought she'd been busy during the summer, but once she started interviewing the teens she was completely booked up with no free time at all. She enjoyed talking to the kids and felt like they gave her honest input. Across the board, it seemed like they all experienced bullying on one site or another, which didn't surprise her. Social media was notorious for people saying things they never would if they were face to face.

The things kids did to get around their parents' rules and safeguards was the appalling part. She found it disturbing that many parents didn't have any supervision at all when it came to social media. She thought of Paige. Aunt Lisa hadn't paid much attention to what her daughter did online. She smiled, knowing with Lilly that would not be the case.

Midway through the term she met with Professor Morris again. "I know it's going to sound like I've been living under a rock and I guess in a way I have," Darcy broached a difficult topic. "But I had no idea there is a thing called sextortion!"

"Ah, yes! Have some of your test subjects been caught up in one of these blackmail schemes?" Her mentor leaned back in her chair, her fingers making a triangle.

"A few. What's worse is some of them know kids who have committed suicide after getting threats that these bottom feeders are going to release their nude pictures or videos to everyone they know if they don't pay them thousands of dollars!"

"Bottom feeders is an accurate name for those scammers. They're vile humans," Professor Morris said.

"Personally, I don't understand why anyone would take nude pictures or videos and send them over the internet in the first place. These kids don't understand that once it's out there it's out there forever."

"No, they don't seem to comprehend the consequences. I'm just grateful there wasn't any internet posting garbage when I went through my reckless youth," Professor Morris said with a chuckle.

"I've never been reckless," Darcy admitted.

"I believe that about you. Trust me, I don't mean to make light of this phenomenon. The sad thing is, those who are targeted think it's the end of their world, when in reality, if they simply ignored the extortionists, the scammers rarely go through with their threats and even if they do, it eventually goes away."

Darcy shook her head. "It's such a waste. The FBI needs to track these people down and charge them with murder."

"I totally agree. It's interesting this has come up during your interviews. How is the rest of it going?"

"Better than expected. I should have all the data collected by the end of January. I figure I'll need a couple of months to write my thesis."

"So, I'll look for it at the end of March, beginning of April?" Professor Morris asked.

"I'll aim for that."

"In that case, carry on," her mentor encouraged, with a bright smile.

The neighborhood, decked out in Christmas lights, depressed Darcy. She stood with the water hose on, trying to keep the palm tree alive. The hopeless wilting plant matched her mood. It seemed wrong to have temperatures flirting with the 70 degree mark in winter. In all the time she'd been here, she'd never shared more than a wave with neighbors. Her life progressed as dry as the California drought. She made a last-minute decision to fly to Lisa and Howard's for the holidays.

Being home, or the closest thing she associated as a home, was salve for her soul. If Lilly's contagious laughter and her cuteness could be bottled and shared it could rid the world of most of the despair that seemed to haunt so many people. The toddler couldn't spend enough time with Darcy and brought her books saying, "Read me, pweeeze!"

"I wish you would come back here for graduate school," Aunt Lisa suggested.

"I'm afraid I'll need to be in a booming city, where I have more opportunities," Darcy explained. Later when she and Howard talked alone, she told him, "I can't risk putting all of you in danger."

"It's been a while since you've had any indications he's around, right?" Howard asked.

"Not since Dallas. Have there been any weird occurrences around here?"

"Nothing other than the vandalism of the farmhouse. Maybe he's given up or he's dead or in jail. You can't live your whole life like this, Darcy. It's not healthy." Howard rubbed the back of his neck.

"I wish I believed that. I think he's afraid to come after me at UCLA." She explained about the four murdered college students and gave him a memory stick with all her research on it. "If anything happens to me, give this to the FBI. They might be able to connect him to at least some of these murders."

Howard nodded and locked it in a small fireproof safe, looking even more worried now than when they began their conversation.

During the winter term she finished her research and wrote her thesis. Spring quarter she took the final class she needed for her Bachelors of Arts degree in developmental psychology. She turned in her thesis to Professor Morris and took a summer internship at the offices of the Los Angeles Department of Children and Family Services. Since she didn't have work experience, she needed this for her application to graduate school.

She hated the job and the brutal commute. What should take twenty minutes, during rush hour took over an hour. The agency was housed in an imposing concrete building on South Broadway where the sounds of traffic were constant. Her job consisted of filing and answering phones. Once in a while, she would go with one of the social workers to drop off a child at their new foster home.

Stories of kids who landed in foster care emotionally weighed on her, giving her a new appreciation for what Yolanda Murphy's life must have been like. It also reaffirmed her initial thought that she held no burning desire to become a social worker. She graduated with honors but didn't go to a graduation ceremony, UCLA mailed her the certificate. In her spare time, she perused the internet, researching schools suitable for her master's degree. Darcy checked UCLA off the list of colleges. Professor Morris hated to see her go but wrote a glowing letter of recommendation.

Los Angeles didn't appeal to her at all.

Too many people. The brown haze hanging over the city depressed her and she missed the change of seasons she'd grown up with. She planned to donate most of her furniture and sell the rest, including her Honda. She wanted to find a research job at whatever college she picked. It had to be someplace she wanted to set down roots.

Sitting at her computer, searching her opportunities once again, Darcy ate Chinese takeout with chopsticks. *Florida? No, too hot and humid, too many mosquitos. Minnesota? No, too cold and too much snow.* She chewed a mouthful of orange chicken and rice. The East Coast kept drawing her in.

Then she found it.

A professor who was looking for a research assistant to help him with studies on intentional human behavior. She read his theory and excerpts from research already conducted. The job entailed investigating negative behaviors of incarcerated people. This posting hit her as a perfect fit.

If David Hobart, PhD at Boston University granted her a way into Bellview, she might be able to find out even more about the Devlin twins and perhaps put an end to her living nightmare.

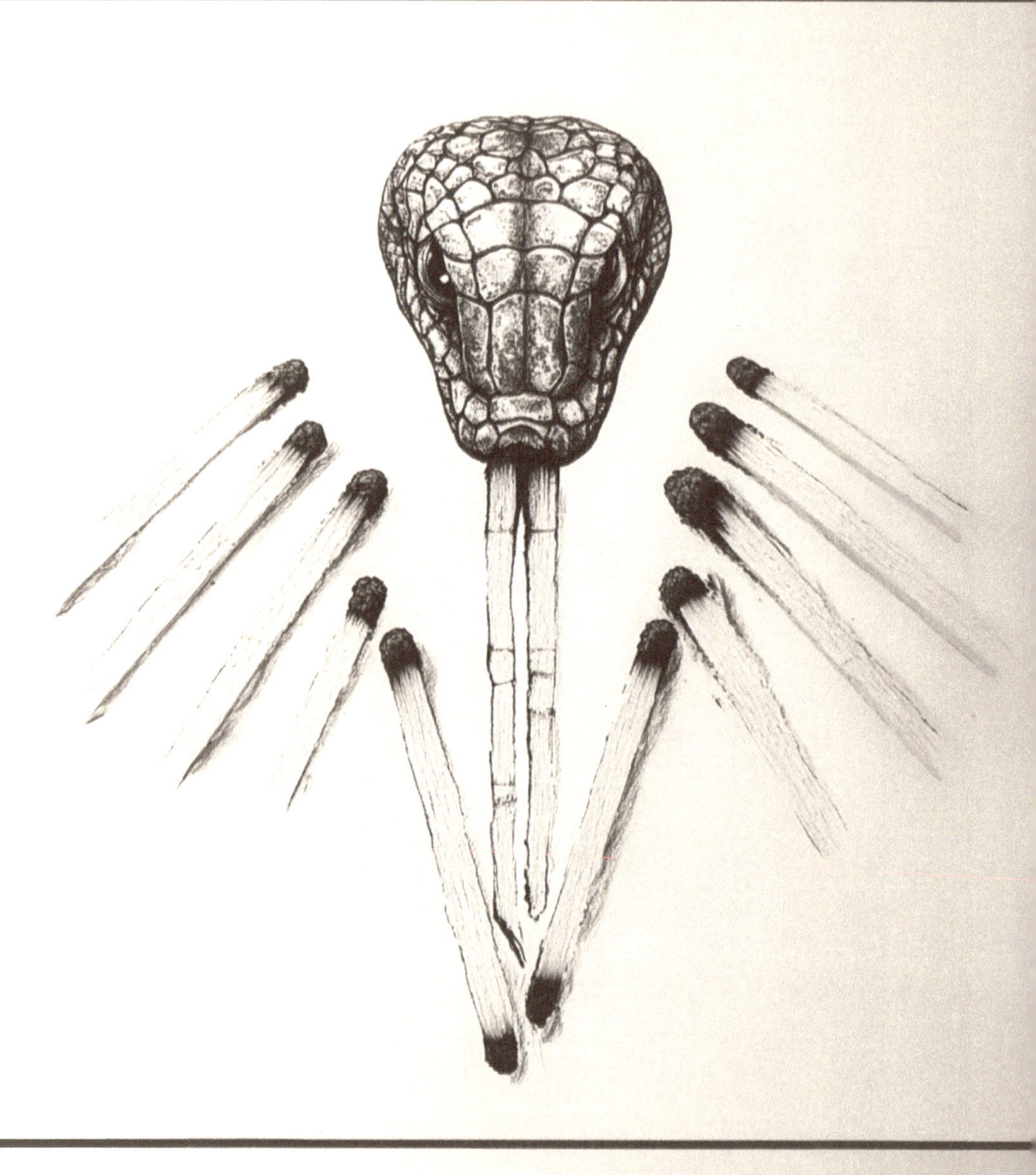

Part 4

Collateral Damage

22

Convergence

The day Darcy Jensen got off the plane in Boston, a pleasant autumn breeze was blowing. From the cab window, vibrant fall colors filled her with a delighted nostalgia and the thrill of a new school year. She saw the town as a cohesive mix of old and new, history and forward thinking, stability and possibility. The modern city grew tall yet was protective of the Revolutionary War landmarks; they were cherished. *Confirmation: Boston is the right decision. I already feel my spirits are up.*

Upon entering her suite at Hotel Commonwealth, the bellman asked, "Would you like the suitcase in the bedroom, ma'am?" He looked maybe nineteen, with a peach-fuzz beard. He'd called her ma'am. *At twenty-four, do I qualify as a ma'am?* She giggled.

"That'll be great, thanks," she said, placing her bag down on one of the brown leather wingback chairs. A cozy reading nook nestled in a bay window promised to be a favorite spot. She put her laptop backpack on the desk the same instant the boy reappeared. She handed him a tip.

"If there's anything you need please let me know." He seemed unsure of himself as he backed out of the room. Probably new on the job. The last few years had forced her to grow up, she didn't have the luxury of acting unsure. It seemed as though she was a decade past nineteen. Darcy looked in the cozy bedroom, warm colored walls, dark cherrywood furniture. The bed looked inviting.

She smiled. *Yes, this will do nicely.* Following a year of living sparsely in California after bouncing around the years prior, she deserved to treat herself to some luxury. At least for right now.

It was a graduation gift to herself.

Once she unpacked she went to the sushi restaurant at ground level. The sun cast long shadows in the golden light. As she ate alone she went over notes for her meeting with Dr. Hobart. She felt prepared, but giving them another look couldn't hurt.

The interview was set up weeks ago. She'd been somewhat shocked when she'd called Boston U to confirm her meeting time and the department administrative assistant spilled the professor's personal business as if it were wastewater. Apparently she lacked the same training as the woman who worked at Bellview.

"You need to be careful around him," Dean Collingsworth's assistant warned in a whisper. "He has a reputation with women. His wife divorced him because of multiple affairs. The department is whitewashing his arrest for domestic violence. He kicked in his ex's front door."

Darcy, of course, had done her own extensive research on the man she hoped to work with. She purchased his books and read them. They were captivating. She found his writing enlightening, while still interjected with humor in the right places.

The more she learned, the more the shrewd little voice in her head said *go this way*. She wanted to be involved in this research for her own reasons.

She'd seen his photograph on the back of his books so she knew he was attractive. She hadn't expected to walk into such a disorganized office. Piles of papers sprawling across his desk formed a treacherous maze, swallowing anything he placed on the desk. He shuffled through several piles looking for her resume.

Darcy took the opportunity to glance around. One end of his two-sided partner desk was under the metal cased window. The half not directly in front of him held a few boxes. His workspace faced an alcove occupied by a green leather sofa. The walls were white up to a drop ceiling with fluorescent lights. Two bookcases took up the remaining space to the door.

What she envisioned about this moment didn't coincide with reality. In fact, the entire non-descript building that housed the Psychology Department didn't fit her image of an East Coast university. The modern architecture was more warehouse than an institution of higher learning.

He found a thick folder of applications and pulling a chair to the side of the desk, motioned for her to sit. "Would you like some coffee, tea?"

"I've got water, thanks." She pulled a bottle from her cross-body bag and took a seat. He returned to his place at the desk, rifling through the folder.

Darcy decided if she was going to hook the research assistant job she'd have to take control from the very beginning. So she spoke first. "I've looked over your proposal and the excerpts you posted of your study. I'm impressed; it's exemplary work. What garnered my attention was your recent decision to broaden your focus to more than strictly the positive intentional behaviors of successful people, that you wanted to explore the intentional negative behaviors of those who have been arrested."

"That's right. As I investigated the variables of inherent and learned behavior, I realized I'd discounted the intentional behavior which also predictably produced negative consequences," David explained.

"Many researchers would have missed that. Did your insight come from personal experience?" The backhanded compliment opened the door to see how he'd react. Given his reputation with women, she needed him to know she didn't intend to fall for his charm. Unlike other fawning fools.

"Do you listen to rumors, Miss Jensen?" David asked, his eyebrows raised.

She couldn't tell if he was angry, embarrassed or neutral. "Not generally, Dr. Hobart. I'm only interested in attaching myself to projects conducted in a professional manner and that have the potential to be of tremendous value to you and society. Whereas I find your theories insightful, I think you are still somewhat shortsighted in the complete picture." She hoped that made it clear she had no intention of sleeping with him.

"Please, Darcy, enlighten me."

She'd irritated him and he meant to take her down a peg.

"Well, David," she responded, deliberately using his first name to keep them on the same level. "You've totally ignored the intentional behaviors of those who weren't sent to prisons but were institutionalized instead. Many of them planned, stalked and tortured their victims and, although they were deemed unfit to stand trial, their actions were premeditated and certainly intentional." It disappointed her when he didn't respond but looked at her resume instead.

"I see here you transferred to six different schools during your undergraduate work. Why so many?"

"I've always sought the best teachers in my studies. That's why I'm applying here for graduate school." She'd anticipated this question and had thought about her answer many times. This history could be considered as flighty and undisciplined.

She couldn't tell him she'd been running from a serial killer who incidentally murdered one of her favorite professors. Saying that would surely bring an abrupt end to any further discussion. This would be a work endeavor, he'd be her boss, not her friend.

"Graduated from UCLA with honors, undeniably a splendid

choice," he said, reading the file. "High praise from your professors. Your thesis, interesting. What were your findings on the impact of social media on adolescents?"

"In a nutshell Professor Hobart," she answered, smiling and being very respectful, "the world has been impacted by social media in both positive and negative ways. For this generation it's been there all their lives. You can't put that genie back in the bottle. Some kids use it wisely. It's super easy for kids to get in trouble with it though. It's a dangerous world. Safety boils down to the need for parents to step up and monitor what their children are exposed to."

"I'll forward you what I've compiled up to this point. Read it over and get back to me," he said.

Her tactics must have worked, she had to be in the running for the job or he wouldn't have bothered letting her look at his research. Back in her luxurious room Darcy printed off the over five hundred pages of Hobart's work in progress, then using a red pen, corrected his numerous spelling, punctuation and grammatical errors. She hoped she didn't offend him too much, but she couldn't imagine the professors she'd gotten to know letting such glaring mistakes go unrevised.

Darcy spent the next four days and nights pouring over David's research. If she wanted this job, she would have to be quick, thorough and efficient. After years of very little sleep, staying up until the wee hours and taking cat naps occasionally wasn't a hardship. Coffee helped. She ordered room service for some of her meals and left the hotel to stretch her legs and go outside for fresh air.

Darcy attached her own insights on how to approach the next phase of research and provided criteria for selecting the prisoners who should be included. She made suggestions on which institutions might be open to their study. Some of this she'd started back in Los Angeles, hoping he would see her efforts as invaluable and hire her.

His surprise when she placed a manuscript box containing her summary and edits on his desk, pleased her.

"You've read the whole thing?" David asked in disbelief.

"Start to finish. I hope you don't mind, I made some suggestions as I went along. When do you want to start on the negative behavior research?"

"I'll get back to you," he said, already examining the red corrections bleeding all over the pages.

Taking advantage of her free time, Darcy decided to be a tourist and take in the sights of Boston. She'd always enjoyed history and Boston was as steeped in it as the tea they dropped in the harbor.

From the Old South Meeting Hall to the Old State House to the trail that Paul Revere rode, ending with several leisurely walks through Boston Common, she loved autumn and the east coast cornered the market on its beauty. It didn't get more New England than this.

It had been a few days since Dr. Hobart said he'd get back to her. She needed to consider the possibility he'd chosen someone else to assist him. She'd pinned all of her hopes on snagging the job and been pretty confident she'd convinced him to give her the position. *What will I do if I don't get it? Should I stay enrolled and try to work with another professor?*

Sick of moving around, she wanted to settle down. Boston gave her the option of a life she might enjoy living. She missed her Aunt Lisa and Uncle Howard and she'd missed Lilly's milestones. Yet she didn't want to move back to the rural mid-west college town. There were so many more opportunities in this city. It felt fresh and vibrant and the restaurants were crazy good and diverse. If she could beat this stalker, she'd ask her small family to move here.

Right then and there, Darcy made the decision that whether or not she got the research assistant job with Professor Hobart, Boston would be her new home. There were plenty of colleges here to support her Master's and Doctorate degrees. If she wrote her thesis on mental illness connected with violent offenders, that might open the doors to Bellview without being Dr. Hobart's assistant. That very afternoon she walked into the Mt. Washington Bank and within an hour, she left pre-approved for a one-million-dollar home loan.

"You know, your financial disclosure indicates you're flush enough to go much higher. Homes in the Boston area can be very expensive. I can rework this for a higher amount," the young mortgage broker had recommended.

"I'll let you know if I need to," Darcy said, signing the document to secure a low interest rate. She inherited the means to buy nearly anything she wanted outright, but the opportunity to establish credit in her own name also created a paper trail her stalker might see.

By the time her Boston loan showed up on the web, she'd be ready and waiting for him.

23
Home Ground

Darcy initiated a meeting with Dr. William Collingsworth, the man to impress in the psychology department. This was the first time she met the chatty administrative assistant. Darcy estimated Marsha to be in her fifties, a few grey hairs caught the light contrasting her mousy brown bob. Of average build, Marsha wore a flowered print dress which reached mid-calve. The woman didn't have time to share any juicy gossip because her boss buzzed and ask her to send Darcy in.

Heavy executive furniture in Dr. Collingsworth's office testified to this man's importance at the university. There was a clear difference between David Hobart and the man in charge. A tall, beefy gentleman, with shock-white hair, Collingsworth deployed an easy smile when he shook Darcy's hand. He gave the impression of friendliness but also seriousness. With a hard swallow Darcy tried to quell her intimidation

She must have answered his questions correctly because at the end of the discussion, he proclaimed, "Welcome to Boston University, Ms. Jensen. Remember, I'm always here to guide you on your path to success."

Darcy choked out a thank you. Outside his closed office door she let out a quiet exhale. She enlisted Marsha's help in finding a real estate agent. It was an intentional step to befriend the gatekeeper of the entire psychology department. Darcy was determined to get and stay on Marsha's good side, and the best way was to make her feel helpful.

"You're too old for the dorms," Marsha said thoughtfully. "Are you looking for a rental, open to a roommate?"

"I'm looking to buy a house."

"That's impressive! Okay, I can recommend Mitzy Goldwin," Marsha rattled off the number. "So, wow! You're buying in Boston?"

"I like it here. I'm still waiting on news about the research position." Darcy shrugged.

Marsha leaned forward and with a delighted expression whispered, "Dean Collingsworth is breathing dragon fire to get Dr. Hobart going on this project again. He's going to have to make a decision in the next week or all hell's going to break loose. I'll let you know if I hear anything." Marsha winked and put her fingers to her lips as if keeping a secret.

Even though classes were full, with the Dean's note of approval, Darcy was able to get into a class on Criminal Psychology conducted by Liz Keller. Later she learned this professor shared a past with Hobart.

Professor Keller was in her mid-forties with a head full of beautiful blonde hair. She reminded Darcy of a young Dianne Keeton. Animated during lectures, Keller fueled interest in her students. Plus, she knew her stuff on criminal behavior.

Often, Darcy approached her after class to ask questions or pick her brain about serial stalkers. Keller came off as welcoming and engaged during these conversations.

They intersected one evening waiting in line at a crowded sea food restaurant. Liz, two places in front of Darcy, waved for her to join her. "I know you," Professor Keller said.

"Yes, I'm in one of your classes, I'm Darcy Jensen."

"I knew I recognized you. Aren't you also an applicant for Dr. Hobart's new research assistant?" Darcy caught a whiff of the alcohol on her breath as she nodded. "I knew you looked familiar. Marsha told me you're perfect for the position." The line inched forward. A moment passed awkwardly. "Are you here alone?"

"As a matter of fact, yeah. You?" Darcy asked.

"Seems so. There's two seats at the bar, do you want to join me?" the professor offered. They side stepped the line for a table, claiming the bar seats. Liz ordered a martini, Darcy a glass of cabernet and a glass of water.

They agreed to share a calamari appetizer and talked. Liz rambled on about what a talented teacher and father David was. Darcy's first glass of wine was still half full when Liz ordered her next martini. They talked about the interesting things to do in Boston while they ate their meals.

Sipping her second glass of wine, Darcy enjoyed their comradery. Liz shared some of the ins and outs of navigating the politics of the Psychology Department. Sharing an Uber home more gossip fell into Darcy's lap.

"I've had a shit day!" Liz huffed. "David got the grant money, I got passed over, once again."

"I'm sorry," Darcy said.

"David deserves it. He's fucking brilliant. I just deserve some too. Please promise me, if you get the position, you'll keep him on the straight and narrow."

"I can easily promise to do so," Darcy assured her.

Liz sucked in deeply. "So many regrets, I missed my only chance to be a mother with David." She let the tears flow, then she sobbed. "I chose an abortion. I told him it was a false alarm. I didn't want to destroy his family! I'm not a home wrecker." Liz sniffed. "Then, Claire comes along and everything blows up anyway."

Darcy told the Uber driver to wait while she got Liz tucked in at home. In the town house Darcy followed Liz to her bedroom, helped her to bed then locked up when she left, pretty sure the confession wouldn't be remembered in the morning.

A few days later she saw Liz in the hall between classes. The professor blushed and acted as if she didn't see Darcy and ducked quickly into her office. Darcy guessed she recollected enough to be embarrassed.

Darcy didn't take it personally. She focused on finding a permanent home. The real estate agent Marsha recommended took Darcy on a tour of a dozen properties, all of which, for one reason or another, came up short.

The woman showed her condominiums and townhomes, but Darcy didn't like the idea of neighbors too close. No one needed exposure to avoidable danger. The trendy areas were just too crowded.

At the end of yet another unsuccessful day of house hunting, Darcy tried to make it clear she didn't want any shared walls with neighbors. She hoped this time the woman would listen. Irritated, she went back to her hotel room and got online.

"If I want this done right, I guess I'll need to do it myself," she said out loud. She cruised the MLS listings for single family homes. The banker's assessment of Boston's expensive housing proved true. She tagged a few in a price range which, despite her inheritance, made her uncomfortable about spending so much money.

Not knowing the city very well, she decided to search the neighborhoods around the university. Then she thought she'd better Google David Hobart's address to be sure to avoid that area; she didn't want him for a close neighbor. She pinpointed his address on Google maps. She zoomed in on a majestic Victorian house with a manicured lot and an inground pool in the back yard.

The blabbermouth in Collingsworth's office tipped her off that his ex-wife had retained the house after the divorce. She'd also been told David rented a flat in a brownstone close to where his ex-wife and daughter lived. She circled the Hobarts' neighborhood on her map with the intention of avoiding the whole area.

For a few hours she scoured properties.

And then she found it.

The perfect home, a smaller version of the one she grew up in. Immediately calling the realtor, she asked to schedule a showing the very next day.

The next afternoon they pulled up to the curb in front of the yellow home with one-story Romanesque columns. If Darcy could, she would have bought it immediately without even an inside tour.

"I didn't realize you wanted something quite so roomy," the real estate woman explained.

"I want something that feels like home," Darcy clarified, following her up the redbrick pathway to the front door.

"Okay, but it's a lot of house for one person. It's got five bedrooms and three full baths plus a main floor powder room. The owners did a complete remodel three years ago. You'll see, it feels like a brand-new home." Ushering Darcy through the stately columns to the leaded-glass entrance, the woman unlocked the door and went into sales pitch mode. "Built in 1889, the home comes with some notable historical significance. There is documentation that Teddy Rosevelt once dined here." Mitzy puffed out her chest while dispensing the urban legend.

"It's obviously been lovingly cared for. The grand staircase is original to the house; they sure don't make them like this anymore. On the initial blueprints there was a wall here. During renovations they removed it to achieve this beautiful open floor plan," Mitzy continued while walking along.

The living room and formal dining room were to the right of a well-crafted staircase which climbed three steps to a landing then turned 90 degrees to the second floor. It was the first thing Darcy saw from the foyer and she loved it.

To the left, behind French doors, was a study with floor to ceiling bookshelves. The thought of perusing Boston's bookstores to fill those shelves with the books she'd lost in the fire flashed in her mind. She contemplated the possibility of living a normal life in this house.

Mitzy moved Darcy through the main floor rooms. The house was completely empty, not even a picture hung on the walls, and it lacked window coverings. Their foot falls echoed as they entered the open dining area flanked with the wall of French doors.

"I love what this couple has done with the design," the realtor continued the sales strategy. "If you want to close off the kitchen, you can keep this as is, but, with a flip of a lever, all these panels fold to the side, opening the space to your formal area. It's the same for the atrium."

The kitchen was spacious with a granite topped island, lined by stools. The fold away doors made it ideal for entertaining. The cabinets were antique and the sturdy lower set was topped with granite. Cream-colored walls and tall windows made the room sunny and inviting.

"As you can see, this kitchen went through a complete renovation with brand new high-end, stainless-steel appliances, but they kept the charm and detail you can only find in homes of this age. The electrical and plumbing have all been updated. There isn't a thing for you to do but move in," Mitzy said, making a sweeping gesture with her hands like a model on a gameshow while the announcer described the grand prize.

"I love it," Darcy approved.

To the left in the kitchen, was a second wall of fold away-doors which opened to the atrium, revealing a breakfast nook and cozy family area done with three walls of windows.

"Perfect for indoor plants. There are eight working fireplaces which have all been converted to gas. And these doors open to the study. When you have them all open, it's like one extensive circle," Mitzy explained. Darcy pictured Lilly on a big-wheel tricycle using it as a racetrack.

Proceeding to the second floor, the real estate agent apologized for a couple of squeaking steps. "You have to expect a few creaks in older homes. I'm sure the stairs can be fixed."

"I don't mind a house with a few creaks." In fact, Darcy liked the idea; that way she would be alerted if someone was on the stairs.

On the upper level were two huge master suites with private baths. The three remaining bedrooms were smaller but washed in abundant natural light.

"What's the story on the owners?" Darcy asked as they concluded the tour of the empty house.

"He got transferred. You know how it is in this economy; you either go where they tell you or you're out of a job. They're very eager to sell. The asking price is $969,000. But you're not obligated to offer the asking price. Motivated sellers often entertain lower offers."

"No. It's a fair price. Besides, I'd rather not be dragged into a bidding war. I would have paid more if that was what they were asking. I want you to put in an offer today contingent on an inspection. This place is perfect. There will be a generous bonus for you if you can expedite the closing on the house."

Two hours later in her hotel room, Darcy got a call from David Hobart. "Are you back in LA?"

"No. I officially enrolled here. I've been taking in the sights."

"Good. I'm calling to offer you the research assistant job. I hope you realize it doesn't pay much." David went on to outline the terms and financials while Darcy did a silent victory dance. "Dr. Collingsworth's secretary can help you with relocation."

"She's already been quite helpful, trust me," Darcy said with a laugh.

"What does that mean?"

"Nothing but she connected me with a real estate agent; when do you want me to start?"

"How does four weeks sound? Is this a sufficient amount of time for you to get settled?"

"I'm sure it will be, Dr. Hobart; I look forward to working on this research." Darcy hung up and immediately dialed her aunt and uncle.

"Put me on speaker," she told Lisa. "I got the position!"

"That's wonderful," they both chirped proudly

"I also put an offer on a house today. It's really beautiful and there's enough room for all of us. Hint hint, you guys would love it in Boston."

"Oh, I don't know," Howard gave a weak protest.

"Tell you what… You make plans to come and see me for Christmas and I'll talk you into it then."

"You can try. But we'll take you up on the Christmas in Boston offer," Aunt Lisa laughed.

"Tell Lilly there are eight fireplaces in my house so Santa won't have any trouble finding her."

With all the pieces of her future falling into place, Darcy slept soundly that night. She dreamed of a safe home and being surrounded by family. She imagined a normal life with friends and fulfilling work.

Her subconscious confirmed that if she wanted all this, she would have to intentionally go after it and work to keep it safe. Dreaming, she formulated a plan to catch the murderous stalker who had robbed her of so much.

Now she fully intended to turn the tide in her favor.

24
Baiting the Nest

Darcy's offer on the house on Melville Avenue was accepted the day after she put in the bid. The inspection found no hidden problems. Motivated by the promised bonus, Mitzy Goldwin called in favors and twenty days later, Darcy became a happy new homeowner. She'd used the days in between to arrange for an alarm company to install a state-of-the-art home security system with cameras and the biggest and best in-house sprinklers in case of a fire.

Hiring a second company, she had a saferoom installed. A sliding bookcase revealed the bullet proof, fireproof safe room door. It operated with a thumb-print entry pad. She purchased a Glock 19 9mm pistol along with a second cell phone to keep in there. All the feeds from her security cameras shown on displays built into a console. With so much extra square footage she'd have to find a new hiding place for the Ruger GP100 Magnum revolver. It only made sense to spread out her weapons.

Then she hired an interior decorator to help her pick out furniture, lighting, linens and essentials to make her new house a home.

On her first day working with David Hobart, Darcy left her semi-furnished home by ceremoniously setting the alarm. She got into her brand new, silver, Hyundai Tucson. She picked it because of its easy maneuverability and it made parking on the narrow streets of Boston less challenging.

Arriving at his office, she once again found the professor in a state of disorganization. "Is everything all right?" Darcy asked, concerned his mind wasn't in the proper place to start discussing research.

"Yeah, I just got into a squabble with my ex. She has a particular talent for pissing me off. Have you gotten settled in an apartment?"

"Actually, I closed on my first house last week; it's close enough to the university to be convenient," she said.

"At your age?" David was astonished. Then he joked, "What are you, independently wealthy?"

"My parents saw to it that financial limitations wouldn't hold me back from pursuing my ambitions."

"I see."

He probably thinks I'm a spoiled, rich kid, but I don't care. She didn't view herself in such shallow terms. If she invested wisely, she wouldn't have to work a day in her life. But without work and contributing something, what was the point of life?

"Let's get started." Darcy opened her laptop and set it on the desk across from him. "I hope you don't mind; I kept a copy of your work in a folder on my computer."

"You were remarkably confident I was going to give you the position." David's tone underscored his perception that she had an arrogant streak.

"Weren't you?" she asked, doubling down with a smile.

David chuckled. "Yeah, you got spunk, kid. You were the best applicant for the job," he admitted. "Okay, moving on... I've obtained permission from Riker's Island, Leavenworth, San Quentin, Attica and Louisiana State pen. From your recommendations about the mental health side, I used my connections to get us into West Haven and Moorehurst hospitals so far. Dr. Collingsworth is still working on Bellview; they tend to be real sticklers up there."

Darcy knew this from experience.

David mapped out their initial visits to the institutions for select inmates. They needed to investigate a broad sweep of criminal behavior from the white-collar variety to the hardened violent type. "Keep in mind, all the study subjects are volunteers. To go along with the questionnaires, we need them to agree to give us blood samples for DNA analysis."

"Are you going to try to prove there is an evil gene?" Darcy asked.

"We're just collecting samples, whatever comes of it we'll include in our published articles."

"Hasn't the majority of the psychology community steered clear of genetic testing?"

"I'm not sure the study will go that way. Dr. Collingsworth wants us to cover all the bases. If we can find a common thread, the ability to predict future behavior is helpful in all sorts of research," he said.

"It might also bring about gene profiling. The reality of that would be scarier than science fiction. Interesting theory, dangerous territory," Darcy voiced her objections.

"Glad you think so. To clarify, we're only collecting samples for storage. No research is earmarked for them except ours. And incidentally, I'm not a proponent of gene profiling, but securing samples is a caveat connected to the grant money."

His mind on the right track now, he continued, "Okay, to be sure we don't miss any of the variables, we need to know the same details about each inmate in the study: background, family history of crimes going back several generations including siblings, parents, extended family; education records, medical records, criminal records, history of drug or alcohol abuse, links to domestic violence, gang activity. It's important that we record which socioeconomic group they come from. We also need to know if they were raised by their natural parents or adopted or lived in any foster homes. Were their formative years with both parents or in a single parent home or were they cared for by grandparents or extended family?"

The two continued to formulate the strategy for the last part of his research study well into the afternoon. The whole time Darcy's fingers flew over her keyboard taking down his every word. Having a check list would be a valuable aid when they were out in the field to ensure the exact same data was collected for each test subject.

"I've done a lot of thinking about division of labor," David announced. "I'm going to have a limited number of days I can travel. I still have classes to teach and my daughter Abby is with me Wednesdays through Saturdays. It's out of the question being away from Boston on those days. I'd like to handle the prisons and have you concentrate on the mental health institutions since that was your idea and a good one, I might add. If we tried to coordinate and travel together, it would end up taking over a year to gather enough data. William Collingsworth is breathing down my neck about this project; claims his reputation as dean of the department is on the line, so we need to show him some quick results to keep the funding going."

"I understand. It's no problem." Darcy was relieved David was allowing her to travel on her own and take the lead in half of the research. Plus, not traveling with him removed the likelihood he'd try to make a pass at her.

"I suggest you go to Moorehurst first. Dr. Andrew Jerrod is the physician-in-charge and he's more cooperative than the chief of staff at Westhaven; it will be easier for you to get your feet wet and get comfortable with the process with Dr. Jerrod. You also need to be aware that many of the test subjects you'll be dealing with will not be able to give their consent and you'll have to obtain permission from a family member or the courts. Sometimes this part can be sticky and you may have to make repeated phone calls and send the consent forms a few times before you get permission to include them as participants," David explained.

"All of those phone calls have to be made from my office land line and all printing and postage for letters has to be handled through this department," he elaborated. "The pencil pushers in accounting want an accurate cost of this project down to the last damn paper clip or we get the grant money pulled back." Then he added a barely audible, "Fuckers!"

"I'd like to call Dr. Jerrod today and see when he has time to meet with me," Darcy said, eager to get started.

"I've put contact information, including the names of the attending physicians, on this stick. You'll also find the university's travel requests, milage reimbursement and any forms you need to submit to Marsha on it. Plus, this contains the standard consent forms and sample letters to send. You can amend those for the various institutions and participant names. If you want, you can do most of your work at home as long as the phone calls and printing and such are done here. All this clear as mud?"

"Yeah, sounds great." By the time she headed home that day, she'd set up a meeting with Dr. Jerrod for Thursday. He'd offered her several days to go over potential candidates for their study. She submitted her travel request to Marsha.

"Is Dr. Hobart traveling with you?" the busybody asked.

"Nope, just me," Darcy answered.

Marsha eyed her suspiciously, "Usually he doesn't trust his research to anyone."

"Maybe he's learning to change," Darcy suggested. She speculated the cynical members of the staff were circulating a betting pool on how long it would take Dr. Hobart to seduce the new research assistant.

Wednesday afternoon Darcy met with David to go over any last-minute details of her trip to Moorehurst, which was in Utah. "You have a $40 per diem for meals, and a rental car has been arranged. Be sure to turn in your receipts to Marsha when you get back—"

Suddenly, the office door flew open and a pretty teenage girl with long blonde hair came trotting in like she owned the place. Dressed in a school uniform, she looked like a picture from a private academy brochure.

"Mom told me to tell you, she knows the arrangement is for you to pick me up at the house, but she said she doesn't want you stepping foot on her property until you sign over the title to her car. She says she's been nice about this and doesn't want to argue." The girl noticed Darcy sitting in the leather chair across from David's desk and asked, "Who's she?"

With a humorless chuckle David conveyed he intended to hold onto his patience, but the vein pulsing at his temple suggested a breaking point was near. "Darcy Jensen, this is my charming daughter, Abigail Hobart," David said, making the introduction.

Then, turning to Abby, he said, "Say hello to Ms. Jensen, my new research assistant. We were close to wrapping up a meeting. Can you have a seat and I'll be with you when we're done here, please."

"He usually hires blondes," Abby told Darcy coldly. Putting in her ear buds, she plopped on the green leather sofa.

David turned his attention back to Darcy and said, "Sorry for the interruption. Do you have everything you need? Any other questions?"

"No. I think I'm clear on the objectives. If something comes up I'm not sure about, I'll call you." Darcy began to pack up her laptop and notes.

"How long are you planning on staying here today, Dad?" Abby quizzed.

"Maybe another hour."

"What you really mean is another three hours," Abby groaned.

"Two hours tops," he promised.

"Can I take an Uber home? I'm starving. I can stop by Swish Shabu's and get us some sushi and tempura," she tempted him.

"I don't mind your being at the apartment by yourself but I don't like the idea of you running all over the city in Ubers," her father objected.

"How about you, Miss Jensen, do you like Japanese food?"

"I sure do; I don't know too many people who don't," Darcy answered as she slipped on a light jacket.

"I wonder if Miss Jensen wouldn't mind giving me a lift, since she's heading out anyway?"

"Abby—"

"You know, Professor Hobart, it wouldn't be out of my way at all. I don't mind. Besides, all of a sudden, I have a taste for some teriyaki chicken and fried rice. Abby can give me directions to your apartment after we eat," Darcy offered, intrigued by this spitfire who reminded her of Paige.

David took his wallet from his back pocket and handed his daughter a credit card, along with a look that, in dad code, *meant we're going to talk about this later, young lady*. "Yeah, why not. Use my card to pay for Ms. Jensen's dinner as well."

"That's not necessary," Darcy objected.

"Of course it is. It's the least I should do. And call me when you get home, Abby, so I know where you are," David insisted.

Abby strapped herself into the seatbelt on the front passenger side of Darcy's new Hyundai and as they pulled out into traffic Abby asked, "Are you sleeping with my dad?"

Darcy scoffed at her boldness and the ridiculousness of her question. "No, and I don't intend to either."

"I'm sure many of his co-workers didn't plan on it when they first met him. How old are you anyway?"

"Twenty-four; how old are you?" Darcy asked.

"Fourteen."

Darcy eased to a stop at a red light.

"He's practically old enough to be your father, ya know?" Abby didn't let up.

"That fact didn't escape my notice," Darcy assured her.

"Are you aware you come off as kind of passive/aggressive?" Abby asked, as if she were asking Darcy her shoe size.

"Humm, is that so? It probably comes from being raised in an overly protective home. I don't mean to appear hostile. I guess I should work on my ability to dazzle with conversation." Of course her defense mechanism radiated passive/aggressiveness. It came from being on high alert at all times.

"Dine in or carry out?" Abby asked as they turned into the parking lot of the restaurant.

"Doesn't matter to me; either way, I'm going to sit down and eat it someplace."

"Then let's dine in. I'm not in a burning hurry to hang out at the apartment alone, but having to entertain myself in Dad's office is about as exciting as watching paint dry."

Darcy smiled as Abby pulled her cell out and sent off a quick text. *So much like Paige.*

When their food arrived, Abby continued her third degree of her dad's new assistant. "So do you have a boyfriend?"

"No. Do you?"

"Not right now; I broke up with my last boyfriend, Ronny, a couple of days ago. He's too obsessed with video games."

"I can see how that might dilute your interest in Ronny." Darcy picked up her chicken with chopsticks.

"How come you don't have a boyfriend; are you gay?" Abby asked.

"You sure ask a lot of questions."

"So you *are* gay!" Abby's eyes sparkled in triumph.

"No, I'm not gay. Not that it's any of your business," Darcy said.

"Well, I figure if you're going to be spending so much time with my dad, I should know more about you." Abby shrugged.

"I see." Darcy couldn't disagree with that tactic. "But the usual questions are where did you graduate, what's your interest in psychology and do you have pets?" Abby smiled and Darcy knew she was winning her over. "I should get to ask some questions too. Like... how come you're so pissed off today?"

Abby laughed. "Isn't it obvious? My parents hate each other and I'm expected to be the parrot who repeats their hateful messages back and forth."

"It was apparent to me; I wanted to see if you knew why you were acting out."

"I'm well aware of my mental health being in jeopardy because of my parents' poisonous relationship," she said shrugging. "They don't seem to recognize the position they've put me in. Isn't it funny, you met me thirty minutes ago and you recognize my plight."

"My cousin went through a similar situation when she was about your age. I talked her off the ledge a few times," Darcy explained.

"Have you ever thought about going into private practice and treating children of divorce?" Abby asked. "You might have a knack for it."

Darcy tried to squish a smile, and replied, like her mother would, "Food for thought."

Half an hour later Darcy dropped Abby off at her brownstone, part-time home. "Thanks for getting me out of there today. You're okay." Abby gave her seal of approval.

"No problem."

As David's daughter skipped up the steps, lugging her backpack into the building, Darcy wondered if Abby was going to turn out all right. The adversarial relationship between her parents could mess this girl up permanently. You'd think a guy with a PhD in psychology would recognize this.

Maybe not.

She hoped Abigail Hobart would come through their conflicts with minimal damage.

25
Born That Way

Darcy's trip to Moorehurst was very productive and, as David predicted, Dr. Jerrod was helpful and engaged. Dressed in a business suit with distinguished white hair, he exuded professionalism.

"You're very lucky to be working with David Hobart; he's an excellent researcher." Dr. Jerrod sat behind a massive mahogany desk. Diplomas, accommodations and awards decorated the office walls. On his credenza, family photos revealed grown children with successful lives and families of their own; one more sign of Dr. Jerrod's accomplishments.

"I read his book on body language and thought it was interesting," Darcy agreed.

"Yes, very insightful. This research on intentional human behavior might be his most important project yet. I'm glad he picked Moorehurst for test subjects. You see, here we've seen some progress with patients that other facilities would usually consider hopeless."

"So you believe antisocial personality disorders are treatable?" Darcy asked with a flush of interest.

"In some cases, yes. Not all. The younger the subject, the better chance we have of success. Our society prefers to label the mentally ill as monsters who should be locked up and forgotten. They don't consider the trauma that caused the illness can be, over time, reversed with kindness and positive reinforcement. There are a lot of misconceptions about pathologies. We've discovered that anxiety often drives violet urges. If you remove the anxiety, you remove the urge."

Darcy raised her eyebrows. The majority of her knowledge on psychopaths indicated there was little to no chance of rehabilitation.

Sensing her skepticism he said, "Don't misunderstand me. I'm not suggesting we set free those who would be a danger to the public. But with a quarter of inmates in the prison system classified as psychopaths, without any psychological intervention, it stands to reason that most of them will be arrested again within five years of release. The number is even higher after ten years."

"Do you think the lack of treatment is a matter of available resources?" Darcy asked.

"That, and lack of knowledge. This is why I'm enthusiastic about this study. If we can understand the why, we can design better treatments, maybe catch them before they turn violent and teach them other avenues of handling their emotions. I see this as a win, all the way around," Andrew said.

Darcy didn't share his optimism. She suspected many victims of crime would agree, sometimes evil was just evil and knowing the why didn't make it less painful. But wasn't that the reason she'd gotten into psychology in the first place? To figure out why people did what they did?

Dr. Jerrod spent the next few days helping Darcy download the files of over one hundred patients who fit the criteria for the study. "It's going to be up to you to get permission for these patients to participate," he told her, as he walked her out of the building. "If you have any trouble, let me know and I'll make some calls."

"I appreciate all your help," Darcy thanked him sincerely.

In Boston, she got busy writing letters and amending the consent forms in her home study while Janet Robinson, the interior designer she'd hired, arranged furniture and decorated.

Darcy left it up to Janet to coordinate the delivery and the setup of her purchases. In the living room she'd chosen a Birch Lane group of a beige and brown sofa and love seat with patterned throw pillows. An accent chair matched the pattern on the pillows. A round cherrywood coffee table and end tables topped with modern lamps completed the space.

The dark wood of her dining table and chairs complimented the end tables in the living room. The style was contemporary with sleek lines, tan, cherry, leather and wood.

The hardest part was finding fine china resembling her mother's. Going off the description Darcy gave her, Janet spent weeks tracking down a set exactly like the Lawrence family once owned. Darcy was thrilled on the afternoon the dishes arrived, she put her work on hold and helped Janet put the dishes in the glass front cabinet.

"I'm so excited you were able to find these," Darcy said, holding up one of the dinner plates to admire the geometric design around the edge. "I can't imagine celebrating the holidays on dishes other than ones like my mom owned."

Janet smiled. "I understand how important familiar objects are in establishing a sense of home. I've worked for many clients during my career and I particularly enjoy working with you, Darcy. You know what you want, which makes my job easier."

Whenever indecisive, Darcy trusted Janet's expertise. In the family room atrium, Janet suggested an oversized red sectional sofa. The plush fabric was so soft and comfy, Darcy looked forward to evenings watching television there. She asked her aunt to send some family photos which she could display on the bookshelves on either side of the fireplace. Several easy to care for house plants softened the bright colors and gave the space a cozy feel.

The upstairs bedrooms were each decorated uniquely. For Darcy's bedroom they chose a four-poster king size bed with an oak finish. Bedside tables with drawers flanked it. Her floral bedspread and drapes accomplished a room with feminine and soft ambiance.

The second master suite they designed to perfection with Aunt Lisa and Uncle Howard in mind. A luxurious maroon and gold duvet drew attention to the king size sleigh bed.

The guest bedroom was freshened up with mission style furniture and a yellow country quilt. One of the other rooms they designated as a workout room and soon had it fully equipped. It could easily be converted to an art studio, if she was able to convince Lisa and Howard to relocate to Boston.

On her final day at the job, Janet stuck her head into Darcy's home office. "Sorry to interrupt, I've finished the last bedroom. Come see."

Darcy followed her up to the bedroom they created especially for Lilly. She put her hand over her heart in appreciation when she saw the white toddler bed, purple sheets and curtains and white furniture. The white shelves were stocked with books and toys age appropriate for a three-and-a-half-year-old.

"Oh, Janet, this is so precious. Lilly is going to love it!" Darcy ran her hand across the silky pastel comforter with happy cartoon unicorns. "I can't wait to have my family visit and see the excitement on Lilly's face when she sees this room."

Her house now felt like a warm and inviting home. Not since her parent's death, had the ground felt this firm under her feet both literally and figuratively.

Darcy went to the department's main office to print the first batch of letters and make phone calls. When she walked by Dr. Hobart's office, she found Abby relaxing on the couch with ear buds in, tapping her feet to the music.

"I didn't expect to see you here today," Darcy said standing in the doorway.

"Teacher's in-service day," Abby explained, turning off her music.

Darcy moved just down the hall to the work area, plugged in her memory stick and punched in the grant code on the printer.

"What are you working on?" Abby asked now standing in the doorway herself. Darcy explained the process, Abby looked bored. "I'm not going to bother you by being here am I?"

"Not at all; I like your company."

"Good. Claire, Dad's last assistant, hated it when I was around. She said I got on her nerves," the girl complained.

"That's not very nice."

"She wasn't very nice," Abby agreed.

For the next few hours, while Darcy made phone calls, Abby helped her address envelopes.

"So Dad put you in charge of interviewing the insane people, huh?" Abby asked, while she ran the envelopes through the postage meter.

Darcy laughed. "He didn't call them insane, but yes, I'll be going to the mental health facilities."

"Aren't you worried about being around psychopaths?"

"Considering four percent of the male population in the United States are psychopaths or sociopaths, I'm around them every day. At least there, I know the person has been diagnosed with ASPD."

"ASPD? What's that?" Abby put the finished mail in a basket to go to the post office.

"Antisocial Personality Disorder. Clinicians diagnose both sociopaths and psychopaths as having ASPD," Darcy answered, adding another reem of paper to the copy machine.

"Four percent doesn't seem like a lot," Abby said.

"If you do the math, we're talking about close to seven million," Darcy explained.

"Oh. Well it's different when you put it that way. Aren't sociopaths and psychopaths kind of the same thing?" Abby asked.

"Yes and no. There's a lot of overlap in traits like lack of empathy and disregard for social rules. Both can be violent. It's generally thought psychopaths are the way they are because of genetics and sociopaths are more a product of their environment. There's other differences, but what fascinates me is that by studying the brain using MRIs and other tests they've found people with psychopathic tendencies have fewer connections in important parts of their brains."

"So they're born that way?" Abby asked.

"Early childhood development plays a big role in it too. Some researchers believe if children at risk are given therapies to increase the connection between the amygdala and prefrontal cortex then their brains can develop the way they should."

"My mom says my dad's a narcissist. Is his brain defective?" Abby asked, as if she were comparing it to the common cold.

"NPD, that's narcissistic personality disorder, is considered treatable if the patient is motivated to change. There's no standardized treatment for psychopaths and sociopaths, mostly because they don't believe there's anything wrong with them. It's hard to treat a person who doesn't think they need to change."

"So, there's hope for my dad, after all?" Abby smiled, tilting her head.

"I don't know if your dad's a narcissist or not. I'm not qualified to make a diagnosis."

"I don't think my mom's qualified either, although she did study psychology. That's how they met, she worked for Dr. Collingsworth. Dad took her out a few times. Mom got pregnant, so they got married. They didn't love each other. Now they hate each other," Abby stated flatly.

"I'm sorry you're having to deal with such an unfortunate situation. But I doubt your parents would be happy about you telling me all their personal business," Darcy warned.

"It's not classified. Mom made sure anyone who would listen knew my dad cheated on her. She tried to ruin him, which is abundantly stupid when you think about it. Financially, she's better off if he has a successful career. She didn't accomplish what she set out to do anyway," Abby said.

Darcy considered what would be an appropriate response and concluded it best not to say anything. She didn't want Abby to tell her more negative things about David. She'd heard enough from other staff members. She would have preferred it if everyone let her form her own opinion about him. So far, he'd been nothing but professional and the more she worked with him the more she liked him.

Just then David returned to the office. He'd wrapped up his last class of the day and the pep in his walk indicated an excellent mood.

"I've got spectacular news!" he proclaimed. "Dr. Collingsworth secured approval for you to go into Bellview!"

"Fantastic! I'll get started right away."

"Dr. Laura Dunham is your contact. Don't expect much help from her; she's not too happy about having someone looking through patients' files. Thank goodness William can be very persuasive."

The following week a meeting was set up.

The whole idea offended Laura Dunham, she granted only a day to choose test subjects. She snarled about proper paperwork then curtly ended the call.

It didn't matter.

Darcy was going to be allowed into Bellview and that was the real reason she'd gotten involved in this project in the first place.

26

Sleep-Over

David took a flight to Louisiana State Penitentiary in Angola and spent a couple of days with the warden to select the study inmates there. Darcy took advantage of his absence to do most of her work in his office.

On the afternoon he was scheduled to return, she was working on updating the spreadsheet of consent forms when her cell rang.

"Hey, where are you?" David asked.

"In your office. How's the search for test subjects going?"

"That's going fine. But I have a problem. There's one hell of a storm rolling in and they've cancelled my flight. I'm supposed to pick Abby up after school today; and when I don't show up, she'll come over to the university. I can't call her because Regina took her cell away as punishment for texting in the middle of the night. Regina's not answering and I don't like to leave her messages. She tends to try to use them against me when I do," David explained.

"Do you want me to pick her up at school?" Darcy asked.

"No. You're not authorized. When I don't show up, she'll call an Uber and show up at my office, mad as a hornet. Will you tell her what's happened and take her to her mom's house? She can explain it to Regina."

"Sure, no problem," Darcy assured him.

Accurate to David's prediction, a half hour later, Abby came bounding into her father's office, madder than a wet cat. "He forgot to pick me up again!" she shouted as she threw her backpack on the couch. "I put that stupid calendar on his refrigerator, with all those color-coded sticky notes to keep him organized, but he still forgets to pick me up!"

"No, he didn't." Darcy relayed David's message.

"Oh classic! Mom's gonna blow a gasket over this one. She'll threaten to take him back to court and tell the judge he's unreliable. This is all she needs to start a bunch of crap again," Abby ranted.

"Would she really do that?" Darcy looked up from her laptop.

"In a heartbeat. I swear she lays awake at night, dreaming up ways to make my dad's life miserable." Abby plopped down in the chair on her dad's side of the desk.

"That's unfortunate."

"Tell me about it." Then Abby seemed to be hit with a wave of inspiration. "I know! You could let me stay with you tonight and she'll never have to know."

Darcy raised her eyebrows at the girl; but seeing the pleading expression on the teenager's face, she gave in. "It's okay with me. I can drive you to school in the morning. But you have to check with your dad." Darcy handed Abby her personal cell phone.

When she got off the call with her dad, Abby said, "He told me to tell you thanks. He saw the wisdom in not pissing off Mom."

"Smart man," Darcy said.

An hour later the two of them entered Darcy's house. She punched the code into her alarm and told Abby, "Make yourself at home. I'll be back in a few minutes." Then she went up to her bedroom to change into a comfortable sweat suit and fast forward through the footage her security cameras captured that day.

As usual, there was no sign of a stalker. She didn't expect there to be; after all, she hadn't felt the hairs on the back of her neck stick up since she'd moved to Boston. At this point, she had encountered no reason to believe he was close by but she checked every day anyway.

When Darcy came downstairs she found Abby in the atrium. "You live in this massive house all by yourself?"

"Yep."

"These your parents?" Abby asked, holding up a picture of Howard and Lisa.

"No, my aunt and uncle. My parents died when I was seventeen," Darcy said.

"Sorry. How'd they die?" Abby asked.

"House fire. Are you hungry? I can make some spaghetti," Darcy offered.

"Sure." Abby answered following Darcy into the kitchen. "Wow, you cook too? You're a woman of many talents."

"Ha, you haven't eaten it yet. You might want to reserve judgment until then." Darcy opened the refrigerator and took out a package of ground beef. "My mom was an amazing chef. I've tried to teach myself to cook since I moved into this house. It has such a first-rate kitchen; I thought it would be a shame if the only appliance I used was the microwave."

"Dad and I eat out a lot. He gets too distracted when he's cooking and burns stuff most of the time," Abby said. Darcy gave a short laugh as she began to brown the meat. In an apologetic tone, Abby continued, "I might have given you the wrong impression about my mom. We're pretty tight. I was just upset when I got to Dad's office today."

"That's nice that you're close to your mom. Parents are important, I miss mine every single day," Darcy admitted.

"I get that. I love both my parents. Dad and I used to be super close when I was younger. Once his second book hit big, he was gone all the time. Mom resented the attention his books got and that's when their marriage fell apart. She's turned it into a competition. I try not to play her game. It's hard sometimes."

"I'm sorry you're stuck in the middle," Darcy sympathized. Movement always helped to process difficult emotions so Darcy asked, "Do you want to set the table? The plates are in this cabinet and the silverware is in the top drawer of the built-in hutch over there."

Abby willingly pitched in, but stopped short with a gasp as she opened the wrong drawer in the hutch and discovered a pistol.

"Don't touch it," Darcy cautioned. "It's real and loaded."

"Why do you have a gun?" Abby asked.

"For protection. I'm a single woman who lives alone." Darcy walked over to the hutch and closed the drawer.

"Did you ever consider getting a dog?" Abby suggested.

"I'm too busy at the university, it wouldn't be fair to the poor animal," Darcy said.

After a filling, not half bad meal, the two of them cleaned up the kitchen and sat down in the atrium to watch television. "My favorite show is Criminal Minds; have you ever watched it?" Abby asked, changing the channels.

"Yeah, it's interesting. I sometimes feel like I see enough real criminals in the files at work. But we can watch it if you want."

Abby laughed.

Around 10:00 Darcy supplied Abby with a fuzzy fleece night gown and showed her to the cheerful yellow guest room. "This should fit you. Bathroom is right next door. There is a brand-new toothbrush and toothpaste in the medicine cabinet. If you need anything, just holler, I'm a light sleeper."

As Darcy turned to leave, Abby said, "Hey, Darcy, thanks for letting me stay with you tonight."

"My pleasure. Sweet dreams, kid."

When the day finally arrived for Darcy to travel to Bellview, she waffled between excitement and dread. Excited because there was the chance she'd talk to Barry and dread for the exact same reason. The facility was in a small town northwest of Chicago. She hadn't been back to this part of her home state since she and Lisa abandoned their apartment.

As the plane made its descent toward O'Hare Airport, she looked out the window. The sprawling metropolis was laid out in a familiar grid pattern. She'd only been gone for five years but it felt like a lifetime. From this vantage point, not much about the city had changed. Yet, everything about her was fully transformed. This realization hit like a title wave of power; she had created a new life from the ashes.

She'd thought about taking a few extra days to drive down and visit her aunt, uncle and cousin. She was so close. She decided it wouldn't be wise to ask for days off so soon after starting the job. Besides, David's stress over the time he'd already lost on the project filtered down to her. Her family would be in Boston for Christmas and for now, she'd make do with that.

Dr. Laura Dunham's silver hair was styled in a textured lob cut, framing her face perfectly. She wore black dress pants with a crisp white blouse under a lab coat, she looked exactly how Darcy pictured her when they'd talked over the phone. She emitted no nonsense vibes.

"This is Dr. Dianna Poe," Dr. Dunham introduced her colleague. "She'll pull the files of the ASPD patients. You can go through them together. Please exercise the utmost care with our patient information. The last thing I need is an expensive lawsuit due to your mishandling of documentation."

Dr. Poe must have sensed Darcy's discomfort, because once they were alone with the files she said, "She can be intimidating, but trust me, her bark is worse than her bite."

"I promise to be respectful of the patients' right to privacy." Darcy put up her hand as if swearing an oath.

"The records are also kept up to date in our computer system, I'm assuming you'd rather put the information on a thumb drive for easy transport."

Darcy took a USB stick from her satchel, twirled it with a smile and handed it over. "That's exactly what I was thinking."

While Darcy quickly read the basics on the patients and chose the ones who met the research criteria, Dr. Poe downloaded electronic copies of the case files of these possible participants. When they began the second batch of patient files, Barry Devlin's name came up. She noticed right off that Dianna Poe was his doctor and her notations about him were surprising. **Patient seems docile, not the type who would commit the crime he is accused of.**

"What can you tell me about this one, Barry Devlin?" Darcy asked, nonchalantly.

"Mr. Devlin is a very interesting patient. He stabbed his mother twenty-seven times and set a fire to cover up the crime, except he got trapped and suffered brain damage from blunt force trauma from falling debris and smoke inhalation. When he first came to us, I didn't think he would improve. But he's made remarkable progress. He still can't walk, so he's confined to a wheelchair. What amazes me is the brain damage has made him very passive."

"Is he able to talk?" Darcy asked hopefully.

"In a fashion; it's garbled and a complete conversation would be difficult. His dexterity with his hands is where he's made the most progress. He makes the cutest little animals out of toothpicks and string. It isn't a fast process, sometimes he will work on one for a whole week," Dianna said.

"Toothpicks?" Darcy asked.

"He asked for matchsticks, but for obvious reasons, we don't let him have those," Dr. Poe explained with a smile. "If you want him in your study I'll sign the consent forms for Barry to be interviewed. He has no apparent next of kin and I'm authorized to oversee his treatment."

"He's never had any visitors? In his file, a twin brother is mentioned," Darcy quizzed.

"Not one visitor," the doctor confirmed. "His brother has never attempted to contact him. I guess it's a myth about twins having a special bond, at least in their case."

Darcy used their office printer and produced the necessary documents for Barry Devlin, which Dr. Poe readily signed. They worked late into the night and before Darcy caught her red-eye flight back to Boston, they agreed she would return to begin the interview process the week after Thanksgiving, assuming Darcy secured at least ten permission forms from patients' families.

It would be a short timeline which in turn created a sense of urgency and a need to be persuasive. She didn't want too much time to go by to give Dr. Durham an opportunity to change her mind.

Barry Devlin would be the first interview.

She'd had an eerie sensation ever since she read his file; she chalked it up to anticipation and brushed it off.

27
Up In Flames

Tired from working on the plane, then barely getting any sleep, Darcy was dragging when she walked into Dr. Hobart's office to update him. Surprised to find Abby and him engaged in some kind of argument, she hung back, not wanting to interrupt.

"Come on, Dad. Mom's driving me crazy. Just do this for me," Abby said.

"No, Abby. I've got you for Thanksgiving and I'm not going to let your mother bully me into switching holidays. If I do it once, she'll try it every time." David clamped the bridge of his nose with his thumb and index finger of his right hand and closed his eyes.

"Okay, then why don't we eat Thanksgiving dinner with Mom at the house? Just because you guys aren't married anymore doesn't mean we can't do some things as a family," the girl said.

"I'd rather stick bamboo shoots under my fingernails," he answered, using sarcasm to soften his point of view. "Besides, you know she's never going to agree to me being there."

"Yes she will. I'll convince her. You two are going to have to learn to be in the same room and get along. I'm going to want to celebrate birthdays and graduations with both of you there. What about when I get married? Are you going to skip my wedding because the two of you can't play nice?" Abby crossed her arms over her chest and plopped down on the couch, pouting.

David let out a feeble frustrated growl. "She will make Thanksgiving the most unpleasant experience she's capable of making it."

"Not if Darcy's there. She won't act up if there's someone besides just the three of us," Abby rationalized. Turning to Darcy, she asked, "Do you have any plans for Thanksgiving?"

"No, but—"

"Then it's settled." Abby picked up the phone on her father's desk and called her mother. Darcy and David heard Regina's muffled protests on the other end of the conversation. The persuasive teenager used the same argument she'd deployed with her father. As usual, by the time she hung up, Abby got her way.

To say Thanksgiving was awkward would have been a colossal understatement.

Inexperienced with baking, using her mother's recipe, Darcy attempted to make her first ever apple pie from scratch. It turned out lopsided and a little too brown on the top. She hoped it would still taste okay. She didn't want to show up at Regina Hobart's house empty-handed.

When she arrived, David wasn't there yet. Facing the she-wolf she'd heard so much about without back up made her nervous. She took comfort Abby was there to make it a little less terrifying.

"Can I take your coat?" Regina, it turned out, didn't embody the woman Darcy imagined. This woman had glossy, shoulder length blonde hair and a pretty face. She wore an attractive earth-toned dress, which came mid-calf on shapely legs.

"Thank you. I made a pie. I hope it tastes better than it looks," Darcy said as Abby took the dessert from her. Regina gave her ex-husband's new assistant a not-so-subtle once over.

"Don't look at her like that, Mom. She's not sleeping with him. She's gay," Abby said, winking at Darcy. The research assistant turned sixteen shades of embarrassed but didn't rebut the girl's statement. To her relief, David rolled in a few minutes later carrying the bottles of wine Regina requested.

"Can I help you with anything in the kitchen, Ms. Hobart?" Darcy asked.

"Please, call me Regina. I've got everything under control, it'll be a few more minutes. Abby, why don't you show Ms. Jensen the house while I get dinner on the table?"

"Come on," Abby took Darcy by the hand as if they were best friends and led her from room to room. "Mom loves showing off the house. She did most of the work herself, well, at least the jobs that didn't need a building permit." In the library Abby continued, "She rented a sander and refinished all the wood floors."

"They're beautiful."

"Over here is one of the guest suites. It used to be Dad's bedroom until he moved out." The décor was masculine with a nautical theme. It made her think of a room one would find in a high-end seaside bed and breakfast.

On the second floor they quickly inspected the master suite and two more guest rooms. "Mom took some classes on laying tile and did all the tile work. I think if all the old pipes in the house hadn't needed to be replaced, she would have installed the tubs and toilets too. She hired professional plumbers to do all that stuff."

The house was spotless until they came to the room with an industrial-looking sewing machine. Bolts of fabric occupied the corners and were piled on a giant worktable. "She's decided she's going to start a custom drapery business. Mom made all of our window treatments. Sewing is something she enjoys," Abby bragged.

Darcy was familiar with the price tag of quality window coverings. She'd just spent a small fortune on them.

Lastly they came to Abby's bedroom at the front of the house. Everything was pink and white and screamed: **a privileged young lady lives here.**

"I haven't heard any yelling, so they must be getting along okay," Abby whispered.

"Did your mom really try to switch holidays or was that your doing?" Darcy asked.

"What do you think?" Abby smiled, wickedly. "I'm not trying to get them back together. That ship sailed a long time ago. I truly think it's time for them to behave in the best interests of their child, Me! Don't tell Dad. He'd hate it if he knew I was conspiring behind his back."

"I wouldn't dream of it," Darcy said, with a laugh. She remembered Professor Nelson saying during a lecture that testing teenagers for pathologies was difficult because most of them would show many traits displayed by sociopaths:

- being manipulative
- impulsive
- engaging in erratic behavior
- prone to being emotional

This was definitely true of Abby Hobart. The girl's actions were a product of her environment. Darcy was optimistic these behaviors would disappear when she became an adult.

Then her research mind pinged her with a new theory: maybe most sociopaths were just people who never mentally and/or emotionally progressed. Maybe they could be fixed by taking them back to what life was like as a toddler and re-teach them how to be a decent human being.

Being pulled down the stairs to join the others pushed that from Darcy's mind.

The meal was outstanding.

Regina prepared the traditional Thanksgiving turkey and stuffing along with yams, green bean casserole, cranberry sauce and homemade yeast rolls. Regina cooked with the same excellence as Lillian had.

Conversation around the elaborately set table lagged through many graceless gaps but always seemed to come back around to Darcy answering questions about herself, which made her feel like a bug under a microscope.

"So David tells me you came from Los Angeles?" Regina asked near the end of the meal.

"I got my degree at UCLA. I'm originally from the Midwest," Darcy answered. She tried to keep her answers concise, without giving away too much information.

"Where in the Midwest?" Regina asked

"The Chicago area." Darcy was sure Regina would continue to drill her until the main meal ended, so she diverted the subject back to her hostess. "I couldn't help but be in awe of all the beautiful fabric in your sewing room."

"I've got my first customer; my divorce attorney's wife has commissioned me to do draperies for three rooms in their home. If she's pleased with my work, I'm hoping she'll refer me to her friends."

"Word of mouth has built many a successful business," David said.

"Well, it's true, what people say to others can make or break you. With any luck, I won't be financially dependent on you much longer." There was a snideness in her tone which caused an uneasy cloud to descend.

"Oh! Dad, I forgot to tell you, I got chosen for the gymnastics team at school," Abby artfully changed the subject, steering them away from unpleasantness.

"That's wonderful! I'm so proud of you," David said.

"Congratulations, Abby!" Darcy said. "What are your events?"

"I'll be doing floor exercise and the balance beam," Abby said.

"You'll need to write a check to cover the cost, David," Regina was back on money again. Her inflection was challenging.

"Just tell me how much," he sighed. David rose from his chair and began to clear the table, refusing to be drawn into an argument. "I'll make a pot of coffee to go with Darcy's pie," he said, sidestepping the bait and the attitude Regina dangled.

Darcy suspected they were simply trying to be kind when they each ate a piece of her off balanced creation. It tasted fine, except the bottom crust needed to be cooked a little more. The pumpkin pie Regina made sat untouched.

When the festivities finally came to an end, Darcy was never so grateful to be leaving a gathering. Abby retrieved Darcy's coat from the closet for her and whispered, "Thanks for coming today. Your being here made them both behave. What are you doing for Christmas?"

Darcy chuckled. "My aunt and uncle and little cousin are coming to Boston; perhaps we should celebrate that holiday at my house, neutral territory."

David walked his assistant to her car and asked, "How much more do you have to do to be ready for the interviews at Bellview next week?"

"Quite a bit. I have to organize all the consent forms I've already gotten and resend any that are still out. I need to input all the information into a spreadsheet so we can be sure we have a balanced group. And I still want to make some notes on the different patients I can refer to during the interviews. I know I'm going to be working right up to the time I walk through the doors up there."

"I'll help. We can work from my office. I agree with you about getting Bellview out of the way first. I'd hate to have Dr. Dunham pull the plug and I wouldn't put it past her," David said.

The team worked all day Friday and Saturday compiling data and reviewing patient files. David left a few times to run Abby to the mall or pick up take-out food to keep them from starving to death. On Saturday evening, he cut out for about an hour to take Abby back to her mother's house. He returned to dive right back into making notes on the various test subjects.

Shortly after midnight when he stretched and rubbed his eyes, Darcy looked up from the computer and said, "You must be exhausted. Why don't you go home and get some sleep?"

"I'd love to, but I wouldn't sleep. I have a consistent case of insomnia," David said.

"And headaches?"

"It's that obvious?" David asked.

Darcy nodded. David located a bottle of pills in his briefcase and washed one down with cold coffee. "If the headache doesn't go away in an hour, I'll call it a night; all right?"

"Whatever you want to do."

David sat back down and returned to the patient files. A few minutes later he said, "That's odd."

"What?" Darcy asked.

"This file, here, the guy, Barry Devlin, likes to make toothpick animals. You've made a notation that he wanted matchsticks. When I dropped Abby off tonight, I stepped on something on the front steps. When I looked closer, I noticed a pile of wooden matchsticks—"

"Call Regina right now and tell her to get Abby and leave the house!" Darcy yelled. Her eyes were frantic with fear as she pushed the phone at him.

"I can't call her at this hour..."

"Do it!" Darcy grabbed her cell phone and speed dialed Abby's cell. It went right to voicemail.

David did as she said and dialed her landline, then said, "I'm getting a beeping busy signal, that's weird."

"That means the phone line's been cut! We have to get over there." Darcy urged.

David gave her a disbelieving look and tried his ex-wife's cell phone. No answer.

"Let's go. We have to get over there right now!" Darcy yelled, pushing him to the door. David drove his BMW faster as Darcy explained what she now wished she'd told him before. She filled him in about the Devlin twins and the professor she believed her stalker killed.

"I Googled you and your address came up for the house on Manchester Road. The matchsticks are a message to back off."

David breezed through the last few sets of red lights at eighty. When he pulled up in front of the house, flames blazed in all the windows. Leaping from the car, David sprinted across the lawn, shouting, "Call 911!"

Darcy made the call, giving the operator the address and begging her to send help in a hurry. David must have determined the first floor was too dangerous to attempt to enter. Instead, he climbed up the flower trellis that led to the roof of the front porch. Darcy ran after him and started to climb up behind him. Abby's screams tore a rip in the night.

"Wait there," David instructed, "I may need you to help me get her down."

At his daughter's bedroom window, David used his elbow to smash the glass. He unlatched the lock and lifted the window frame, then climbed inside. Seconds later, he reappeared with Abby in his arms. The girl, crying hysterically, begged him to go back for her mother.

"I'm going to lower you down to Darcy." He instructed her to hold tight to his hands as he eased her off the roof. Darcy clung to the trellis and was able to catch the girl around the waist but the weight of both of them caused the makeshift ladder to give and they tumbled to the ground with a thud.

Abby cried out in pain.

"Are you all right? Let me look at you," Darcy told her, checking Abby for injuries and burns. One side of the girl's hair looked singed, but she didn't see any blood.

"I think I broke my ankle," the teenager cried. Darcy took off her coat and wrapped it around the girl who was wearing a thick pair of wooly socks and a flannel night gown. She led Abby, hopping on her uninjured foot, toward the street, out of harm's way. Even there on the other side of the street the heat of the fire reached them, the power of it carried on waves of roaring sound and hot wind.

Emergency vehicles screamed and flashed their way into the neighborhood. Fire trucks screeched to a halt in front of the house. Their red lights created a whirlpool of hell rotating around them, sucking them deeper into a living nightmare.

Darcy looked up at the burning second floor. David Hobart was nowhere to be seen. He'd gone back in to rescue his ex-wife.

"My parents are in there!" Abby screamed to the firefighters who were already deploying ladders and hoses. One firefighter with a hose scaled the ladder to the porch roof and began dousing the flames while a second fearlessly climbed through Abby's window into the inferno.

Darcy felt as if she was reliving the night her parents died. She was experiencing the horror through Abby's eyes. She hadn't actually seen her own house burning. It still felt like a horrible dream with big chunks missing.

Tears cascaded down Darcy's face as she held Abby tight and whispered reassurances that everything was going to be all right.

28

Barry Speaks

At the hospital, Darcy sat in the Emergency Room waiting area, visibly shaking. She'd ridden in the ambulance with Abby. She'd stayed with the girl until they took the teenager up for x-rays. Darcy witnessed when they wheeled Regina past Abby's cubical; the nurse pulled the curtain quickly. Abby hadn't seen her mother covered in burns, hooked to beeping machines when they rushed by. Darcy witnessed David running alongside Regina's gurney, holding a rag against a bloody gash on his forehead.

Sometime later, a nurse called Darcy's name and informed her Abby had been admitted and gave her the room number. Entering the dimly lit hospital room, she saw Abby, peacefully lying in the bed, asleep. An oxygen mask covered her nose and mouth.

At her side, David held his daughter's hand, his own were heavily bandaged. His head was hanging down sorrowfully. She saw the blood-stained strip of gauze covering that wound on his forehead. He looked up at the sound of Darcy's steps. His eyes were red from smoke and most likely from crying.

"Her ankle's not broken, bad sprain. She has a second degree burn on her back. She'll be able to come home in the morning. They've given her a sedative," David relayed wearily.

"Regina?" Darcy asked, softly.

David shook his head no. "She didn't make it."

Darcy put her hand to her mouth to muffle her sobs; uncontrollable tears flowed.

"She wasn't stabbed. That's inconsistent with your serial killer profile," he pointed out, confused, bordering on angry, not sure what or where to land in regards to the horrific story he heard rushing to save his daughter.

"He wanted it to look like an accident, not a murder." Darcy suddenly felt numb. How had she missed the signs he was close by. "David, I'm so sorry. I never intended to put you and your family in danger."

"I don't think you would ever intentionally put anyone in danger. Can we talk about this tomorrow? I'm exhausted."

Darcy nodded and whispered, "I'm so sorry." She left the hospital in a cab and went back to David's office. She stared at Barry Devlin's file for hours; then she booked a flight online. She made plans to head up to Bellview that very day to talk to Barry. She didn't bother routing her travel arrangements through Marsha. She gathered up the files they'd been working on and her laptop and packed them in her satchel. She sat down in David's chair, took pen to paper and wrote:

> David and Abby,
>
> I'm so sorry. I never meant for any of this to happen. I hadn't had the feeling that I was being followed since I was in Dallas, Texas, 2 years ago. I always got those feelings when he was close, so I assumed he was in prison or died.
>
> Everyone treated me as if I was imagining it. I even told the police about it once. They put me on Prozac, which I quit taking. There were times when I thought they could be right. Maybe I was losing my mind. There are too many coincidences for me to believe that Larry Devlin is not behind this.
>
> I'm going to Bellview to talk to Barry Devlin. I have to get this settled once and for all. If anything happens to me, there is an envelope I want you to give to the police. It's in a fireproof safe in my study behind the painting of Versailles. The combination is 5-25-45. I need to find the answers I'm looking for. I hope you can forgive me for the pain I've caused.
>
> With my deepest regrets,
> Darcy

She folded the note in half and wrote David's name on the front, leaving it on his desk where he was sure to see it.

She grabbed her belongings and locked the door behind her.

Dr. Poe escorted Darcy to the day room where a dozen or so patients in varying degrees of lucidity were entertaining themselves. Some dabbled at craft tables while others wandered around aimlessly. A few simply stared off into space, oblivious to all around them. Barry's wheelchair was at a table. He was focusing on a box of toothpicks and spool of string.

"Barry, this is Darcy Jensen. She's going to sit and talk with you for a while. Is that okay?" Dr. Poe asked. Barry nodded without looking up from his handiwork so Darcy scooted a chair up in front of him on the other side of the table.

"How are you today, Barry?" she asked. He didn't look up or answer.

"I'll leave you to it," Dr. Poe said. "Let me know when you're ready for the next candidate."

Darcy was relieved when Poe left the room. Darcy recognized his facial characteristics. He was definitely a Devlin. But the rippled burn scars and brain damage left his features twisted and grotesque.

"Barry, can you look at me? I came a very long way to see you," she coaxed softly.

Her former classmate slowly raised his head to peek at her, from lazy half-mast lids.

His eyes flashed with recognition!

There was a hint of a smile on his contorted lips.

"You remember me, don't you? Do you know my name?" she asked hopefully.

After a minute, with extreme difficulty, he managed, "Toria."

"That's right," she whispered in praise. "Victoria. Do you remember your brother Larry?"

The patient scrunched his forehead with a frown and looked back at his toothpicks.

"Barry, look at me," she tried to regain his focus. He raised his head and she stared him in the eyes, still as azure blue as they ever were.

Suddenly, a memory hit her!

"Can I see your hands?" She gently took hold of his hands and flipped them over palms up. There was no visible scar where Barry cut his hand with the box cutter in Miss Rogers' class. The cut had required seven stitches and would be recognizable; there was no such injury. Darcy's heart beat hard in her chest, her ears buzzed; the disfigured young man before her was not Barry Devlin at all, this was Larry!

"You're Larry aren't you? You didn't hurt your mother and set the fire; Barry did. Did he make you put on the bloody clothes? Did he set you up?" Darcy's mind was racing. Barry intentionally left his brother in the house to die. He'd taken his brother's identity.

A tear slipped from his eye. He started to shake his head.

Suddenly the young man became agitated. He smashed his toothpick creation and in a strangled voice moaned, "L…L…Larry makes!" he repeated over and over, crushing his sculpture until nothing was left of the design. Broken splinters of wood stuck in his hand.

"Oh, Larry, stop. It's okay!" she groaned. She took his hand and gently pulled out the toothpicks, trying to use a soft voice to sooth him. Now she understood why her mind never wrapped around the concrete evidence of Larry's violent behavior. This explained everything.

"I'm going to make this right, okay Larry? I'll be back to see you again soon," Darcy promised. She tenderly touched the side of his face. He shook his head and tried to say something but couldn't get the words to form properly. His eyes filled with tears as he slowly raised his hand to cover hers.

Her heart was breaking for him. It must be torture for him to have lost the ability to talk. Larry was sobbing now. An orderly rushed over.

"He's going to have to go to the medical wing. He is prone to seizures when he's agitated," the hulking Jamaican orderly explained in a thick island accent.

The patient reached out his hand to Darcy as the attendant wheeled away and repeated, "No, no, no! Ooo Ong! Ong!"

In Dr. Poe's office, Darcy was surprised the doctor didn't give her the third degree about what just happened. Instead, she seemed more concerned about Darcy's welfare than her patients. "I'm so sorry. I can see you are shaken by Barry's sudden outburst. It can be very unsettling to witness when you aren't around such hysterics on a regular basis," Dr. Poe said.

"Does he get emotional very often?" Darcy asked

"From time to time they all have their meltdowns. We'll need to watch him closely for a few hours. It might be best if we postpone finishing any other interviews until the end of the week, once one has an incident, the others seem to pick up on the anxiety," Dianna suggested.

Darcy was relieved going back to Boston was Dianna Poe's idea. She quickly agreed.

She needed to get home to tell David what she'd discovered.

This changed everything.

29
Home Invasion

Darcy was on the first flight back to Boston, which arrived at Logan International Airport around 11:00pm. In her car she powered up her cell phone and placed it in the docking cradle. There were two voice messages from David. **"Darcy, it's David. I got your note. We need to talk. I wish you would have told me all this before. But hey, I might have thought you were a little off too, so I can understand why you didn't. Anyway, like you predicted, the investigators are calling it an accident, blaming faulty wiring for the fire. I know that isn't right. The building inspections certified the electrician's replacement of the old knob and tube crap. Everything met modern building codes, every step of the way. Call me when you get this message."**

The second message was shorter. **"Darcy, it's David again. I wish you'd pick up. Call me, please."**

Darcy used voice assist and said to her phone, "Call Dr. Hobart." The line for David's phone went straight to voicemail. Waiting for the beep, Darcy left this message: "David, it's Darcy. I went to Bellview, I just got back to Boston. I need to talk to you too. Please come over to my house, I'd rather we talk in person than over the phone."

Darcy couldn't imagine what David was going to say when she told him about the switched identities. She needed his help to convince the police and Bellview that Larry was the one locked up in maximum security while the real killer was on the loose. Darcy was focusing solely on this identity swap, despite the Hobart fire, her gut was too tired to remind her it was set by the stalker, her brain too obsessed with setting an innocent friend free.

Somehow thinking she knew the twins had switched places overrode the reality that it didn't matter who was the stalker, the stalker knew not only what city she was in now; he knew the people she was spending time with, and therefore it was nearly a certainty he knew where she worked and where she lived.

Exhausted, Darcy unlocked her front door and punched in the code on her alarm to disarm it and set it again. She secured the entrance behind her. In her study, she dropped her satchel on her desk and locked up Barry Devlin's file in the fireproof safe. She'd only slept three hours in the last two days.

Drained, she shuffled to the kitchen and fixed a bowl of cereal. She hadn't eaten for over twenty-four hours. She wasn't hungry but forced herself to eat, so tired even sugary loops tasted like cardboard. Halfway through her last spoonful, the squeak of someone on the stairs pierced her ears, the quiet sound shattering the silence. Tiny hairs on the back of her neck and on her arms twitched to attention.

Her security system had sent no alerts, none at all; that didn't matter, she trusted her gut.

With heart racing, she set the cereal bowl on the counter and tiptoed to the built-in cabinet where she kept her Smith and Wesson .40 pistol. Darcy eased the drawer open, hoping to do it soundlessly. It scraped slightly. In her alerted state it sounded loud enough to be heard outside.

The gun wasn't there, it was gone!

Thinking quickly, she turned off the kitchen light and as her eyes adjusted to the darkness she crept into the atrium room. She snatched the cordless landline phone from its cradle, pushed the activate button… no dial tone sounded. The battery was new. Had the phone line been cut?

Darcy froze and listened intently. All she heard was her own heartbeat and breathing, both of which she tried to slow down. She inched her way to her office door. If she could make it to the satchel she'd left on the desk she'd have her cell phone and her .38 revolver.

The glow from the streetlights confirmed her bag was right where she'd put it. A small sense of relief fluttered through her. As quietly as a whisper, she made her way into the room. Fumbling through the satchel she couldn't locate her phone or her gun.

Then it hit her, because of fatigue and being distracted, she'd left her phone in its holder in her car. Where was the gun?! She'd taken it from the glove box when she got in her car at the airport. Hadn't she? Yes, she remembered doing it. She always immediately put the gun in her bag whenever she got in the car from a place she couldn't take a firearm, even before clicking the seatbelt. She searched frantically, panic rising, knowing she was making too much noise. *Where the hell is it?*

The distinct CLICK of a revolver hammer being cocked startled her and she jumped back away from the desk.

"Looking for this?" A chilling voice came from the shadowed corner of the room. Slowly, a man's silhouette emerged. His tall frame was dressed all in black. A hoodie and ski mask hid his face. Her gun was pointed right at her. Darcy's chest went tight. She struggled to breathe. Dizziness threatened.

No, no, no! Get a grip on your emotions.

Panic and die. Use your brain!

Closer to the door than he was, she calculated her odds of getting away. She took a step forward. "If you pull that trigger, my neighbors will call 911 faster than you're blinking right now!" She growled it, trying to muster as menacing a sound as her shaking voice allowed.

"We don't need this anyway," he snarled. Popping open the cylinder, he dropped the bullets in his hand and put them in his pants pocket. He tucked the gun in his waistband at the small of his back. "I have other plans for you."

She took another step toward the door. The intruder was on her instantly, his hands around her throat. Darcy screamed as he shoved her against the wall. With all her might she turned her body to the left and pulled down on his right forearm, at the same time, she thrust her other palm under his chin and pushed him off her. She ran for the front door.

He grabbed her hair jerking back as she grappled with the locks. Pain burned on her scalp. With one stiff-armed heave he launched her across the foyer. She hit the wood floor and slid. The next thing she knew he was on top of her.

Pulling her arms behind her back, he worked a zip tie around her wrists. She balled her hands into fists but was unable to stop him. She screamed. Dizzying sickness accompanied the blow to her head from the butt of the gun.

When she came to, duct tape was plastered over her mouth and her ancles were secured with it also, strapped to the legs of a dining room chair. Her wrists, still cinched with a zip tie, were behind the back of the chair. Darcy's shoulders ached and her head throbbed. A warm trickle of blood ran down her face. The masked man was pacing the foyer, a gleaming eight-inch kitchen knife in his hands.

He noticed she'd come around. He spun and marched over to her. "Are you going to shut the fuck up now?"

Darcy cast her eyes down in defeat and nodded submissively. Her mind whirled, she needed a way out of this. *Think logically, ignore the torturing throb resonating through my body and swallow my fear, for a start.*

He squatted down; their eyes fixed on one another. She knew those eyes; they were not the eyes of the boy who kissed her. She pulled tactics from David's book on body language and kept her expression mournful. When what she really wanted to do was claw his eyes out.

"If you scream, I'll gut you like a fish. Do you understand?" He said it in a snake-like whisper as he ran the blade of the knife up the side of her face. Darcy nodded.

The tear of the tape being pulled off felt like it took skin with it. Darcy gasped, sucking in air, her eyes watered sending uncontrollable tears down her face. *All the better if he thinks these are tears of fear*, her mind took in every object around her.

Looking him in the eye again, in an even voice, she said, "You can take off the mask now. I know who you are."

"I don't care if you know who I am; you're going to be dead in a little while anyway. This was for all those security cameras you've got deployed around here." He ran his hand over his head lowering his hood, then pulled off the stocking cap. It was Barry Devlin, no doubt in Darcy's mind.

"There you are," she said, unable to hide at least some of her rage. "Why? Just tell me why you feel the need to come after me?" Behind her back, she flattened her palms, which were sweating already, and gently slid her hands around to try to free one of them.

"Why? Do I have to explain it to you? You couldn't leave it alone, could you Darcy? Or should I call you Victoria? You couldn't just go on with your life and forget about us."

Her senses tingled on high alert. "You started killing long before I started looking for you, mostly girls who looked like me."

"Why do you think that is, Victoria?" he asked.

"You're the one with the superior mind, explain it to me," she said, intentionally taunting him to get him emotional, hoping that would cause him to get sloppy and open up an opportunity of some kind.

"You fucking tease, you're doing it right now! That whole coy game you play!" The blade of the knife was at her throat, his words sheathed in a vicious tremble.

"My concern has been misunderstood. I'm one of the only people who cared about you and your brother!" Her right hand slid from the zip tie, finally. She wove her fingers together, so he didn't know her hands were free. Her shoulders screamed in pain, the fight to keep from bringing her hands around to relieve the stress on her shoulders was all consuming for a few seconds.

He blew out a hateful sigh, stepping away. "Toying with our emotions is what you call caring?"

"I didn't toy with anyone. Why are you doing this, Barry? It wasn't enough you butchered your mother and framed Larry for it?" Darcy wiggled her toes in her boots. Devlin hadn't thought through his bondage strategy. Certain now her feet would slide easily from her tall boots, she tensed with readiness. She needed to bide her time and wait for the right moment. Hands free, she could stand and slip out of her boots in an instant... if she could get him off guard enough to give her those precious seconds.

"Is that what you think?" He threw his head back and laughed sadistically, sending shivers up her spine. "Oh Victoria, you disappoint me! You never did learn to tell us apart!"

Darcy was confused. "What are you talking about? I saw your brother's hand; he doesn't have a scar. You're the one who cut yourself with the box cutter. You're the one who freaked out when the circulatory system project went bad. You're Barry!"

"I'm Larry you stupid cunt. For most of the science project you worked with Barry. We swapped back and forth. You see, my pussy of a brother couldn't deal with Sean and his stupid whiney mouth. So after that first day, I did the majority of the work on both projects. In class you worked with Barry so he could just give you vapid yes answers as you took over like the pushy bitch you are. Over the computer, you were talking to me."

Darcy's jaw tightened as this new revelation sunk in. "So you're your own alter ego? That's fucked up," she said. Thinking back on all the times they worked together, how could she have miss they were swapping places? "But...Why?"

"Oh that's easy. I actually liked the solar system project better. Plus, ***my*** name was going to be on our entry. I wasn't going to leave it to Barry to mess up our chances of going to the state finals."

"So I was talking to you the night of the fire?" Darcy asked.

"That's right, genius," Larry laughed.

"Who killed your mother and set fire to the house?" Darcy asked.

"I'm the one who stabbed her, but my stupid brother started the fire," Larry answered.

"But the police said he practiced killing techniques on the neighborhood pets; that the dead animal parts were found in Barry's bedroom," Darcy argued.

"Jesus! You really aren't that bright, are you? Who do you think told them it was Barry's bedroom?"

"You heartless bastard! You let Barry take the blame for everything," Darcy said, anger rising with each of his revelations. Larry was breathing hard now; she was getting to him. Her adrenaline was running high. A trickle of sweat ran down her back.

This was a tight-wire of emotion and strategy.

Anything could set him off, anything could distract her.

"You don't have a fucking clue what you're talking about. I loved Barry. I tried to save my brother from a brutal beating. There was no plan to murder my mother." His voice became high pitched as his words came faster.

He paced the floor again.

"When I logged off the computer that night, I went upstairs and she was beating Barry with a fireplace poker. Our mother caused his head trauma. What was I supposed to do? I grabbed a knife and stopped her. Barry had her blood all over him because he was on the floor half beat to shit when I stabbed her." He took a deep breath and continued. "When I realized I'd killed her, I stripped out of my clothes and threw them in the fireplace. When I went to wash up Barry started the fire to burn my bloody clothes. I was going to help him get cleaned up too, but when I came back upstairs the whole house was going up in flames. He was hugging her and crying like a baby. I was trying to get him to safety but he kept fighting me! The flames became too intense. The upper floor was collapsing on top of us." Larry's voice cracked and he turned his back to her.

Seizing the moment, Darcy raised her knees, freeing herself from her boots and was standing in her stocking feet next to the kitchen island. When Larry turned to face her, his eyes widened, Darcy grabbed a bar stool and swung it like a softball bat.

"How did you..." Larry was saying as the legs of the stool connected with his chest, hurling him backwards.

Darcy made a mad dash for the stairs.

If she could make it to her saferoom where she kept a second cell phone, she'd be able to call for help.

30
Guns & Spiders

Whizzing past Larry at full speed, Darcy hit the stairs, only to slip on the landing, crashing to her knees. She ignored the injury and scurried up the remaining stairs on all fours, like a toddler. Larry's footfalls came loud and fast, right behind her.

Darcy reached the top and slid into her bedroom, slamming the door with all her might. She caught Larry's hand in the process. She wasn't sure if the audible crunch was the wood of the door or the bones of his fingers. He howled like a scalded dog and stepped back.

"You fucking bitch!" he yelled.

Darcy threw her body against the door and locked it. She maneuvered the bookcase which disguised her saferoom entry and had only just placed her thumb on the access control panel when Larry exploded through the top of the bedroom door. Wooden casement splinters flew like shrapnel everywhere.

Darcy screamed as Larry slammed her body to the floor, knocking the wind out of her. Dazed, she lay on the floor gasping for air.

"Well, well, what do we have here?" Larry inspected the open safe room. "Outstanding! You've just given me the means to replay your death over and over again. I'm impressed Victoria!" He came back into her bedroom and flipped on the overhead light.

Darcy managed to sit up. Terror rushed through her like an icy blast of Chicago winter wind; matchstick spiders were lined up all around her room. Dozens of them! It was exactly like in the nightmare when she was seventeen.

Larry was holding her Glock and her emergency cell phone. "Geez, Victoria! You sure have a lot of guns around here. You must be paranoid or something." He laughed as he dropped the phone to the floor and crushed it under his foot. Then he ejected the magazine from the gun and put it in his pocket.

Darcy coughed; her lungs were accepting air again. She scooted on her butt toward her nightstand. "Don't bother, I found that one too," Larry grabbed a scrub bucket from her adjacent bathroom and dumped the contents on the floor, metal clanging, gun parts spewed all over. He'd disassembled the guns he'd found. He opened her bedroom window and threw out the two unloaded guns he couldn't break into parts. They hit the ground with a thud two stories below.

Darcy looked at the gun pieces on the floor and did a quick calculation.

He's missed one!

Like a darkening storm, Larry walked slowly toward her. "Now you're going to give me what you should have given my brother." She struggled and kicked as he raised her off the floor and threw her down on the bed.

"Stop fighting me!" he barked, as he tried to tie her ankle to the bedpost with rope he'd left on her pillow. Darcy kicked with anger-fueled force and knocked him backwards before he tightened the knot. She rolled off the bed away from him, landing on the other side, her movement scattering matchstick spiders.

"You say you love your brother, then why did you blame all your crimes on him? Explain it to me, I don't understand!" Breathless from the effort, she sucked in air while trying to get her ankle out of the rope before he could come at her again. That's when she noticed the topaz ring on her left ring finger.

"They told me he was going to die!" Larry was saying. "For weeks after the fire they told me not to get my hopes up, his injuries were too severe. By the time he started to improve, it seemed too late to change my story, and all the blame was on him, leaving me free." Larry shrugged, as if that explained everything.

"What the fuck is this?" Darcy tugged at the ring which refused to budge off her finger.

"It belonged to my mother. Just a little reminder of what calculating cunts all women are."

"So because she mistreated you that gave you permission to go on a killing spree? You set the fire that killed my parents and my cousin!" Darcy said, her words quivering with rage.

"The news reported it as an accident, something about a frayed electrical cord. I was surprised to hear your cousin also died in the fire; you were supposed to die, not Paige. I didn't even know she was at your house that night. Everyone else was collateral damage."

The jubilance in his voice infuriated her. "She was in the bed right next to me! She liked to sleep with a pillow over her head."

"That explains why I didn't see her," he said, his eyes wild with intensity.

"How many did you kill?" She had to keep him talking to distract him. She slowly stepped toward her ruined bedroom door.

"Hard to say. I didn't keep a running count," he answered, proud of his accomplishment. "And I'm good at getting away with it."

"You killed those four girls at UCLA and my professor in Austin," she accused, still tugging on the ring.

"Now you're sounding more like the brainiac I used to know. Someone died every time you ran from me. Three died when you transferred to UCLA and resurfaced. I got the message; you figured it out."

Darcy was only a foot away from her escape route. "Yeah, I figured it out. I was surprised you didn't have the balls to come back to LA after me. I guess you were too scared of getting caught."

"No, I was being patient, waiting for the perfect opportunity. Tell me, Victoria, are you still a virgin?" he said as if her chastity belonged to him.

Finally, with a forceful twist the ring slid off her finger. Darcy threw it at him and bolted three steps toward the door. He moved faster than lightening; capturing her, smashing her into the wall. She saw the knife in his hand right before he drove it hard into her left shoulder.

She shrieked in agony. He pulled his weapon out, which was just as excruciating as when it went in.

"Oh no you don't. I'm not done with you yet! We're going to fuck and then fuck more even slower. Then I'm going to burn down your gorgeous house with you in it," he sneered.

"You're a monster," Darcy hissed.

"How can you say that after I made you all these cool spiders? They are going to sacrifice their lives for you. It's going to be prettier than a birthday cake when it all goes up."

Darcy glared at him. "I'm not going to let you start one more fire." She summoned all her strength and kneed him in the groin; he landed with a thump on the floor. Darcy tried to run, but he grabbed her foot, toppling her. Her face hit the floor, hard. She fought to stay conscious, knowing she would surely die if she passed out. Laboring to move, Darcy used her right arm to crawl across the floor. She didn't make it far. Larry drove the knife into the thigh of her right leg.

"Help me! Somebody, help me!" she screamed at the top of her lungs. Survival adrenalin pulsed through her and she found power she didn't know she had; she coiled her good leg and kicked him square in the face. The cracking sound it produced let her know she'd broken something. It gave her enough time to drag her injured body across the wooden floor, out into the hall. She kept calling for help every inch of the way.

She'd almost made it to the bookshelf where she knew her last hidden gun was stashed in what looked like a vintage copy of War and Peace, when she heard him step out behind her. She looked over her shoulder at him; his nose was pouring blood; she'd hurt him badly. His cheek bone was at an odd angle, it swelled instantly and was turning black and blue. He seemed disoriented.

Struggling, Darcy pulled herself up into a cockeyed standing position and stared into the face of her stalker. "That's right, let me get a good look at you. You're not as cute as you were when you were fourteen," she told him, trying to fight off the urge to give in and just pass out. "Especially now that I broke your face."

As she pulled the fake book off the shelf, he stumbled toward her and thrust the knife into her stomach. Searing pain rocketed through her and she let out a bloodcurdling scream for all the victims and all her anger. That scream gave her power and she screamed again in fury!

He shoved the topaz ring he'd scavenged from the floor into her mouth. "Choke on it, bitch!" he growled.

She wasn't going to let him win. She grabbed her Ruger GP100 Magnum revolver letting the box fall to the floor and spit out the ring, hitting him in the eye. At the same time a thunderous crash resounded as someone kicked in the front door.

David Hobart stood at the bottom of the stairway. Darcy saw the frantic look in his eyes; he must have heard her screams. With one hand covering his injured eye, Larry turned his attention down the stairs to the foyer where the professor was taking in the situation. Darcy harnessed her opportunity, she raised the gun and fired three rounds, hitting her mark every time. Then she slumped against the wall at the top of the stairs.

Everything happened in slow motion.

The ear-splitting crack of the gunshots clouded her hearing as Larry Devlin staggered backwards and tumbled down the stairs, crashing through the antique railing mid-way and crumpling at the landing. He thumped to the floor at David's feet. In muffled tones, she heard David on his cell calling for help.

Covered in blood, she leaned against the wall and hobbled down the stairs. Her arms extended, she trained the gun on the evil twin, in case he moved a muscle.

Darcy lost her footing on the last three steps and slid down on her ass, her gun never moving from her target.

"Is he dead? Turn on the light; I want to see him," Darcy heard herself say. David flipped on the foyer chandelier. They both evaluated the condition of the intruder.

"He's still alive; help is on the way, Darcy," David's voice came through a clogged-up ringing of her ears. The next thing she knew, David was by her side, uttering reassurances, the same ones she'd used to comfort Abby… that everything was going to be all right.

Darcy stared into Larry's cold blue defiant eyes. Blood leaked from the bullet holes in his throat, chest and groin; blood trickled from his mouth. One of the balusters had impaled his right torso and he gushed blood in a pool on the floor of the foyer. Yet he fought for life with hatred clear in his expression.

"Don't you move, psycho," she threatened.

Larry gurgled some unintelligible response to her threat.

"I hear the sirens, Darcy, give me the gun... come on... let go. They're almost here." David's arms were around her, supporting her. She let loose of the gun.

She felt energy draining from her body. "Don't let that son-of-a-bitch die in my house. This is my home now." Crying, she tried her best to hold on for the paramedics. Her vision began to dim and, far off in the distance, she heard David calling to her, "They're here, Darcy. Wake up! Can you hear me! You have to fight! Wake up!"

Everything went black for a second and then she heard her mother's laughter. The sun warmed her face. Dad laughed too! They were in the gardens at Versailles, misbehaving and splashing water at each other from one of the ornate water fountains.

A sudden jolt of fire passed through her body and she heard some strange voice announce, "We have V-tach people. Stand by with the paddles; we need to get her in the OR before she bleeds out."

She tried to ask, "Is Larry dead? Is it over?"

Then, she heard her father say, "Victoria, look here, smile for me." A flash bulb went off and he took her picture.

Then everything seemed to float and go dark.

40

Aftermath

David Hobart looked at his watch; he had two hours until time to pick up Abby at gymnastics. His mind flashed to the sticky note she'd placed on the refrigerator calendar: **4:30.** He rubbed the back of his neck. The migraine that began during his meeting with Agents O'Sullivan and Grant hurt less, now it ached instead of throbbed.

His cell rang, startling him. Looking at the caller ID, he groaned. "Dr. Hobart," he answered, attempting to sound professional.

"David, how are you?" William Collingsworth's voice sounded a bit too cheerful for David's comfort. He knew why his mentor and boss was calling and he wasn't ready to listen to the older man's guidance.

"I'm well, except this isn't a convenient time to talk. I'm about to step into a meeting," David said.

"Are you on campus?"

"No, I'm with a real estate agent, getting ready to look at a condo. My lease is up next month," David lied.

"We need to schedule a time to talk about your project. I can understand why your research has stalled again, first with Regina and now the awful business with Miss Jensen. But it's that time of year when the grant givers want to see where you stand." William had lost his peppy cadence.

"I know." David feigned annoyance they'd been unable to schedule this by now. "We've been missing each other. Maybe we can get together next week." In truth David was actively avoiding Collingsworth.

"Monday morning, first thing, in my office." This wasn't a suggestion; it was an ultimatum.

"First thing Monday, I'll see you then," David confirmed. They ended the call.

Since coming to terms with how his lies caused so much mess,

David despised deception, but in this instance, it bought him some extra time.

William Collingsworth was a solid boss and without him, David's career path would never have led him to the enormous success he'd achieved. If not for the department head, David's research on intentional human behavior would likely still be in the drawer where he'd stashed it after Claire bailed on him. *Wouldn't it be better if it had never saw the light of day?*

It had been two months since David's research came to a second halt, the night the house on Manchester Road went up in flames, then twenty-four hours later, he'd kicked in the front door of Darcy Jensen's house and witnessed her put three bullets in Larry Devlin's body.

He still suffered nightmares. Maybe that was why his insomnia was worse; he didn't want to dream any more. He didn't want to see Regina's horrifically burned face or hear her painfully whisper again, "I'm sorry for everything, David. Take care of Abby." He'd tearfully begged her to hang on for Abby's sake. Just as his ex-wife breathed her last, he vowed to put Abby first for the rest of his life.

He was doing his best to keep that promise. Regardless of what he perceived as her faults, Regina had been an exceptional mother to Abby. Now David's only priority was Abby and her mental health. Grief being an individual experience for everyone, he watched her carefully.

During the initial shock of losing her mother, Abby withdrew. She underwent periods of anger, deep sadness and anxiety. Overwhelmed by feelings of helplessness, David reached out to a former student now in private practice as a grief counselor. Abby begrudgingly agreed to sessions with Sarah Cramer.

Earlier that week Abbey had finally opened up to her father.

She'd said, "I didn't think I could talk to you about Mom, given the toxic relationship you two shared. Talking with Sara is helping. She told me you're seeing her for counseling too." They were sitting in a booth at a diner, having breakfast.

"I am," he'd confirmed. "I'm grieving too. I'm working through some issues, guilt, anger, fear. I'm so afraid I'm going to handle things wrong with you and irrevocably screw you up."

Abby smirked. "You're not screwing me up, Dad."

"What a relief. Grief is a very different path for everyone, Abby. There's no right or wrong way to travel it. I just want you to know, no matter what, you can always talk to me. You're not alone," David compassionately told his daughter.

Her eyes rimmed with tears. "I understand that now."

They did a few counseling sessions together, which brought them emotionally closer. Abby sometimes shared a memory of Regina with David. She'd laugh or on occasion cry, and this was healthy. They were establishing a new normal. It wasn't always smooth. But David was determined to be a better man, a father Abby always felt secure counting on. The loving and supportive father she deserved.

Remembering the assignment Abby tasked him with before she left for school, David went to his computer and began perusing real estate listings for condominiums. His apartment was much too small for the two of them. They'd agreed they didn't want to live in a single-family house.

Abby came up with the non-negotiable criteria for their next dwelling. Their unit couldn't be higher than the third floor. It must be a newer building with a sprinkler system and fire escapes. It needed to have at least two bedrooms with a private bath for each and an office where David could work from home rather than spending so many hours at the university. An open floor plan was preferable. And most important, it must be pet friendly, she wanted a puppy.

David found several that met or exceeded Abby's list and had scheduled showings for the weekend. After breakfast on Saturday (their new routine), they'd tour the properties together. This was Abby's life too and he wanted her to feel involved, to know she was listened to. The entire time he'd been booking condos viewings Collingsworth's words echoed in his ears like an unwanted song stuck in his head. *And now, this awful business with Miss Jensen.*

David opened the **Darcy** file in his Word Documents. Darcy's Uncle Howard had given him the memory stick she'd entrusted to him. David copied it to his computer. It held the same information he'd taken from Darcy's safe in her study; the one she'd told him to give to the police should anything happen to her. He'd followed her instructions the night she was brutally stabbed.

He'd read all the evidence she'd collected a hundred times; the proof that Larry Devlin was stalking her. He'd memorized the photographs of the women she'd suspected were murdered by her former classmate.

He'd stared at the composite drawing of the suspect in the murder of the UCLA students and he'd instantly recognized him as the man he'd watched dying in Darcy's foyer. He'd never forget the face of the monster who'd tried to burn Abby alive. David was glad Darcy's wish came true that night. When the paramedics arrived, Larry Devlin was still clinging to life. He died en-route to the hospital and not in her front foyer.

By the time the second ambulance arrived to transport Darcy, police were swarming all over her house. David wanted to go with her to the hospital but the head investigator told him as the only witness he needed to remain at the crime scene for questioning.

That's when he remembered the envelope Darcy mentioned in her note. Because of that package and the videos in her safe room, the police were able to see and hear what happened while piecing together the de-evolution of Larry Devlin, the serial killer. Everyone believed her story now. Larry, not Barry, was the evil one.

The surveillance videos with him confessing to her, gloating to her, proved to be the evidence that closed the case.

Larry never got to light his matchstick spiders.

Every time David thought about it, a chill ran up his spine. If only someone had believed Darcy years ago, so much tragedy would have been avoided.

David added to that file as the investigation unfolded: all the articles dealing with the case, as well as the obituaries.

David inserted Darcy's original memory stick in the port and began copying over the new information he'd collected. First, the articles about the fire that destroyed his home and killed Regina. Next, he saved the ones about the intruder who'd broken into his research assistant's house and how she'd shot him.

The next batch comprised the joint task force investigation. This case was national news. So many files: The Boston Police and FBI announcing an abandoned stolen car discovered the day after the break in and linking it to Devlin and the killings. The killer's stolen laptop and evidence found on the hard drive, the searches Devlin conducted and his methodical stalking. The encrypted file Larry created "scrapbooking," which was like keeping a trophy from some of the murders he'd committed. All the pictures of his matchstick creatures were somehow leaked to the press creating a firestorm of curiosity and publicity surrounding the case.

The Matchstick Monster was front-page news.

Sadly, he was destined to gain the same notoriety as Bundy, Dahmer and Gacy. One clever reporter pieced together Darcy's connection to Bellview and Barry, culminating in Larry's driving need to stop her.

Dr. Laura Dunham, of course, reacted poorly to the exposure the story generated. She threatened disciplinary action but relented after a lengthy conversation with sweet-talking Dr. Collingsworth. This increased David's indebtedness to William.

David's stomach turned, bile rising remembering all those creepy matchstick spiders. Larry had been a fool to underestimate Darcy and that facilitated his undoing. David had to admit, he'd underestimated her as well. Killing someone hadn't made his previous list of her abilities. He was glad she had that hidden skill.

The nightmare was over now.

David put Darcy's memory stick in an envelope and slipped it in his inside coat pocket. He grabbed his car keys. He needed to leave immediately to be on time to pick up Abby. On the drive over to her school, David thought about all the lives Larry Devlin had turned upside down. All those families who lost loved ones at his hands.

The killer had confessed to Darcy dozens of victims and that was caught on security recordings; but many of the details died with him. Would they ever be sure of exactly how many people he killed or how many fires he intentionally set? Those families now included people right here in Boston.

David spotted Abby in the crowd of schoolgirls waiting for their rides. As he pulled up to the curb she gave him a sunny smile. This was a good day. She would continue to have bad days; but the frequency was diminishing.

"You're the third parent to pick up, you get a gold star," Abby said as she fastened her seatbelt.

"How did you do? How's the ankle?" David asked.

"It's good. I did a dismount today. I'm not gonna lie, I was a little scared at first but it feels fine," Abby said.

"Fantastic." As they pulled out of her school campus, David asked, "Do you mind if we go to Spaulding before dinner instead of after?"

"That's fine," Abby said.

As they drove through the wintery narrow streets, Abby changed the subject to the condominiums her father was supposed to investigate online. He handed her his phone where she inspected the listings he chose. David was happy for the distraction; he resolved to put his troubling thoughts behind him, at least until they got where they were going.

As they walked into the room they visited almost every night, Lisa announced, "You're just in time, we're celebrating!"

Lisa, Howard and Darcy were all holding plastic cups with sparkling grape juice. Lilly balanced a sippy cup. Howard poured two more from a bottle that looked like champagne.

"What's the reason for the party?" David asked.

Darcy, in particular, was beaming when she gave him the news. "Dr. Poe called! Barry is being transferred to Wingate in Brighton next month. Here's to you, Dr. Hobart, for all your help!" Darcy raised her cup and they all clapped.

"I didn't do that much; I only made a couple of phone calls." David bowed away. "You're the one who proved he shouldn't be locked away in a state facility with criminals. I'm glad Dr. Poe finally figured out Barry was creating the toothpick animals to try to tell her about Larry and what he'd done."

"Well, regardless, his care is covered by the state. They have an impressive program there for brain injured patients. With the dexterity he has in his hands, maybe he can learn to write and communicate. I'll re-teach him how to read myself, if I have to," Darcy said.

"You're incredible," David said, shaking his head in disbelief.

"I knew that the first time I met her," Howard said laughing.

"Me too," Abby agreed, toasting Darcy. "How come we're not drinking real champagne?"

"I can't mix the medication they have me on with alcohol," Darcy explained. "You two showed up early tonight; what's up?"

"Dr. Collingsworth called me this afternoon," David began.

"I'm sure I know why," Darcy laughed. "The annual tribunal of funding is about to commence."

"Exactly. I don't know what to tell them. Do we submit it with only the positive aspects or do we continue to investigate the negative behaviors before we call it complete?"

"What does your gut tell you, Dr. Hobart?" Howard asked.

"I think I've seen enough evil for a while. I want to submit it as is. I'll still share credit with Darcy as a researcher," he said.

"You can give me credit as an editor, that's all I did on the positive behavior portion of the project. I agree with you about leaving out the negative intentional behaviors. I don't think we want to produce a textbook for budding psychopaths. So, have you given up on the idea of looking for the evil gene?" Darcy asked.

"You told me it sounded like something that might backfire. We didn't have the chance to collect any samples from the prisons or mental health facilities, so..."

"I'm glad we didn't. Technology and science don't look before they leap. Just because we can, doesn't mean we should. What if, a decade from now, your initial research was developed into some kind of DNA profiling that judges people just by genes? The Devlin twins started out with duplicate genes. What if they both possessed the same gene that's labeled evil? What if, given the opportunity, one would act on it and the other would choose not to, but because he possessed the bad gene, he's labeled a criminal, without ever breaking the law? They both could have been institutionalized as toddlers. For life."

"That doesn't seem too farfetched to me," Abby weighed in.

"Eventually, someone will do research on it but it won't be you and me," David confirmed his decision.

"I think that's wise. Why add insult to injury?" Howard gave his opinion. The room fell silent for a moment. They all felt the weight of those who were lost, strangers as well as loved ones.

Howard broke the tension. "David, I've been meaning to thank you for calling me about the storefront you saw for lease. I looked at it the other day and it might be perfect for my gallery."

"Does that mean you've decided to relocate to Boston?" the professor asked.

"Yes," Lisa confirmed. "After almost losing Darcy, I can't bear the thought of being over a thousand miles away from her. Plus, she's going to need taking care of when they release her from here next week."

"Next week?" Abby asked, excitedly.

Darcy smiled broadly. "Yup. Of course, I'll still have to go to physical therapy. The good news there is, I'll be doing that at Boston University's Physical Therapy Center, so I'll be back on campus."

"What do you think you want to do now, Darcy?" David asked.

"I don't know. Although I'm not opposed to staying on as your research assistant if you have some other hazardous project you'd like to labor over," Darcy said with a wry smile.

David put up his hands, as if warding off evil, with a surprised expression. "I think I'll take a break from research for a while, if you don't mind."

Darcy pointed her finger at him and began to laugh; everyone else joined in on the laughter.

Smiling, David shook his head at his own obliviousness. "Yeah, I see what you're doing; you intentionally set me up as the punch line for your warped humor."

Darcy put her hand over her mouth, laughter tears streamed down her face. When she gained control she said, "Oh man, I haven't laughed that hard in years!" She put her hand over her heart. "I've made some decisions..."

"You're going to get a fearless guard dog?" Abby interrupted. Everyone laughed again.

"I guess I should take that under consideration, but no, I'm going to start on my master's degree next semester, maybe go on for a PhD. I'm thinking about working with patients with brain injuries, like Barry's. It is one option."

"Are you still interested in criminal behavior?" David asked.

"I don't know. It fascinates me." Darcy shrugged as if apologizing. David took the envelope from his breast pocket and handed it to her. She recognized the thumb drive immediately and held it to her chest.

"I only ask because SSA O'Sullivan and Grant from the FBI came by to see me again this morning," David told her.

"That's interesting, Agent O'Sullivan called me today, wanting to set up a time to come and talk with me next week." Darcy was soberly serious now. "We've been over everything completely, multiple times. I can't imagine what else I can tell them."

"They wanted my opinion as to your fitness and willingness to join the FBI," David informed her.

Darcy's mouth dropped open. She smoothed her hair back off her forehead. "What did you tell them?"

"The truth," David said. "You're the smartest, most intuitive person I've ever met. When you set your teeth into a task, you'll work like a dog to accomplish what you're given. Of course, I also told them you have your own way of thinking and I couldn't possibly predict if that career path would even interest you."

"Wow," Darcy breathed. "To be honest, I've never ever considered a career in the FBI."

The possibilities bounced around her brain. *Is this something I want? Maybe I'd be good at it. My gut is saying yes.* She'd have to wait and see what Agent O'Sullivan had to say.

"Food for thought," Darcy muttered. "Food. For. Thought."

ABOUT THE AUTHOR

Dawn Hogan indulged her love of words as an English major at the University of Alabama in Huntsville. Now she lives there with her ever-supportive husband Ralph, their youngest son Christopher, and Zero the cat, who clearly believes he's the household deity. She has three other grown children, and as a reward for that insanity, she has two beautiful granddaughters. With a background ranging from admin in the tech sector to running a photography studio (until "bridezilla" became a literal job hazard), Dawn's resume is nothing if not eclectic. She's also clocked in plenty of volunteer hours at her kids' schools and sports teams, mostly driven by the lure of cookies.

Since 2004, Dawn has been perfecting her writing craft, skillfully dodging household chores along the way. After a mountain of rejection letters taller than her cat's ego, she finally saw her debut novel, *Unbroken Bonds*, hit the shelves in 2021. She's also penned two short stories: *My Dear Mrs. Packard* in the *Feisty Deeds* anthology and *Sand Dollar* which will appear in an upcoming anthology on grief. Dawn readily admits that crafting a short story can be tougher than churning out a 300 page novel. Her sophomore effort, *Intentionally*, proves she's no one-hit wonder.

A proud member of the Women's Fiction Writers Association, Friends of the Library, and Sisters in Crime, Dawn keeps herself well-integrated into the literary community. For tales of her latest escapades and musings, swing by DWHogan.com. You can also connect with her on Facebook as D.W. Hogan author, Instagram @dawnhoganauthor, Threads, Bluesky, X, and Goodreads, where you'll find a delightful mix of cat photos and book reviews.

All Books lose some wonderful scenes at the mercy of the **evil editor's** slashes ….

For an exclusive look at cut scenes from this book, the publisher is offering **a free ebook** that contains the full childhood and school scenes from our main character and more of how our villainous villain was formed.

Please email our director, and you will be sent your copy, and no, you do not have to join a mailing list to get it! This is a straight up gift for fans.

Email: **director@vanvelzerpress.com**
and tell us you want
the missing scenes from ***Intentionally.***

Author's Note & Acknowledgements:

It's often said, as writers we should create a novel we would like to read. That is exactly what I did with Intentionally. I have always been fascinated with the inner thoughts of serial killers. What happened to them to make them so messed up? Are they a product of their environment or are they born evil? I have to credit the television series Criminal Minds, in part, for my obsession.

This book evolved from a vivid dream I had about a psychology professor who was studying intentional human behavior. I began writing Intentionally for the NaNoWirMo 2012 challenge. Since then, the book has received it's share of rejections. After a complete rewrite and the shift to the research assistant, Darcy, as the protagonist, it finally found a home at Van Velzer Press. I immensely appreciate the editing staff there, especially Trish Lewis, for her enthusiasm, direction and expertise.

I confess, I am a total research geek. I went down months of rabbit holes looking up the most credible information there is on identical twins, serial killers, so-called evil genes and resources pertaining to every aspect of this story. So, if it's in the book, rest assured I looked it up.

My husband, Ralph, likes to tell people about the night he came into the kitchen and found me measuring a butcher knife. "What are you doing? He asked. "Research," I answered. To this day, he claims he sleeps with one eye open! He is first, and always, the person to which I owe my gratitude. Without his patience, encouragement and support, I would not be an author. I'm grateful to my family for their belief in me, my kids, my siblings and my mom as well as the extended family. I love you all.

Being a writer is a solitary endeavor. It can be a very lonely and discouraging business unless you have a community. I found mine at the Women's Fiction Writers Association (WFWA). They keep me connected, motivated and accountable to my goals. I might have given up if not for them. I've recently joined Sister's in Crime and will be attending Killer Nashville, where I hope to connect with even more like-minded authors.

To my readers, I'm grateful beyond measure that you devote your time to reading my books. I love to connect with you. Being invited to your book clubs and asked to speak at your events has been a privilege and a joy for me. I read every email and review you write. You make the work involved well worth my devotion to the craft of writing. I thank you, from the bottom of my heart!

Dawn W. Hogan

Love Books?

SUPPORT AUTHORS – buy directly from independent publishers. This puts more royalty dollars into the pockets of your favorite author – and gives them time to write their next book.

Visit us for links to our other books as well as many other vibrant publishing companies to
find the book for you.
Send a note to join our **Book Launch List.**

Director@vanvelzerpress.com

These ARE The Books You've Been Looking For.

Vanvelzerpress.com

www.ingramcontent.com/pod-product-compliance
Lightning Source LLC
Chambersburg PA
CBHW030412310726
48979CB00002B/388